D0032522

BENDING THE
PAW

Diane Kelly

St. Martin's Paperbacks

This is a work of fiction. All of the characters, organizations, and events portrayed in this novel are either products of the author's imagination or are used fictitiously.

First published in the United States by St. Martin's Paperbacks, an imprint of St. Martin's Publishing Group.

BENDING THE PAW

For information, address St. Martin's Publishing Group, 120 Broadway, New York, NY 10271.

www.stmartins.com

ISBN: 978-1-250-19739-9

Our books may be purchased in bulk for promotional, educational, or business use. Please contact your local bookseller or the Macmillan Corporate and Premium Sales Department at 1-800-221-7945, ext. 5442, or by email at MacmillanSpecialMarkets@macmillan.com.

Printed in the United States of America

10 9 8 7 6 5 4 3 2 1

ACKNOWLEDGMENTS

Many, many thanks to the talented team at St. Martin's Press who make these books happen. Thanks to my editor, Nettie Finn, for your invaluable insights and suggestions. You're a joy to work with! My gratitude also goes out to Allison Ziegler, Kayla Janas, Sara Beth Haring, Sarah Haeckel, Talia Sherer and the rest of the St. Martin's crew for everything you do to connect books and readers.

Thanks to designer Olya Kirilyuk and illustrator Allen Douglas for creating such a delightful cover for this book!

Thanks to my agent, Helen Breitwieser, for all you do to advance my writing career.

Thanks to my fellow writers and friends who have encouraged and supported me along the way in more ways than I can count. Y'all are the best!

Thanks to Colonel (Retired) Patricia A. Mance for suggesting the title for this book.

And finally, thanks to you readers who picked this book. Have fun as you chase down clues and bad guys with Megan and Brigit!

ONE

ST. VALENTINE'S DAY MASSACRE

The Slasher

He reached over to the wooden block of serrated steak knives on the kitchen counter and yanked one out, clutching it in his fist. He slashed and slashed, and the blood splashed and splashed. Over the walls. Over the countertops. Over the floor. Over skin and clothing and shoes.

When he finished his bloody business, a little brown face looked up at him from the doorway. The French bulldog's eyes went wide as she tilted her head in question, wondering about the strange events taking place in the kitchen of her home. She issued a soft whine. He tucked the thick roll of bills into his jacket pocket, zipped the pocket closed to keep the cash secure, and reached down to give the dog a quick pat on the head. "Don't worry, girl. Everything's going to be all right."

TWO

HOME IS WHERE THE HEART STOPS

Fort Worth Police Officer Megan Luz

"What do you say, Megan? Shall we form a pack?" Seth, my hunky, blond, broad-shouldered firefighter boyfriend was down on one knee in the foyer outside the police chief's office, the place where we'd first met. Our K-9 partners, Brigit and Blast, sat beside him. Brigit was an enormous German shepherd mix with an abundance of fur and even more attitude. Blast, on the other hand, was a sweet, submissive yellow Labrador. All three gazed anxiously at me, Brigit and Blast with big brown eyes, Seth with sexy green ones.

"Yes!" I burst into happy tears as Seth leaned forward and slipped the beautiful brushed-gold ring on my finger. It fit perfectly. The round diamond glittered in the dim after-hours light.

As he rose from the floor, I rose from my chair. We wrapped our arms around each other and held tight for a long moment, our chests pressed together, our hearts beating in syncopated rhythm. Appropriate, given that it was Valentine's Day, a holiday in which hearts factored heavily. Not wanting to be left out of our love-fest, the dogs nudged our knees with their noses, trying to force their way between us.

I released Seth and wiped my eyes with my fingers, unable to stop smiling. I glanced at my watch: 9:15. My mom and dad would still be up. "Let's go tell my parents."

"They're not out celebrating Valentine's Day?"

"They've been married forever, and Mom's got classes in the morning. They probably got each other a card and ordered a pizza." Despite having conceived five children, my parents weren't exactly romantic, at least not in the traditional sense. They were too busy for poetry and picnics in the park, and too budget-constrained to splurge on expensive gifts for each other. Theirs was a solid but practical kind of love, expressed through laundry services, mowed lawns, and shared laughs.

Seth eyed me. "Think we'll take each other for granted like that someday?"

I slid him a smile. "If we're lucky."

We made our way to the elevator, rode down to the ground floor, and headed out to the parking lot, where we loaded our furry partners into his seventies-era blue Nova with orange flames down the sides. We aimed for my parents' house in Arlington Heights, an older neighborhood in Fort Worth where both I and popular folk singer John Denver had graduated from high school, though he'd preceded me by approximately five decades and had later escaped the brutal Texas summers by moving to Colorado. My parents' three-bedroom, two-bath wood-frame house could use a fresh coat of paint, but no matter how many times my father looked at the house and commented that he needed to go to the hardware store for painting supplies, he always forgot about the task once he'd crossed the threshold.

I used my key to unlock the front door, and Brigit and Blast trotted in ahead of us humans. As usual, they headed straight for the kitchen, hoping to steal what remained in the bowl of kitty kibble my mother maintained for her three indistinguishable orange tabby cats.

The dogs having cued a greeting, my dad appeared in the kitchen doorway. Thanks to his Latino heritage, my father had dark hair and warm brown skin, both of which he'd passed on to me. Thanks to time, his hair bore some silver streaks, more with each passing year. "Hey, you two," he said. "There's leftover pizza if you want any."

Seth and I exchanged a knowing glance.

"Thanks," I said. "But we've already eaten."

We entered the kitchen to find the dogs with their heads shoved into the cat bowl, and my mother and my sister Gabby at the table with their homework spread out in front of them. Gabby clutched a handful of her dark hair as she struggled with pre-calculus. My red-haired, Irish-American mother was elbow deep in books on the Great Depression, working on a history paper for one of her college courses. She'd recently returned to school after taking a break of nearly three decades. She was living proof that it's never too late to achieve your dreams and go after your goals.

While the two still had a way to go on their schoolwork, they'd made quick work of a large heart-shaped box of chocolates. Only three pieces remained, and two of those had small bites taken out of them. Rejects.

I reached out with my left hand, turning it to and fro to catch the light from the fixture over the table, and grabbed the last remaining intact piece of chocolate. Neither my mother nor my sister noticed my ring. *Good thing they aren't aspiring detectives.* I took a bite of the candy.

Dark chocolate-covered coconut. Yum! I eyed my sister. "Is this candy from T.J.?"

"Don't ever mention that name again!" Gabby broke down into a blubbering mass and bolted from the room.

Apparently, my question had been a wrong one to ask. I looked to my mother for answers.

"Gabby and T.J. broke up today," she said. "He met some girl at a debate tournament and called things off."

So my little sister had been dumped, not only on Valentine's Day, but also on the day I'd gotten engaged. *Talk about bad timing.* "I'll go talk to her." I turned to Seth. "I'll be back in a minute."

Dad pulled open the fridge door. "That'll give us guys a chance to have a beer." He retrieved a couple of bottles of Shiner Bock and handed one to Seth.

I walked down the hall to the room Gabby and I had shared before I left for college. I rapped softly on the door. "Can I come in, Gabs?"

"Only if you promise not to tell me there's more fish in the sea!"

While our mother and father had always tended to the physical needs of my siblings and me, they weren't necessarily the best at responding to our emotional needs. Like many parents, they relied on stale platitudes in an attempt to quickly resolve problems they didn't have time for rather than truly listening and empathizing. That's why, when I'd been frustrated by my childhood stutter, I'd ended up pounding rocks with a hammer on the back patio, why I'd disappeared into books where other children suffered but found creative solutions to their problems, or didn't solve them but learned to live with them. Bibliotherapy had done wonders for me. Still does.

I opened the door, stepped into the room, and closed the door behind me. Though my twin bed remained pushed up against the far wall, the space was all Gabby's now and she'd covered my bed with books and rumpled clothing she'd been too lazy to toss in the hamper. My sister lay facedown on her bed, her pillow over her head. How she was getting air was anyone's guess. I sat down on her bed next to her, and rubbed my hand up and down her back. "I'm sorry, Gabby. Breakups stink."

She spoke into her mattress, her voice muffled. "I thought T.J. really cared about me. I'm so stupid!"

"You're not stupid," I said. "Teenage boys are. You have any idea how many of those idiots I deal with every day?" Between fistfights, vandalism, and car accidents, teen boys kept the Fort Worth Police Department busy, that's for sure.

Gabby rolled onto her back. "T.J. *is* sort of stupid. He stayed up all night playing Fortnite a few weeks ago, and then he overslept and missed most of his shift at work. They wrote him up and said if he was late again he'd be fired."

"See?" I said. "Total moron." *I'll be in trouble for that statement if they reconcile.*

She pushed herself up and clutched the pillow to her chest like a security blanket. She turned her red-rimmed eyes on me. "When do boys stop being stupid?"

"It takes a long time," I told her. Seth had been stupid, too, near the beginning of our relationship. Thanks to a father he'd never known and his young mother abandoning him with her parents when he was a child, he suffered severe attachment issues. When he'd developed serious feelings for me, he'd felt vulnerable and called things off. I'd been stunned and heartbroken. Of course, he'd later grown a pair, faced his feelings, and come crawling back with his tail between his legs. In the meantime, I'd had some fun with a sexy mounted sheriff's deputy who rode a black horse named Jack. I reminded Gabby of the incident.

"But Seth didn't dump you for someone else," she said. "Besides, he came to his senses and begged you to forgive him."

"True. But if he hadn't, I would've had some fun seeing who else was out there." Okay, so that was just a variation of "there's more fish in the sea," but at least I'd added a personal anecdote. "You'll want to be free once you head off to college, anyway," I added. "You'll meet a cute boy every time you turn around. You'll have way more fun if you're not stuck in a relationship."

Her face brightened at the thought. She sniffled and blinked to dry her eyes. She reached out a hand to take mine and give it a squeeze. "You'll be a really good mom someday."

Her words warmed my heart. "I hope so."

As she moved to retract her hand, her fingers brushed my engagement ring. She looked down, spotted the diamond, and sat bolt upright on the bed, her eyes wide and mouth gaping, T.J. and his betrayal promptly forgotten. "You're engaged? Since when?"

"Since twenty-three minutes ago. Want to help me plan the wedding?"

"For sure!" Fueled by a renewed faith in romance and a fresh sense of purpose, she bounced out of bed and bounded to the door, yanking it open to holler down the hallway. "Mom! Dad! Megan and Seth got engaged!"

I followed her as she sprinted to the kitchen.

Raising his beer in tribute, Dad put his other hand on Seth's shoulder. "Welcome to the family, Seth. You'll be the son I never had."

Dad seemed to have forgotten an important fact. "You've already got three sons," I reminded him.

"I know," he said. "But none of them are handy like Seth is."

It was true. Seth might not have received a lot of encouragement or affection from his grandfather, but at least the old coot had passed on his aptitude for fixing things.

My mother stood, a big smile on her face. She gave me a hug before embracing Seth, too. "I'm so happy for you two!"

As the news sunk in, though, her smile faltered and she bit her lip. I suspected I knew why. With two of their sons and my mother in college, my parents had no spare funds to pay for a wedding, fancy or otherwise.

"Don't worry," I told her. "We're going to have a simple ceremony and reception. Nothing big and expensive. Besides, we're adults with jobs. We'll pay for it ourselves."

Seth slid me some side-eye. "We will?"

The grin tugging at his lips made it clear he'd been merely teasing, but I elbowed him gently in the ribs anyway. Might as well start this engagement off letting him know who's boss. "Of course we will."

My dad looked from me to Seth. "Mom and I can scrape together something to help out. Maybe cover the flowers and the cake?"

"That would be perfect." I leaned in and gave my father a kiss on the cheek. "You'll give me away, won't you?"

"Heck, yeah," he said. "I've been trying to get rid of you for years."

I knew better. I'd seen his eyes grow misty when Gabby had dropped the news of my engagement.

Mom pulled out her planner and opened it, uncapping a pen. She'd never been very organized, but returning to school had forced her to develop better habits. She held her pen poised over the notebook. "What date are you planning on?"

"We haven't gotten that far yet." I'd been engaged less than an hour. *Sheesh*. I glanced over at Seth. "Maybe early fall?"

Seth shrugged. "Or we could just go down to the courthouse tomorrow."

I'd never been the type of girl who dreamed about her wedding day but, still, I wanted my family and friends to share in the celebration. Besides, the courthouse was where people got divorced, or arraigned, or sentenced, or summoned to serve jury duty. It wasn't exactly a romantic place. "You know that's not happening, right?"

"It was worth a shot."

My mom closed her planner and recapped her pen. "We don't need a date to start looking at wedding gowns and mother-of-the-bride dresses. Why don't we start first thing Saturday morning?"

"Works for me."

Gabby chimed in, "Me, too."

After another round of hugs and amid death glares from my mother's cats, Seth and I departed and headed back to my place. I was dying to tell my roommate Frankie the exciting news, but unfortunately she was out on a date with her boyfriend Zach. Only her cat, Zoe, was home at the moment and, while I adored the sassy little beast, sharing the news with my feline housemate would not be the same as sharing it with my human one. The fluffy calico met me, Seth, and the dogs at the door with an insistent "meow?", demanding to know where we'd been and why we weren't petting her already. I gave her a scratch under the chin and a "Hey, girl," before stepping inside.

In the living room, Seth pulled me to him for a soft warm, kiss that was clearly a prelude to something more. Unfortunately, that kiss was rudely interrupted by my phone blaring the "Pink Panther" theme song. It was my special ringtone for detectives Audrey Jackson and Hector Bustamente, two of the investigators from my station.

Seth groaned as I gently pushed him away. "Ignore it. You're not on duty tonight."

"Not officially." But as a K-9 team with a special set of skills, Brigit and I could be called at any time to assist in police matters. Besides, the detectives had taken me under their wings and taught me lots of invaluable investigation techniques. I'd never blow them off if they needed me. I reached into my purse and retrieved my phone. The screen indicated it was Detective Jackson calling. I touched the icon to accept the call. "Hello, Detective."

Her voice was barely more than a whisper. "I'm at a crime scene. A grisly one. Can you and Brigit get over here?"

So much for basking in the glow of my engagement. "Of course. Where are you?" I slid my hand into my purse and rummaged around for a pen and notepad. As Detective Jackson rattled off the address, I scribbled it down. "Got it. I'll be there ASAP."

Seth groaned again as I ended the call. "What is it this time?"

"The detective used the word 'grisly.'"

"A murder then?"

"Most likely."

He sighed. "I should've realized what I was getting myself into when I fell for an aspiring detective."

"Right back at you."

Seth was not only a firefighter, but also a member of the city's bomb squad. Blast was an explosives detection dog. Like Brigit and me, Seth and Blast could be summoned any time there was an explosion or bomb threat. Being continuously on call was an occupational hazard we both faced.

I leaned in and finished our kiss. Not to be crass, but if someone had been killed, they weren't going to be any less dead if I took four seconds to kiss my fiancé one final time.

When I pulled back, Seth reached for the doorknob. "Go get 'em, girls."

As he left, I ran to my bedroom and changed into my uniform at warp speed. Brigit and I were back out the door in two minutes flat and climbed into our specially designed K-9 squad car, me in the front and Brigit in her carpeted enclosure behind me. I nearly backed into Frankie and Zach as I reversed out of the driveway. I pulled my cruiser up next to them in the street, and Zach unrolled his window. Frankie leaned over from the passenger seat, putting her head next to his, her bright blue hair a contrast to his dark military cut. Though Zach had been a paratrooper in the army and served in Afghanistan like Seth, the two hadn't met overseas. Rather, they'd been introduced when serving reserve duty at the joint base on the west side of town. Seth and I had set Zach and Frankie up, and our matchmaking attempt had proven quite successful.

"Where are you going?" Frankie called. "We were hoping you and Seth might want to hang out and watch a movie with us."

"Detective Jackson called me and Brigit in."

"Say no more," she said, waving us off. She knew time was of the essence if Brigit and I had been summoned when we were supposed to be off duty. "We'll catch up later."

By then, I'd have even more than my engagement to catch her up on, though girl talk and a grisly crime would make an odd combination of topics. I could only wonder what, exactly, I'd have to tell her about the investigation Detective Jackson had summoned me to. The term "grisly" could cover a lot of ground. Smashed skulls. Gaping exit wounds. Severed limbs. *Eek.* Every cell in my body squirmed at that last thought.

My furry partner and I headed off, and a mere five minutes later we turned onto May Street, the siren silent on our cruiser but the lights flashing. Like many of the neighborhoods in my south-central beat, the area comprised a mix of older houses in need of work, charming renovated homes, and new construction built on the proverbial gravesites of older residences that had been neglected too long to be economically updated and instead had been razed. Though it was too dark for me to easily read the house numbers, I didn't need to look at the address I'd jotted down to tell which house Detective Jackson had called from. The yard was cordoned off with yellow crime scene tape. A Hyundai Kona SUV sat in the driveway beside a red Ford Fusion sedan. A Fort Worth PD cruiser, Detective Jackson's unmarked sedan, and a crime scene van were parked at the curb.

After making a U-turn at the next intersection, I eased my squad car into the lineup, retrieved Brigit from the back, and attached her lead. As I turned my attention to the house and my eyes adjusted to the limited outdoor lighting, I could see the place was one of the renovated structures, a single-story house sporting a coat of paint that bordered the line between yellow and green, like the inside of a not-quite-ripe avocado. While the trim bore classic white paint, the door was painted an attractive, contrasting bright red.

My former partner, Derek "The Big Dick" Mackey, stood on the sidewalk just outside the cordon tape, a clipboard in his hand. Looked like he'd been assigned the task of maintaining the scene, documenting those who moved in and out of the perimeter. Derek had red hair, bulging muscles, and big cojones, at least in the metaphorical sense. I had no idea how big his boys were in actuality, and I had no interest in finding out. Once upon a time, I'd used my Taser to send a well-deserved jolt of electricity to his groin region. The lewd bastard had made one crude joke too many and I'd lost my cool. Luckily for me, while my use of my Taser on my partner was grounds for dismissal, so was Derek's unprofessional language. Derek was buddy-buddy with the chief, and the chief didn't want to see his golden boy lose his job, so he'd had no choice but to let my offense slide, too. He'd reassigned me to work with Brigit. Though I'd resisted at first, sure the dog would be a burden, I'd soon learned she was the best partner an officer could ask for. She was hardworking and incredibly intelligent. While she was a sweet pet off the job, on duty she could summon her inner wolf to convince a suspect to quickly surrender. She'd saved me time, energy, and even my life.

Derek scoffed and smirked. "Well, well," he said, his breath creating a fog in the cold night air. "If it isn't the hairy bitch and her dog."

Thanks to a recent waxing at the salon, I was only as hairy as I was supposed to be and, frankly, being called a bitch by The Big Dick was an indirect compliment. It meant he considered me formidable. I didn't bother to greet him, just gestured for him to hand me the clipboard so I could sign myself and Brigit in.

"It's a bloodbath in there," he said. "Someone must've got their throat slit from ear to ear. Probably looked like a Pez candy dispenser when it was all over." He ran his index finger across his throat and threw his head back, imitating the device.

Though his creepy description caused fresh dread to slither up my spine, I ignored him once more. He was trying to psych me out. *Jerk.* Besides, from the way he'd phrased things, it sounded like he hadn't got a good look at the victim or victims. Rather than the usual blue paper booties made to prevent officers from contaminating a crime scene, Derek handed me a white pair made of heavy-duty impermeable Tyvek intended to protect the wearer from biohazards. *Not a good sign.*

I slid the booties on over my tactical shoes and wagged my fingers. "Give me four for Brigit."

Derek handed me four more booties. I slid them over Brigit's paws, securing them with short stretches of cordon tape I laced around the tops. When I finished, the dog resembled an Old West saloon girl wearing thigh-high stockings. She didn't seem to like the feel, and lifted her paws up and down in an awkward prance, but at least she didn't use her teeth to try to pull them off. I lifted the cordon tape and ducked under it, leading my partner along with me.

As Brigit and I approached the house, Detective Jackson opened the front door and stepped out onto the porch to brief me. She wore a navy pantsuit paired with a cream-colored turtleneck, professional yet utilitarian attire. Her usual perky braids were gone tonight, her hair instead left natural, framing her face in loose black curls. As one of the few female detectives in the department, she served as a role model for me. She was also a mentor, having pulled me into earlier investigations once she learned that I hoped to become a detective one day and she realized how determined and hardworking I was.

While my eyes went straight to a small, jagged crack in the front window-pane, her eyes apparently went straight to my ring. "You're engaged," she said, keeping her voice low.

Leave it to the eagle-eyed detective to notice. I shifted my gaze to meet hers. "As of an hour ago."

"Then I should apologize for my timing."

"Not necessary." After all, she was not the one who chose tonight to commit a heinous crime.

"It's ugly in there," she warned, getting down to business and giving me a pointed look that told me to prepare myself. "Blood everywhere. Try not to step in it."

I swallowed the lump in my throat and squeaked, "How many victims are there and how do they look?" Knowing what to expect would make it would be easier to cope when I saw the body or bodies.

"Your guess is as good as mine."

Huh? "I don't understand."

"The amount of blood tells me it must have come from more than one person. But as for victims? Whoever they were, they're gone now."

"Gone?" I repeated. "What do you mean?"

"There's no bodies. A married couple lives here, Shelby and Greg Olsen. The wife came home from having dinner and drinks with her single coworkers and found the kitchen covered in blood. Her husband's cell phone and wallet were lying on the floor. Both he and his car are missing. It's an older-model Volkswagen Jetta. No OnStar service. They bought it used for cash."

In other words, there was no tracking device placed in

the car by a lender intent on monitoring the location of its collateral, no immediate way to locate the car.

Jackson exhaled sharply. "I've sent out an alert to all departments in North Texas to be on the lookout for the vehicle. With any luck, someone will spot it."

It seemed odd a married couple wouldn't spend Valentine's Day together. A happily married couple, anyway. Could the two have been having problems? Often, when a person was killed, especially in their own home, the culprit was the spouse or another family member who resided with them. "The couple didn't celebrate Valentine's Day together?"

"No," Jackson said. "Mr. Olsen is an assistant manager at a movie theater. Since Valentine's is a big date night, he had to work this evening. That's why Shelby went out without him. He texted her an hour ago to let her know he was heading home. That's the last she heard from him. Shelby's coworker, Regina, followed her home. Regina was going to pet sit while the Olsens took a trip to Fredericksburg this weekend."

Fredericksburg was a quaint town in the Texas hill country, known for its scenery, wineries, and charming bed-and-breakfast accommodations. The town would provide the perfect romantic getaway for a couple who'd been forced to postpone their Valentine's Day celebration.

The detective went on. "Shelby was going to introduce Regina to the dog tonight and show her what to do. But when they came inside, they found the kitchen covered in blood."

"So Mrs. Olsen was with other people all day?"

"She says she arrived at the office around eight thirty, ate her lunch in the break room, and was with coworkers from the time she left work until now. Regina is still in there with her."

"Could it be a burglary gone awry?" Burglars sometimes became killers when they were caught in the act and panicked.

"Again," Jackson said, "your guess is as good as mine. The only things Shelby has noticed missing are her husband's green winter coat and her own purple hat and scarf. They were all hanging on a coat rack inside. My guess is the attackers might have taken them to cover up the fact that their clothes were covered in blood. Shelby says Greg often makes the cash deposits for the movie theater. I spoke by phone with the other manager on duty tonight. He confirmed Greg made a deposit of around twelve-hundred dollars late this afternoon. It's possible Greg was targeted because he has access to the theater's safe. Shelby said he mentioned a couple of weeks ago that he thought he might have been followed from the theater to the bank, but he couldn't be sure. He didn't give her any details about the car or who was in it. The other manager working tonight said Greg mentioned the incident to the general manager, too, but said only that it was a silver or gray vehicle. He didn't get the make or model, or a good look at who was inside."

"You think whoever came here planned to force Greg back to the theater after it closed to swipe the cash?"

"Exactly. Of course it's just a theory at this point. Greg has no history of violence. For now, we're operating on the assumption that he was the victim, not the perpetrator. We'll have to run labs on the blood to know for sure. We've got officers stationed inside the theater in case anyone shows up to rob the place, but if that was the original plan my guess is they won't go through with it. Anyone with a half a brain would realize that we'd be on to them."

True. But a lot of criminals were like the scarecrow from *The Wizard of Oz*. No brain at all. At this point, it seemed the only thing that we could conclude for certain was that Mrs. Olsen didn't kill her husband. Not herself, anyway. There was always the chance she'd hired someone to do it, or that someone with an interest in seeing Mr. Olsen meet his maker had taken it upon themselves to do the dirty deed.

Jackson went on. "We need to figure out what happened in there, where whoever was in that kitchen went after they left the house."

That was the detective's cue for us to go inside and see if we could trail from the crime scene to the escape route. Of course, by "us" I really meant Brigit. Her nose was an incredible tool. I was merely along for the ride, to interpret her signals and make sure she didn't inadvertently follow a trail across a busy street or into a dangerous situation. Yep, while I was referred to as her handler, I was really more of her sidekick and caretaker.

Detective Jackson turned to open the door, and I held tight to Brigit's leash, keeping her close by my side. We followed the detective into a boxy foyer. A wide, open doorway sat to the left. A temporary plastic curtain had been affixed to the doorway to shield the room from view. The curtain swung forward slightly as we closed the front door, creating a gap that gave me a glimpse into the living room before it fell back into place. A heavy brass coat tree had fallen over onto the floor, one of its hooks causing the break I'd seen in the front window. Beyond the coat tree, a crime scene technician crouched with a flashlight to search for evidence on the floor, which was hardwood and dotted with faint, bloody paw prints.

Jackson motioned for me to follow her down the hallway to the right, which led to the bedrooms. As was routine procedure, she'd moved witnesses out of the primary crime scene to prevent them from further contaminating the evidence.

The door to the first bedroom was open. A number of cardboard boxes were stacked in the back corner, all of them marked with the words GUEST ROOM. The bedroom was spare and unadorned, the only furniture a queen-sized bed covered by a colorful crocheted afghan and a short, empty bookcase. A full-figured, thirtyish Latina sat on the edge of the bed. I took her to be Regina. Her arm was draped over the shoulders of a tall, willowy woman with silky-straight strawberry blond hair. The woman's face was blotchy and tear-stained, much like Gabby's had been only minutes before. I pegged her as Shelby Olsen. Shelby looked to be in her late thirties, slightly older than her coworker. She wore black heels with a black pencil skirt and a fitted pink sweater, stylish office attire. She clutched both her cell phone and a French bulldog, and stared down at the floor in front of her as if in a daze. When the dog spotted Brigit, she wagged her tail, raised her smushed snout, and issued a friendly greeting: *Yip-yip!*

Brigit, who'd been trained to ignore such distractions when on duty, cast a quick glance the dog's way, offered one side-to-side swish of her tail so as not to be rude, and looked up at me, awaiting instruction. Shelby Olsen looked up at me, too, her blue eyes wide with worry.

Detective Jackson stepped over to the woman and gave a quick introduction. "Mrs. Olsen, this is Officer Megan Luz and her K-9 Brigit. They're going to see if they can trail from the kitchen and determine where whoever was in there went next. Okay?"

Shelby nodded. I didn't bother with a direct greeting and neither did she. There was no need for formalities in this horrific situation, and the sooner Brigit and I got to work, the sooner Detective Jackson could figure out what had happened here.

The detective escorted me back down the hall and past the curtain, where she gestured to another wide doorway at the rear of the living room. Through it, I could see into the nicely renovated kitchen. The countertops were white quartz with gray-blue streaks running through them, the backsplash was a busy blue-and-gray mosaic tile, and the floors were durable vinyl plank in pale gray arranged in a herringbone pattern. But the stylish remodel job was overshadowed by the fact that every single surface seemed to sport splashes, puddles, or pools of blood.

Shortening Brigit's leash to keep her right by my side, I led her through the living room. The Olsens had an inordinate number of framed photographs on their walls and bookshelves, their smiling faces amid ever-changing backdrops evidencing many happy times spent together in a variety of vacation locales. They'd posed in front of the Cloud Gate sculpture in Chicago, commonly known as "The Bean." In front of the fountains at the Bellagio Hotel and Casino in Las Vegas. At the rim of the Grand Canyon. While Shelby's straight, strawberry-blonde hair gave her a distinctive look, her husband had no especially distinguishing features. Average height, average build, average looking with a clean-shaven face and medium brown hair. By all appearances, the two were living the happily-ever-after every couple hopes for. Shelby was already distraught, but I could only imagine the inconsolable grief she'd feel once this initial shock wore off. Seth and I had only just become engaged, but already I couldn't imagine my life without him. I didn't even want to think how I'd feel if he'd been senselessly and violently taken from me.

I continued to the kitchen threshold and stopped to take a closer look. Up close like this, I could see the term "bloodbath" had been an understatement. My leg bones seemed to melt as I took in the image, and I had to put an arm on the door jamb to support myself.

The room looked like a lesson in forensics, displaying every type of bloodstain pattern possible. Impact angles with spear-shaped ends and tails that showed the direction in which the blood was traveling at the moment of impact. Cast-off patterns with round spots becoming increasingly oval-shaped as they traveled in a line, showing where blood was cast off from a swinging object, in this case most likely a sharp instrument used to stab Greg Olsen. Contact patterns where a bloody object, such as a shoe, came in contact with an otherwise unstained surface. A dotted line of blood drops marking the path a bleeding person or an object dripping blood took across a room. The most disturbing pattern however, was the one on the far wall near the table. The large volume of blood surrounded by flow patterns, radial spikes, and droplets indicated a high-pressure arterial spurt, very likely from a slit throat. The thought brought my hand reflexively to my neck as I swallowed hard, not wanting to imagine what it was like to suffer such an injury.

The blood displayed various degrees of viscosity. Some of the thin spatter on the walls, refrigerator, stove, and dishwasher had dried completely. Other spots on flat surfaces had dried around the edges, but remained wet in the center, forming miniature domes due to surface tension. The various puddles and patterns were designated with numbered plastic evidence markers, thirty-seven in all. Given the volume of blood, I reached the same conclusion Jackson had, that the blood must have come from more than one source.

A cell phone lay in one of the puddles, its screen shattered. Beside it lay an open wallet. The corners of a couple of one-dollar bills peeked out from the cash compartment. Two plastic cards were nestled into the card slots. The face of a smiling but otherwise unremarkable man with brown hair peered out from a driver's license tucked behind the clear plastic window. His eyes seemed to lock on mine. My stomach squirmed as if trying to hide behind another organ and my vertebrae turned from bone into ice cubes.

The fallen phone, wallet, and blood spatter told a tragic tale, a sad, sickening story involving a sharp blade plunged repeatedly into a human body during a wild struggle. The footprints and paw prints on the floor told a story, too.

Around the perimeter of the puddles and angling to the door that led to the garage were footprints indicative of women's high heels. The sole under the ball of the foot formed a triangular shape, while the tips of the heels left small dots a few inches behind. Two of the triangles were elongated, telling me that Shelby's feet had slipped in the blood. Footprints facing in the opposite direction led out of the kitchen, fading with the distance as the blood wore off the sole of the shoe. The pattern told me that Mrs. Olsen had entered the kitchen, run to the door to look in the garage for her husband or his car, and returned to the living room when she failed to find him.

Other footprints appeared around the kitchen, too, despite the fact that someone had evidently tried to erase them by running a mop over part of the floor and smearing the blood and prints. They seemed to have abandoned the effort mid-task, either realizing it was futile or panicking and wanting to leave the scene as quickly as possible. The mop leaned against the counter. Judging from the patterns of the remaining footprints, there appeared to be three different sets and, judging from the size, all three likely belonged to men. One set, presumably, was Greg Olsen's. It looked like he'd been outnumbered, two to one. Not a fair fight. But criminals don't care about fairness. Distinct bloody paw prints appeared all around the kitchen, the little bulldog having run rampant through the crime scene. I wondered what the dog had witnessed here, wished she could tell me, felt glad her life had been spared.

My gaze moved about, seeking a weapon among the blood and the numbered plastic evidence markers but spotting none. A single steak knife appeared to be missing from the block on the counter, though, an empty slot evidencing its absence. *Had one of the attackers held Mr. Olsen while the other took the knife to him?* I didn't want to think about it. But I had to. A professional investigator had to face their cases head on, no matter how difficult that might be. There was no room for squeamishness. If I wanted to make detective some day, I'd better get used to it.

The bloody scene was eerily similar to photos taken at the Saint Valentine's Day Massacre in Chicago on February 14, 1929. I'd seen pictures in my criminology textbooks in college, the horror muted only slightly by the fact that the photos were in black and white. Today was the anniversary of that horrific event. In a barbaric act of gang warfare, seven members of the city's Irish North Side Gang, which was led by George "Bugs" Moran, were lined up against a wall and mowed down by Thomson submachine guns. Al Capone, who led the South Side Italian crime syndicate, was suspected of orchestrating the executions as part of a ploy to control the profitable but illegal gambling, prostitution, and bootlegging trades

in the city during the days of Prohibition. The only sur-
vivor of the shootings was a dog named Highball, who
was visibly shaken at the violence he'd witnessed. This
scene, too, was nothing short of a bloodbath, a modern-
day Saint Valentine's Massacre with a dog, once again, as
the only witness. But while the long-ago crime had never
been solved, I was determined to do whatever I could to
ensure this one would be.

As I stepped into the kitchen, a floral fragrance met my
nose. A dozen red roses in a glass vase sat on the kitchen
table to the right. A white ribbon with red hearts was tied
around the top of the vase. A heart-shaped Mylar balloon floated above it, the shiny surface reading ALWAYS
AND FOREVER. I cringed. *So much for that sentiment.*
Shelby's husband must have brought the roses home for
her. A small pink gift bag adorned with tissue paper sat
on the table, too.

A particularly large pool of blood seeped over the edge
of the tabletop, releasing a slow drip onto the floor below.
Had someone approached Greg Olsen from behind and
slashed his throat as he placed the roses on the table?
An open jugular vein would explain the blood spurts that
appeared on the walls and cabinets. Had the men whose
footprints appeared about the kitchen followed him in
from the garage, or might they have already been waiting
in the house?

The technician who'd been collecting blood samples
from the various pools and puddles stepped back to give
my partner and me room to work. I had no way yet of
knowing exactly what had happened here, but whatever
had occurred had been violent and vicious, brutal beyond
belief. Brigit, too, took in the scene, though while I relied predominantly on my eyes to assess the evidence, my
partner relied primarily on her nose. She sniffed at the

blood on the floor in front of us, moving from one puddle to another and back again. She sniffed the puddles on each side of the dishwasher before turning her attention to the one in front of it again, as if comparing scents. Fortunately, she didn't knock over the yellow plastic marker, which identified the puddle as number 23.

Given Brigit's behavior, I suspected that particular pool of blood might have been from a second person, perhaps an attacker. The volume of blood would be typical of multiple victims. Still, even with all three people involved in the incident being potential sources of the blood, the amount splashed about the room seemed extraordinary. Without enough blood, the body couldn't transport oxygen to the brain and other organs, and they'd soon begin to fail. But only time and lab results would give us an accurate body count.

Once Brigit had gotten a good sniff around the room, I issued the order for her to trail. The dog lowered her snout again, inhaling with more purpose now as she searched for the scent trail that would tell her where the people had gone. She led me a few feet in one direction, before going back in the other, probably following the path the killers had taken as they attacked their victim. After performing this improvised two-step, she trotted straight to the door at the back left of the kitchen, which stood ajar. I noticed damage to the drywall behind the door, a tell-tale circle indicating where the doorknob had impacted the wall. Someone had shoved the door open, either to get in or to get out, or had bumped up against it, hard. Someone had also dragged something through the blood, leaving a long smear.

Both the smear and Brigit continued through the door and into the one-car garage, which contained miscellaneous lawn-care tools, a garbage can, a recycling bin, and a member of the crime scene team, who was dusting the wall-mounted door opener for prints. As I followed behind her, Brigit sniffed along in a roughly rectangular pattern, outlining a compact automobile. The smear ended in a still-wet puddle where the trunk of the car presumably would have been. Brigit spent extra time at the back of the garage and on the far side before circling back around and sitting to tell me the last of the trail ended where the driver's door would have been if a car had been parked in the garage.

Just to be sure, I asked the crime scene technician to open the garage door.

"No problem." He pushed the button on the wall with the small end of his fingerprinting brush and the door rambled its way up and over our heads.

I led Brigit over to the open doorway and ordered her to trail, but when she did, she retraced the same rectangular track as before, lingering again where the trunk and passenger doors would have been before returning to the driver's side of the car. Her behavior told me that whoever had been in the Olsens' kitchen had left via a car that had been parked in this garage, and that the person or persons had spent some time at the rear of the car and the passenger door. The fact that Brigit had lingered in those areas told me the scent was stronger in those specific spots.

I bent down, looked my partner in the eye, and praised her performance. "Good girl!" Knowing she'd expect payment for her services, I reached into my pocket and pulled out three liver treats, feeding them to her one by one.

My partner and I went back into the house. Detective Jackson motioned for me to follow her to the corner of the kitchen to give my report privately.

We huddled in the corner and I filled her in. "Whoever

was in this kitchen left in a car that had been parked in the garage." I told her how Brigit had paused where the trunk and passenger doors would have presumably been, assuming the car hadn't been backed into the space.

Jackson thought aloud. "So the people who'd been in the kitchen put something in the trunk and one of them climbed into the passenger seat and one into the driver's seat."

"Looks that way."

As far as the "something" that might have been put into the trunk, my gut and the smear pattern told me the some*thing* was most likely a some*one*. I still wasn't sure what had happened here, but one thing was certain. Cupid wasn't to blame for what had happened. It would take more than an arrow to cause this amount of carnage.

THREE
MAKING SENSE OF THE SCENTS

Brigit

The kitchen had been an interesting place to explore. There'd been blood all over. Brigit knew what blood was. In her time working with Megan, they'd come across blood at some of the crime scenes. She'd smelled blood on dead squirrels and frogs she'd rolled on, too. Most of the blood here smelled the same, but one puddle smelled different from the others. She could scent the smells of three people in the kitchen and the garage. One of the smells was very strong. The same smell seemed to be in the living room and hallway, though more faint. That person must live here. The smells of the other two people she scented were very weak, but she could still distinguish them. Her nose told her that the little dog had been in the kitchen, had run through the blood on the floor. Her nose also told her that there was a box of peanut butter-flavored doggie treats in the pantry. She'd been tempted to paw at the door to see if Megan might give her one, but she knew better than to mix business with pleasure. She was on duty now, and she had to stay on task.

Part of Brigit envied the tiny beast. Brigit was too big to fit nicely on Megan's lap. She'd tried several times without success. But being able to curl up on a person's lap is where Brigit's envy ended. The poor thing had a smushed snout rather than a nice long one like Brigit. A flat nose like that wouldn't be much use in scenting. But she supposed it didn't much matter. The dog seemed to serve the same purpose as a toy. Whether she could scent well wouldn't much matter. Yep, all in all, Brigit was happy being a big, furry working dog.

The fact that her partner had already paid her in liver treats told Brigit that she'd completed the tasks she'd been brought here to perform. Still, Brigit stood dutifully beside Megan just in case her partner needed her again. She wished she could get out of these weird booties, though. They felt strange on her feet and legs.

FOUR
SLASH AND SPLASH

The Slasher

He had to ditch the car. *Quick.* By now, law enforcement would be looking for the black Jetta. If he was caught driving it, he and his partner in crime could face prosecution and serious prison time.

He turned into Marion Sansom Park, which sat in the northwest part of the city and bordered Lake Worth. The sign at the entrance stated that the park was open from dawn until dusk, but he ignored it, driving down the entrance road in the darkness. He kept the headlights off so as not to draw attention to himself, only a small flashlight stuck out the open window to show him the way.

The park was hilly, rugged, and craggy with scrubby trees and brush. Serious mountain bikers came here to ride the challenging trails, which had names like Thunder Road, Gangster, Lone Wolf, and Rocket Loop. The trail he sought was known as the Dam Drop. The trail flanked the tall concrete structure that held back the waters of the west fork of the Trinity River, forming Lake Worth.

When he reached the parking lot, he looked around for the trailhead and drove onto it, the tines of the prickly pear cactus and the limbs of the scrubby mesquite and cedar trees scratching along the sides of the car. At one point, the car got hung up on a small outcropping of limestone, but he managed to rock it free.

When the trail narrowed too far for him to proceed any farther, he cut the engine. He ripped open a small foil packet containing a pre-moistened wipe and cleaned the steering wheel, gear shift, and door handles. He pulled up on the trunk release, and the back opened with a pop. He wiped the trunk release clean, then tucked the wipe in the front pocket of his pants.

He grabbed the trash bag of bloody shoes and clothing from the passenger seat, and headed to the dam overlook on foot, being careful not to overstep. He hurled the shoes and clothing over, sending them as far out into the water as possible. Scurrying back to the car, he raised the trunk lid and wrangled with the heavy, incriminating contents, dragging it down the trail, too. Pulling the steak knife from his pocket, he gutted the evidence, letting it fall into the lake below where it would become food for fish, a tasty treat for turtles. He followed it with the car keys, listening until he heard a satisfying *splash*.

Relief washed over him as he hurried back down the trail on foot, the beam of his flashlight bouncing. In minutes he was out of the park, striding past the entrance to Camp Carter, a YMCA facility where local youngsters attended summer camp. He passed the Carswell Federal Medical Center, a minimum security healthcare facility for female inmates, taking deep breaths in an attempt to calm himself. Another mile and he was back in civilization. He passed a bus stop, but kept on going. He knew the city buses had security cameras. He also knew that once the car was found, the police might assume the killers had caught a ride at the nearest bus stop. They might review the footage from the bus cameras. He continued walking for a couple more miles before approaching a stop where three women awaited a ride. They were probably employees of the stores in the nearby strip mall that had just closed up for the night.

He kept his face down, looking at his phone, avoiding eye contact. He didn't want to risk any of the women getting a good look at his face and being able to identify him later. He needn't have worried. They, too, stared down at their screens. Nothing short of a nuclear explosion would have gotten their attention.

His respiration and heart rate began to slow as realization sunk in. *We've gotten away with murder.*

FIVE
BLOOD, SWEAT, AND TEARS

Megan

"Mind sticking around?" Detective Jackson asked me. "Can't hurt to have another set of eyes and ears on the case."

"Of course." She didn't have to ask me twice. The opportunity to watch her in action, to see a murder investigation unfold, wasn't one that came along often. It would be a great, if grim, learning opportunity for me.

We stopped at the curtain to remove our booties and dropped them into the trash bag the crime tech held out to us. Brigit danced a little jig, glad to be bare pawed again.

The three of us returned to the guest room, where Jackson returned her attention to Shelby. "I'd like to interview you alone. Would it be all right if we sent Regina on her way?"

Shelby nodded, and the other woman rose from the bed. "If you need somewhere to stay tonight," Regina told her, "call me. You're welcome to sleep at my place. I can come back and pick you up if you want. You can bring Marseille, too."

Marseille must be the dog's name.

Shelby looked up at her friend. "Thanks, Regina."

I walked the woman to the door, advising her to stay on the paved pathway out front and to check out with Derek. "Don't tell anyone the details of what you saw in the house," I warned. "It could jeopardize our investigation."

"Can I call our boss?" Regina asked. "She'd want to know that Greg's missing. Some of Shelby's work will need to be reassigned if she doesn't make it into the office tomorrow."

It was only fair to give their boss a heads-up so she could shift any time-sensitive matters to another staff member. "That will be fine. Just no specifics. She's an attorney, right? She'll understand why we have to be cautious in legal matters like this."

Once I was back in the guest room, Detective Jackson addressed Shelby. "It would help if we could identify the shoeprints in the kitchen, determine if any of them belong to your husband. Can we see his other shoes?"

"Of course." Shelby stood, still holding tight to her phone and cradling the dog. She tilted her head to wipe an escaped tear off the shoulder of her pink sweater.

She led the way down the hall, the detective and I following her. We passed a small bathroom and another bedroom that had been turned into a media room. A thick, light-blocking curtain covered the window. A big-screen TV took up most of one wall. Two recliners fitted with swivel trays and cup holders faced the screen. The loose vinyl on the seats said the couple had owned the chairs for some time, watching many a show from them. An assortment of DVDs filled a rack designed specifically for such media. Other racks sat empty, with boxes marked SCORSESE, SPIELBERG, ABRAMS, EASTWOOD, KUBRICK, COPPOLA, and TARANTINO on the floor before them.

The Olsens appeared to own every movie made in the last three decades.

Shelby glanced back and caught me looking into the media room. "Greg studied film at the University of Oklahoma. He's a total movie buff."

Their bedroom at the back of the house featured a king-sized bed with a shiny brass headboard and a whimsical polka-dot comforter. Boxes marked MASTER BEDROOM sat about the perimeter of the room. More candid photos of the couple sat on the night table and dresser, while a decorative piece of metal scrollwork that read ALWAYS AND FOREVER hung above the headboard. Shelby placed the dog and her phone on the bed, and opened the closet door. Like many of these older houses, this one had limited closet space. The rod was crammed tight with clothing, mostly hers from the looks of it. While her shoes resided in a pocketed bag that hung over the closet door, her husband's footwear lay jumbled in the bottom of the closet. Still holding onto her dog, she reached down and matched a pair of tennis shoes before standing and handing them over to Detective Jackson.

The detective turned the shoes upside down and ran her gaze over the soles. I took a look over her shoulder. The wear pattern was typical of someone with moderate pronation, meaning the wearer tended to walk with their weight shifted to the inside of their foot. While the tread was clearly visible on most of the sole, it had been worn flat on the inside ball of the foot.

Jackson pointed down at the floor of the closet. "Mind if I look at the other pairs?"

Shelby sniffled and dabbed at her nose with a tissue she'd pulled from her pocket. "Anything that will help."

Jackson knelt down, and I crouched beside her. She matched another pair of shoes and turned them soles up. While these shoes showed less wear, the pattern was the same. Moderate pronation. Two other pairs confirmed the finding. The detective lifted the tongues on each of the pairs to check the size, and lined the shoes up along the floor with the soles facing up. She rose and I stood, too.

Jackson turned to Shelby. "Wait here until I come back. I'm going to send a tech here to take some photos and bag these shoes. He might have some questions for you."

"Okay."

We headed back to the foyer, where Jackson pulled back the curtain and addressed the crime scene tech with the flashlight. "Get some pics of the shoes in the master bedroom, then bag them as evidence."

"Yes, ma'am."

I ordered Brigit to lie down and stay in the foyer. Detective Jackson and I slid clean booties over our shoes. We returned to the kitchen, where we crouched and compared the wear patterns on the footprints to what we'd seen on Greg Olsen's shoes.

I kept my voice low as I pointed to one of the prints. "The wear pattern on this print is the same as on his shoes." I moved my hand to indicate another. "That one, too."

"Mm-hmm." Jackson stood and turned to address the tech collecting blood samples in the kitchen. "Got a measuring tape?"

The tech opened the plastic toolbox he'd situated inside the pantry where it wouldn't come in contact with the blood. At the bottom of the pantry sat a large bag of fancy dog food, the top rolled over and secured with a clip to keep it fresh. After retrieving a measuring tape, he handed it to the detective. She put a finger under the tab and pulled it out. She measured the most complete print, which was eleven

inches long. "Looks to be a size eleven. That's Greg's size."
Using the tape, she measured the other two sets of prints.
"We've got what look to be a size twelve and a size nine and
a half, too."

"The size twelve has mild supination," I said, noting
the narrow strip of wear on the outer part of the sole.

Jackson stood and called out to the tech. "Process the
wallet. I want to know what's in it."

The tech complied with her order, coming over and
carefully using small tools and tweezers to open the wallet. "There's two singles and one five-dollar bill in the
slot." He used the tweezers to gently pull out the two
cards. One was a debit card. The other was a Visa credit
card.

Jackson turned to me, raised an index finger, and circled it in the air. "What do you make of all of this?"

I looked around. "It looks like the victim put up quite a
fight. It also looks like it could be personal."

Those who killed for non-personal reasons, such as
theft, usually made things easy on themselves, hurting the
victim only as much as was necessary to get what they
came for, or to ensure the victim wouldn't survive to
identify them. A bloodbath like this generally indicated
the attack was personal in nature, rooted in rage at the
victim. Of course, there were exceptions to every rule.
If the attackers had, in fact, targeted Greg Olsen for the
theater's cash, Greg might have fought back harder than
his attackers expected, or he might have injured them in
the brawl, which could have caused matters to escalate.
Until the blood samples were processed, we'd be unable
to tell how many people had lost blood in the altercation,
or extrapolate how badly each of them had been hurt. But
the multitude of footprints indicated the trio had danced
a fairly intricate, and probably murderous, mambo. The

fact that Greg's wallet had been left behind also seemed to indicate that they hadn't come here to take it. Then again, his wallet contained mere chump change. Maybe they'd been furious he'd had such a small amount of cash and made him pay the price with his life, or maybe his wallet had simply fallen out of his pocket as they wrangled.

Jackson angled her head in the general direction of the master bedroom and whispered, "You get any sense that she's involved?"

I tossed the idea around in my mind. Shelby had an alibi. She'd gone straight from work to dinner and drinks with coworkers. She couldn't have killed Greg herself. Sometimes a jealous lover in an extramarital affair did away with their paramour's partner. But there appeared to be at least two attackers here, not just one. Of course, it wasn't unheard of for a husband or wife to hire a hit man to kill their spouse. The contract killers portrayed in movies were expert snipers who could whisk in and out of buildings undetected, as if made of magical vapor and shadows rather than flesh and bone. That kind of hit man rarely existed in real life. In most such situations, hired assassins were bumbling guys named Bubba or Snake found guzzling cheap beer in sleazy dive bars. Their lack of training, planning, skill, and discretion led to many of them being apprehended and charged, along with their clients, for homicide.

I shared my thoughts with the detective. "Think she could have paid someone?"

"Maybe. If we don't get other plausible leads, we'll take a look at their bank accounts, see if there's any evidence she made a large cash withdrawal to pay for a hit. But for now, let's check out their social media." She whipped out her phone.

I followed suit, pulling out my cell phone and searching the woman's name on various social media sites. There were several people named Shelby Olsen, but her strawberry blonde hair was easy to spot in her profile pics. Just as the photographs in their home depicted two people in a happy marriage, so did the posts on Shelby's social media. In fact, some could only be described as sappy, such as the pics of her gazing adoringly at her husband with the caption *How lucky am I to be married to such a great guy? #Always&Forever #ARealLoveStory.* At noon, she'd posted a pic of herself eating lunch in her office break room with the caption *You're never too old for PB&J!* At 5:27, she'd checked in on Facebook at The Library Bar downtown. An hour later, she'd posted a group selfie with her coworkers on both Facebook and Instagram. She'd posted two more pics approximately an hour apart. In one, she and Regina were raising frozen margaritas. In the other, she and another woman held up conversation hearts that read BE MINE and I'M YOURS. In all of the photos, she'd been wearing the same black skirt and pink sweater she still wore.

I thought out loud. "The dog had clearly run through the blood, but there wasn't any of it on Shelby's clothes. Do you think she cleaned the dog's feet before she picked her up?" Having the presence of mind to clean the dog's feet before she picked her up could be a sign that she had known the attack was coming, that she wasn't as flustered by finding her kitchen full of blood as she would've been if it were a complete surprise.

Jackson raised a noncommittal shoulder. "Maybe the dog licked the blood off herself."

Ew. The detective had a point, though. As icky as it might be, it would be natural for the dog to clean her paws.

After we'd taken a good look at Shelby's accounts, we ran searches on the major social media outlets for Greg Olsen. We found nothing. He appeared to have no accounts.

"Let's ask Mrs. Olsen some more questions, see if we can learn anything else." Jackson held out an arm to invite me to return to the couple's bedroom where Shelby was waiting.

Brigit and I took a position just inside the master bedroom door, while the detective pulled a stool from Shelby's dressing table and situated it next to the bed where Shelby sat with Marseille on her lap, her shoulders slumped as if she were trying to curl into a sitting fetal position. Jackson perched on the edge of the stool, leaning toward the woman.

"I'm going to have to ask you some difficult questions, Shelby. Okay?" Detective Jackson reached out and took Shelby's hands in hers in what to the untrained eye would appear to be an act of support and concern. In actuality, it was the detective's way of getting a peek at Shelby's forearms, to see if they bore any defensive injuries to indicate her husband had fought back against her. For all we knew, Regina could be in on things and could have lied to the detective to cover for herself and her friend. Jackson raised her arms a few inches and rolled her wrists slightly, turning Shelby's wrists inward where they would be visible. Shelby's skin was smooth, though, no marks to be seen.

"I don't mean to offend you," Jackson continued, "so please don't take any of my questions personally. Keep in mind that I don't know you or your husband, and that I have to be as thorough as possible so we'll have the best chance of figuring out what happened here and finding Greg." With that, she released Shelby's hands.

Shelby worried her lip between her teeth. "Do you

think Greg was taken for ransom? Do you think whoever took him will call?"

While I could understand the woman wanting to retain some hope, with all the blood we'd seen in the kitchen it seemed questionable whether her husband was still alive. Ransom demands were rare but, then again, so were kidnappings. Most often, attackers left their victims behind and hoped they hadn't also left incriminating evidence. Dealing with an injured person or a corpse was a big burden, and the risk of being caught with a hurt or deceased victim was one most criminals wouldn't take. Besides, judging from their vehicles and their modest home, the Olsens didn't appear to be particularly wealthy people, the type kidnappers would target.

Jackson released a long breath. "It's impossible to know at this point, Shelby. We'll just have to see how things play out."

Shelby nodded and swallowed hard.

Jackson glanced around as if looking for something. "Do you have a landline?"

"No," Shelby said. "We didn't have one installed when we moved in. It didn't seem to be necessary."

"I understand," Jackson said. "If you happen to get a call on your cell phone from your husband, or someone who claims to have your husband, call the department immediately, even if they make threats and tell you not to contact law enforcement. All right?"

Shelby nodded again.

"We'll look into the theater angle," Jackson said, "figure out if your husband might have been targeted for his access to the safe. But we need to consider other potential suspects, too. Is there anyone your husband doesn't get along with? A family member or coworker? A neighbor, maybe?"

"He doesn't have much family," Shelby said. "He's an only child. His father and mother divorced when he was little. His dad never came around much, and his mother passed from cancer three years ago. He hasn't mentioned any problems with coworkers. He would have told me if there were. We've never had any trouble with our neighbors here, either."

"What about friends? Buddies?"

"He hasn't had a chance to make friends here yet. He was just transferred to Fort Worth from Oklahoma City three months ago."

"Is that why you've got all those boxes in your bedrooms?"

"Yes," Shelby said. "We both started our new jobs right away, so we haven't had time to finish unpacking yet."

The detective tried another tack. "What about a customer at the theater? Anyone complain, cause a scene? Did they have to throw somebody out for any reason?"

"If anything like that happened, Greg never mentioned it."

"What about you two? Have you and your husband had any marital issues?"

Shelby looked taken aback. "Me and Greg? No. We get along very well. We've been very happy together."

"Do you two owe anybody money?"

"Not a dime," Shelby said. "We paid off our student loans and our cars years ago. We pay our credit card bill in full every month, and we don't have any other loans."

"Does Greg gamble?"

"No."

"Do you?"

"No."

"Either of you use street drugs?"

Shelby shook her head. "No. Never."

"Engage in any other illegal or risky activities?"

"No."

Jackson went on to ask about Greg's usual routine, and whether he had varied from it recently.

"His work schedule is irregular," Shelby said. "He and the other managers trade off covering evenings and weekends and holidays. He puts in some overtime, too. But when he's not at work, he's usually running errands or at home. He doesn't socialize a lot."

I'd guessed as much from his lack of social media accounts.

"Does he belong to a gym?" Jackson asked. "Or any clubs or organizations?"

"No."

Jackson exhaled slowly. "Is there any chance he could be romantically involved with someone else?"

"No." Shelby shook her head emphatically. "He'd never do that to me."

Don't be so sure about that, I thought. The department received plenty of disturbing-the-peace calls when a shocked wife discovered her husband hadn't been faithful and confronted him about it, often at a hotel or on his mistress's front porch and, just as often, at the top of her lungs.

"All right," Jackson conceded for the time being. "What about you? Are you involved with anyone?"

"No!" Shelby jerked her head back as if the mere insinuation were a slap in the face. "I love Greg. I'd never cheat on him!"

"Understood." Jackson raised her palms in a conciliatory gesture. "Has anyone expressed a romantic interest in either of you? A neighbor or friend? Maybe a coworker who engaged in some harmless flirtation on the job? Anyone seemed jealous?"

"Greg never mentioned anyone, and everyone at my office is very professional."

"So you've never had any issues with anyone there? An argument? Maybe a boss that got too handsy?"

"No," Shelby said.

"Where do you work?"

"Fritz and Winkleman. It's a law firm downtown. I'm an executive assistant to one of the junior partners."

Jackson jotted another note before her gaze traveled the room. "Have there been any signs of anyone trying to break in here recently? Maybe a screen missing, or scratches around a lock?"

"Not that we noticed."

"What about a key?" Jackson asked. "Do you keep one hidden outside somewhere? Maybe a spare somewhere in the garage?"

"No. Our only keys to the house are on our key chains with our car keys."

Jackson gestured around the room. "You two own this place?"

"We're renting."

Jackson readied her pen and notepad. "I'll need your landlord's contact information. I need to find out if they left a key hidden somewhere outside."

Shelby reached over to pick her phone up off the bedspread. Using her thumb, she typed in her password and pulled up her landlord in her contacts list. She held the display out to show Detective Jackson, who jotted down the landlord's name and number.

"Have you had any work done around here lately?" Jackson asked, circling her pen in the air to indicate the house. "Plumbers? Electricians? Lawn guys? Anything along those lines?"

"Our landlord gave us a form to fill out when we

moved in so we could document damage and things that needed repairs. He hired a handyman to fix the things we'd listed on the form."

"What things?"

Shelby looked up in thought. "The outdoor faucet on the back patio. It had a drip. The door to our bedroom was off kilter and wouldn't shut right. Something with the hinges, if I remember right. One of the ceiling fans didn't work. The motor had burned out. The handyman replaced it."

"What about the damage behind the door that leads from the kitchen to the garage?"

Shelby's brow furrowed. "What damage?"

Jackson referenced the damage I'd noted earlier. "It looks like the knob punched through the drywall."

Shelby took a shuddering breath. "I never noticed it before. That must have happened while we were gone today."

"The front window, too?"

"Yeah. That was my first clue that something was wrong. Regina and I noticed it when we were coming inside."

Jackson glanced around the room a second time. "You've got that nice TV in the media room, but do you have any other valuables visible around the house?"

"Like what?"

"Jewelry," Jackson said. "China. Silver. Maybe electronics or guns?"

"I've got a pair of diamond earrings Greg bought me for our tenth anniversary, but the stones are small. He only paid two-hundred dollars for them. We don't have any guns or silver, only everyday china. We've each got a laptop but they're cheap ones and we share a tablet but, other than the TV, that's it as far as electronics."

I noticed she used the term "we" quite a bit, and spoke as if Greg were still alive. These facts could provide further evidence of her innocence. When a person had been involved in the death of someone else, and knew that person was no longer alive, they sometimes inadvertently referred to that person in the past tense.

Jackson asked some follow-up questions in an attempt to determine possible motives for an attack and means of entry, though none of Shelby's responses yielded useful information. When the detective finished, she said, "Okay if I take Greg's laptop with me and have a look, see if there's anything on it that could point to a perpetrator?"

"Of course," Shelby said. "Anything that will help."

"Then you won't mind me taking your computer, too, right?" Jackson said. "It's routine in matters like this to consider anyone close to the victim as a potential suspect."

"I understand," Shelby said. "The sooner you can rule me out, the sooner you can focus on whoever really hurt Greg."

"Exactly. I'll also need something with Greg's DNA on it, maybe a comb with a hair on it or a cup or toothbrush he's used."

Fresh tears welled up in Shelby's eyes. "Our laptops are in the media room." She stood from the bed. Lest Marseille escape the bedroom and run amok through the blood again, I offered to hold the pup while Shelby collected the items for the detective. She handed the dog to me. The little thing was surprisingly heavy for her size. She was like an adorable, bug-eyed anvil. I took advantage of the situation to ask about the dog's paws. "Marseille looks clean. Did you wipe her feet?"

"No," Shelby said. "I didn't think to do it."

Looked like the detective was right, that the dog might have licked her paws clean herself.

Shelby went down the hall to their home theater and returned clutching two laptops to her chest, their tangled cords gripped in her other hand. After laying the computers on the bed, she disappeared into the master bath, emerging with both a comb and a toothbrush in her hand. Jackson called for the crime scene tech to bring an evidence bag. The man who'd been working in the kitchen came to the living room and held an open bag out to Shelby. Her hands shook as she dropped her husband's comb and toothbrush into it. She handed the laptops over, too. He slid the computers into larger plastic bags for safekeeping.

The items secured, Jackson asked, "Do you know your husband's computer password?"

"It's the word 'always' in all caps, followed by the 'and' symbol, the number four, and the word 'ever' in lower case."

ALWAYS&4ever. The same phrase on the balloon in the kitchen and posted on the wall over their bed, though modified to include a special character, a number, and a combination of upper-case and lower-case letters to comply with best practices for passwords. My guts squirmed again. If my fears were correct and Greg Olsen was dead, their "forever" hadn't lasted long.

Jackson jotted the password down on her pad and held it up for Shelby to read and confirm. Shelby looked the notation over and nodded.

"What about his phone?" Jackson asked. "What's his login?"

"Zero four two six zero eight," Shelby said. "April 26th, 2008 was our wedding date."

Jackson jotted that password down, too, as well as Shelby's computer password, before looking up again.

"Where do you and your husband maintain your bank accounts?"

"Chase," she said. "Same as the theater. Greg opened a personal account for us there after he started working for Take Two. It made things more convenient."

"Any chance your husband withdrew money for your upcoming trip?"

"I don't think so," Shelby said. "We normally use our debit or credit cards to pay for things. We don't carry much cash around with us. But I can check on my banking app." She worked her phone again and held it out to show the detective her screen. "There's been no recent withdrawals. See?"

Jackson took the phone, leaned forward to run her eyes over the screen, and reached out a finger to scroll down. From my vantage point, I could see the screen over her shoulder. It showed a current balance of $27,456.89 in the Olsens' checking account. *Not too shabby.* It also showed a list of recent transactions on the Olsens' account. The transactions included payments to their cable provider and the gas company. They'd used their debit cards at Walmart, Target, and several grocery stores, including Kroger, Albertsons, Tom Thumb, and Whole Foods. Dollar stores, too. Quite a number of times, in fact. They must be the type of couple who shopped more frequently rather than stocking up on items.

Jackson murmured in agreement with Shelby. "Mm-hmm. No recent cash withdrawals."

Jackson continued to scroll, looking back through several months' worth of data. I was pretty sure she was taking advantage of the situation to see if there was any evidence of a large cash withdrawal that Shelby might have used to pay a hit man. But rather than a large withdrawal, she noted a sizable deposit. "You got a windfall in early December. Just over thirty grand." She looked up at Shelby for an explanation.

"That was profit from the sale of our house in Okla-homa."

"I see." The detective handed the phone back to Shelby. Sitting back, Jackson asked a final question, one with horrific undertones but one that had to be asked nonethe-less. "Does your husband have any birthmarks or tattoos? Piercings? Scars? Moles?" In other words, did he have anything on his body that would help the police readily identify him if they happened to find a corpse?

Shelby swallowed hard. "He had his appendix removed when he was fourteen. It left a diagonal scar below his belly button." She ran an index finger over the right side of her own abdomen to indicate where the scar would ap-pear on her husband. "He also has an outie."

"Outie?"

"His belly button. It sticks out."

I knew from my forensics classes in college that only around ten percent of the population had belly buttons that protruded outward. That fact could be helpful in identifying Greg's remains, assuming we found them and they weren't too decomposed.

"Anything else?" Jackson asked.

Shelby shook her head.

"That's all my questions for now," the detective said. "I know it can be difficult to remain on site under these circumstances. If you'd like a ride somewhere, Officer Luz would be happy to take you."

"No, thank you," Shelby said. "I want to stay here in case Greg comes back."

There seemed to be little to no chance of her husband returning, but who could blame the woman for wanting to maintain some hope?

Jackson turned her attention to Brigit and me. "Thanks for your help, Officer Luz." She looked down at my partner. "You, too, Brigit."

That was our cue to leave. I turned to Shelby. "Take care, Mrs. Olsen. I'm hoping for the best."

Her lips quivered and her eyes welled with fresh tears. All she could do was nod in acknowledgment.

Brigit and I exited the house, went down the porch steps, and headed over to sign out with Derek. He held the clipboard and pen out to me, but yanked the pen back as I reached for it, smirking at his lame prank. *Jerk*. I pulled a pen from my breast pocket, grabbed the clipboard firmly, and scribbled my name and Brigit's. While I normally let my K-9 partner tell me when she needed to relieve herself, she'd also been taught to urinate on command in case we'd be stuck inside for prolonged periods of time. I gave her a subtle hand signal and she lowered her hindquarters, releasing a puddle around Derek's feet.

He looked down as we headed off, jumped back to get out of the urine, and stamped his feet to clean them. "Damn dog!"

SIX
TRAIL TO NOWHERE

Brigit

Brigit had heard the words "damn dog" before, and she could tell by the tone that the big man who smelled of sweat and onions hadn't liked her pissing on his shoes. But she didn't give a rat's ass. The guy had never been nice to her. Besides, Megan sneaked another liver treat out of her pocket and discreetly fed it to Brigit. The dog knew the treat meant she'd been a "good girl," no matter what the smelly man said, and Megan's opinion was the only one that really mattered to her.

Although Brigit didn't fully understand exactly how she'd helped Megan and Detective Jackson tonight, she was smart enough to know that when she'd tracked her way around the perimeter of the car that was no longer in the garage, it had been helpful to them somehow. She could tell that something bloody had been put in the back of the car, could smell the same blood from the kitchen concentrated in that area, could smell the man whose scent was all over the house and on the computer and comb the woman with the little dog had given to Megan's boss. The icky smell of the automobile exhaust had faded some, but it was still relatively strong. The car hadn't been gone long from the garage. She wondered if Megan would find the bloody car and if she'd get to chase whoever was inside. Brigit liked to take humans down, show them who was really boss.

SEVEN
LYING LOW

The Slasher

He handed the desk clerk the driver's license and the prepaid credit card. He looked down at his phone again while the young Latino man input the information into the hotel's computer system. He didn't want the clerk getting a good look at him, either.

"Is the address on your license current?" the clerk asked.

"Mm-hmm."

"I see you're local," the guy said, a hint of question in his voice as he slid the driver's license across the counter.

Fortunately, the Slasher had anticipated the question and had an excuse at the ready. "Renovating my house. Don't want to live with the noise and dust."

"I don't blame you. I renovated the kitchen in my condo last year and it was a mess."

The clerk ran his credit card through the system and handed it back over the counter along with a key card for his assigned room. "You'll be in two-thirteen. House-keeping comes once a week. There's a continental breakfast in the lobby every day from six to nine. Wifi password is 'welcomehome.' Laundry room is on the ground floor next to the fitness center. If you need anything else, just call down."

"Thanks."

The Slasher slid the key card into his back pocket and the credit card into his wallet. Hiking his backpack up onto his shoulder, he headed to the elevator and rode up to his room on the second floor. The hotel was one of those long-term places you could stay for weeks at a time at a reasonable rate. He planned to hide out here until things settled down and he could safely show his face in public again.

He slid the key card into the slot and the lock released with a click. He stepped inside and closed the door quietly behind him. The room was a bare-bones studio, with a full-sized bed, one nightstand, a table with two chairs that served as both dinette table and desk, one arm chair, and a television. The kitchenette and bath were small, but sufficient for his needs.

After setting his backpack down on the bed, he went to the window and used the stick attached to the thick curtain to move it aside. The room looked out onto the parking lot and the highway frontage road beyond. *Ugh.* He wouldn't have much fun watching traffic going by. Too bad he hadn't thought to ask for a room with a view. But it was too late now. He didn't want to go back down to the desk and make an issue of it, have to show his face again. Besides, if he turned his head to the right and put his face up against the glass, he could just make out the edge of the upper deck of the football stadium at TCU to the east. This room and this view would be his world for the next few weeks. He might as well get used to it.

EIGHT
TAKE IT TO THE BANK

Megan

The morning after Valentine's Day dawned unseasonably warm but overcast, the pleasant temperature and gray sky matching my mixed-up, half-happy and half-somber mood. I'd barely slept last night, both excited about my engagement and also wondering what had happened to Greg Olsen, whether he was recovering from his injuries or giving way to them somewhere.

Frankie shuffled into the kitchen as I poured coffee into my travel mug. Her spiky blue hair stuck up in all directions as she cradled Zoe in her arms. Frankie and I had met quite some time ago, when she'd roller skated in front of my patrol car and I'd nearly run her over. She'd been crying over the boyfriend who'd just dumped her, and her tears and emotion had blurred both her vision and judgment. It was a Code D—damsel in distress. While police protocols provided for the mere issuance of a safety warning in such situations, the implicit code among women dictated that I help her even the score with the man who broke her heart. I'd taken Frankie into my cruiser, driven her home, and prevented the loser ex-boyfriend from taking the television she'd helped pay for. Soon thereafter, I replaced him on their lease. Brigit and I had been living in a tiny studio apartment and needed a bigger home with a yard. Coming across Frankie that day was pure kismet, happy happenstance for both of us, and we'd since become the closest of friends.

She placed Zoe on the counter, along with her food bowl. Not the most sanitary of practices, but the only way to prevent Brigit from stealing the kitty's food. Once Frankie had filled Zoe's bowl with crunchy kibble, she turned her attention to me. "You were out late last night."

I affixed the top to the mug, making sure it was on tight so hot coffee wouldn't spill in my lap as I patrolled my beat. "It was a very unusual crime scene."

Frankie paused at the refrigerator, her hand on the door. "Unusual how?"

"There was enough blood to coat an entire kitchen."

She grimaced, as if picturing the scene. "Yikes."

Yikes, indeed. "There was also no body."

"No body? How could there be no body?"

"That's what we have to figure out." Toying with my roommate, I lifted my mug with my left hand, tilting it to and fro as I raised it to my lips, making sure my ring glinted in the early morning sunlight streaming through the window.

Frankie cast me an odd look at first, no doubt wondering about my strange behavior. But when she spotted the diamond on my ring finger, her face burst into a broad smile. "You're getting married?"

A smile spread across my face, too. "I am."

"Oh, my gosh!" She shut the fridge, stepped over, and took my hand to get a closer look at my new engagement ring before enveloping me in a warm hug. "That ring is gorgeous. I'm so happy for you two!"

"Thanks."

When she released me, she said, "I'm so happy for *me*, too."

"You are? Why's that?"

She performed a mock cringe, grinning all the while. "Because your engagement makes it easier for me to tell you that I'm moving out at the end of the month."

"You are?"

She beamed. "Zach asked me to move in with him."

"Wow! That's great, Frankie." With her previous boyfriend having proved to be a total jerk, I was glad she'd found a guy who appreciated her and treated her right. Looked like Valentine's Day had been eventful for both of us. I pulled her into a second hug, this one to celebrate her change in relationship status. I'd bet dollars to donuts that Frankie and Zach would be following Seth and me down the aisle before too long. "The timing is perfect," I added. I'd assumed Seth and I would have to find a new place of our own once we were married but, with Frankie on the way out now, he could move in here with me. The house wasn't big, but it had two decent-sized bedrooms and a nice yard for the dogs. As a bonus, it was conveniently located within just a few minutes' commute to the police and fire stations where we worked. Still, the news made my heart ache just a little. In light of our irregular work schedules, Frankie and I sometimes went days without seeing each other. But the time we'd spent together here had been fun, and I'd always known she was there for me if I needed her. I was going to miss her.

She rounded up a coffee mug for herself. "The closet in my bedroom is bigger than yours. You better claim it before Seth moves in."

"Good thinking." I was crazy about my fiancé, but there are some things a woman should never sacrifice for a man, including her independence, her dreams, or her closet space. I grabbed my keys, bade Frankie goodbye, and reached out to ruffle Zoe's ears. "See y'all later."

Detective Jackson waylaid me shortly thereafter as I checked in at the police station, silently summoning me to her office with a quick wave of her hand. She wore the same suit she'd had on last night, which said she had yet to return home. She also wore a slack-faced, heavy-lidded expression, clearly operating on little to no sleep. Brigit and I followed her down the hall, my partner's toenails tapping out a rhythm as we made our way. As Jackson slid into her desk chair, I closed her door behind me.

"There was no word from Greg Olsen overnight," Jackson said, though her tight face had already told me as much. "No contact from anyone claiming to have kidnapped him, either. If the attackers decided to take Greg for ransom, they might have changed their plans when they realized they'd be unable to provide proof of life if Shelby asked for it."

Even though I'd had the same thought, that Greg might have died at his attacker's hands, hearing it out loud from Detective Jackson made it more real. I didn't want to accept it, to believe that there could be such brutality in the world. "You think there's any chance he could still be alive?"

"The odds are against it," Jackson said on a sigh. "But I've been surprised a time or two. The lab has expedited the blood analysis, but there were so many separate samples that it's going to take a while. I hope to know something by the end of the day. Until we have the results, we need to keep our minds open."

With any luck, some of the blood would match a person already in the criminal database and we'd readily identify the culprits, make a quick arrest, and find out exactly what had happened to Greg Olsen last night. A prompt resolution might make for a boring investigation, but it would give Shelby some closure rather than leaving her in a state of emotional limbo.

"What about his car?" I asked. "Has anybody spotted the Jetta?"

"Nope."

Darn. I'd hoped to hear there'd been some progress.

She gestured to one of her wing chairs. "Pull up a seat. I ran over to the theater late last night and the manager gave me the login information to access their security feeds. I've watched the past week's footage several times, but nothing has caught my eye. I want you to look over the video footage from yesterday and tell me if you see anything suspicious."

Over the next hour, we scoured the camera feeds, trying to identify anyone who appeared to be plotting to rob the theater, who'd zeroed in on Greg Olsen as a means for carrying out the theft. From an outside camera feed, we saw Greg's black Jetta pull into the theater parking lot as he arrived for work at a few minutes before noon. Only a few other cars were in the lot, mostly minivans and SUVs, mom-mobiles. When Greg climbed out of his vehicle, a sick feeling filled my gut. We were watching what was very likely the last day of this man's life.

Greg reached into his car to retrieve his sport coat. The jacket was bright yellow with black trim and the theater company's black-and-white clapboard logo over the breast pocket. He slid into the garment and began walking toward the theater. We followed along until he entered the building and Jackson switched the feed to an interior camera that provided a wide view of the lobby. At that time of day, only a handful of customers were in the theater, mostly mothers with young children taking in a matinee cartoon. In recognition of Valentine's Day,

heart-shaped helium-filled Mylar balloons floated above
the ticket-takers podium. My mind went back to the balloon I'd seen in the kitchen last night. Greg must have
brought it home for Shelby from the theater.

Greg walked through the lobby and toward a door in
the back wall next to the concessions stand. The door was
situated between a life-sized cardboard cutout of The
Rock from an upcoming movie and a claw machine filled
with cheap stuffed animals.

Greg typed in a code on the security keypad, opened
the door, and disappeared through it. Jackson switched
to another camera feed that showed Greg had entered a
short hallway with doors on all four sides, including
the one he'd just entered. He used a key to unlock the
door at the back, which led to a large office divided into
three cubicle spaces that were overseen by yet another
camera. He took a seat at the modular desk in the center
cubicle and logged into his computer. After spending a
minute or two checking his e-mails, he stood, retrieved
a handheld radio from his desktop, and clipped the device onto his belt. Jackson continued to switch feeds as
necessary to track Greg as he exited the office, closing
the door behind him. He locked the office, slid the key
back into his pants pocket, and walked through the door
to the right, which took him behind the concessions
counter.

We continued to follow him for the rest of his shift.
It was no easy feat with the theater being a multiplex
with long hallways and numerous rooms. We sped up
and slowed the feed as needed to assess the images.
He stopped to speak with a female employee who was
running a carpet sweeper through a hallway. He was approached by a gray-haired couple taking in an afternoon
show, and he pointed down the hall to direct them to the

correct theater. He sat alone at his desk and performed tasks on his computer.

At 4:03 according to the time stamp, a blonde woman with glasses entered his office. She, too, wore the theater's signature sport coat. The two conversed briefly before Greg used a key to unlock a closet in the corner and reveal a floor-mounted safe inside. He knelt down, punched in a series of digits on the keypad, and opened the safe's door. He removed a vinyl zippered bank bag. After closing the safe and locking the closet, he donned his coat, slid the bag of cash into an inside pocket, and zipped it up.

The two ventured out of Greg's office and into the lobby. A young couple, probably high school or college sweethearts, stood in line at the concessions stand. Both wore sneakers, jeans, and hooded sweatshirts. Both had straight dark hair and medium brown skin that pegged them as likely having Latin, Asian, or Middle Eastern roots. Both carried backpacks. The girl was exceptionally tall, her stature nearly equal to that of the boy. Both of them towered over the others in line and fell only a few inches short of the life-sized cardboard cutout of The Rock. As a fan of Dwayne Johnson, I knew he stood six-feet-five-inches tall. Given their relative heights to the cardboard cutout, I'd peg the boy as roughly six foot two, the girl at five ten or eleven. The boy glanced over at Greg and the manager in the blazer, continuing to eye them as they walked across the lobby and out the door together. He didn't look away until the line in front of him advanced without him noticing and the girl he was with shoved him forward.

I tapped the key to freeze the feed and pointed to the boy and girl. "What about those two?" As tall as the girl was, she must have big feet. A man's size nine-and-a-half would be the same size as a woman's eleven. *Could her feet be that big?*

The detective issued a mirthless chuckle. "The boy grabbed my attention the first time around, too. I thought he was watching Greg and the manager. But look again."

She reversed the tape by twenty seconds and resumed the feed. This time, as Greg and the manager exited the office, Jackson pointed to a busty girl in a tight sweater and high-heeled boots who'd exited the ladies room and traversed a similar course to that of Greg and the manager. While Greg and the manager headed outside, the girl stopped just inside the doors to greet a young man who'd evidently come to meet her at the theater.

"So he was just checking out the other girl." No wonder his date shoved him.

"That was my conclusion," Jackson said. "His date's too, from the looks of it. But maybe I was too quick to write him off."

We continued to watch. The manager walked Greg out to his car. They stopped next to it and appeared to be engaged in a short conversation. She reached out and gave him a pat on the shoulder before taking a few steps back. *Hmm.* The touch could be merely congenial and harmless, or it could indicate something more. Hard to tell without being able to hear their accompanying conversation. She waited nearby as he reversed out of his parking place and drove off to make a deposit at the bank. *Was she simply following security protocols, or was there more to it?*

We sped up the feed until we saw Greg's car return a few minutes after 5:00. He parked and came back inside the theater, once again removing his coat and hanging it on the hook in his office. He proceeded to work in his office on administrative tasks. The blonde female manager came to his office and bade him goodbye around 5:30

before leaving the theater. Another manager in a bright yellow blazer arrived a couple of minutes before 6:00 and greeted Greg in his office, the lights reflecting off the shiny forehead exposed by his receding hairline.

Jackson pointed at the man on the screen. "That's the manager I spoke with at the theater late last night."

We advanced the footage at a rapid pace. The theater filled with couples, some of them coming in together on double dates to see seasonal rom-coms and romantic adventure movies, while others opted for a horror flick. Jackson was right. Valentine's was a busy night for theaters. The theater raked in an abundance of cash, so much so that Greg and the other assistant manager made several rounds of the ticket booth and concessions, collecting cash from the registers lest the tills overflow. We slowed the feed to look for anyone who might have been eyeing them as they rounded up the funds, but nobody caught our attention. Greg and his fellow assistant manager returned to their shared office, counted the take together, and documented the amount in the theater's online bookkeeping system. When they finished, they stored the funds securely in the safe.

We sped up the pace, only to slow it again when the tall couple's film ended and the moviegoers left the theater en masse. The evening was fully dark by then, and the outdoor feed showed the couple making their way across the parking lot, which was illuminated by light posts spaced about the medians. They stopped to wait at the bus stop along the street. A bus rolled up a minute or so later and they boarded, disappearing from view as the bus drove out of camera range.

Nothing else on the camera feed caught my attention. When Greg left the theater at 9:12, he exited among a throng of moviegoers who had caught the early-evening shows. Nobody outside seemed to be paying Greg or his car any special attention as he climbed in and drove off. Then again, it was dark and the image was grainy. Someone could easily have been waiting out of camera range, too.

I turned to the detective. "Is there any way to identify the young couple? Did they pay for their tickets or snacks with a debit card? Or maybe they have one of the theater's preferred customer cards." Seemed every business signed people up for some kind of loyalty program these days.

Jackson brought up the footage showing the couple's arrival at the ticket booth. The camera was situated over the ticket sellers' heads, looking down at the windows. The wide-angle image showed the boy pulling out his wallet. The girl reached into her purse and removed her wallet, too. They flashed cards at the cashier. Jackson stopped the feed. While the program had no zoom feature, the two of us leaned in, improvising a close-up. Unfortunately, the lighting in the booth reflected off the plastic, creating a bright circle that obscured the cards themselves. Still, I could tell from the barely visible edge of the girl's card that it was not the same bright yellow as the Take Two Movie Maniac card in my wallet.

"It's not a customer card," I said. "Maybe a college or high school ID so they can get the discounted student tickets?"

As quickly as the two had pulled the IDs out of their wallets, they returned them. The boy paid cash for their tickets, took his change, and the two stepped away to go into the theater. Jackson reversed the feed and slowly went through the interaction a second time, stopping the feed frame by frame to see if we could get a better look at the IDs. No such luck.

"The card isn't purple," Jackson noted. "So they don't

appear to be TCU students. The cards were probably issued by a local high school or junior college." She went back to the feed that showed them at the concessions stand. The boy paid cash there, too.

The colleges would have too many students to make it easy to identify the two. "Any point in me checking with the high schools near the theater to see if the staff can ID the couple?"

"No," Jackson said. "Not yet, anyway. Seems like a weak lead and your time could be better spent elsewhere." She picked up the receiver from her desk phone. "I'm going to check with the captain, see if he'll let me borrow you this morning."

She placed a quick call to Captain Leone and obtained his okay to pull me off my regular beat so that I could serve as both her chauffeur and an extra set of ears and eyes. She'd get no complaint from me. Investigating a major crime like a possible murder was what I lived for. *Ironic, huh?*

She glanced at her watch. "The bank just opened. Let's go."

She grabbed her suit jacket, slid into it, and gave me a quick update as we walked out to my cruiser. Though Brigit's sniffing skills would not likely be needed this morning, my K-9 partner came along for the ride. She'd be bored at home, and I'd miss having my furry partner by my side. She'd become like an extension of myself, much like the way married couples became a unit. Just like Shelby and Greg, Brigit and I had an always and forever relationship. Well, hopefully not "just like" Shelby and Greg, with the way this case was shaping up.

Jackson, Brigit, and I headed for the Chase Bank branch nearest the theater. As I turned a corner, I asked the detective whether she'd been in contact with the couple's landlord.

"Spoke to him late last night," Jackson said. "He said he always changes the locks when he gets a new tenant in one of his rental units. He's used a lockbox that hangs from the doorknob a time or two so that he could leave keys for a repairman, but he never leaves keys out where just anyone could get their hands on them. Doesn't want the liability if someone gained access. He gave me the name of the handyman who worked at the house after the Olsens moved in. Neither the landlord nor the handyman have a criminal record."

"So you've crossed them off your list of potential persons of interest?"

"For now. The landlord insisted on coming out to the house first thing this morning. Fortunately, he's agreed to arrange and pay for the cleanup. That's one less thing Shelby will have to worry about."

Specialized crews trained in biohazard remediation were required to properly clean and sanitize crime scenes. Their services could cost an arm and a leg. The last thing Shelby needed to deal with right now was cleaning up the place. I was glad the homeowner had agreed to take on the expense. Still, I wondered about the lockbox. "Could someone who'd accessed the lockbox have made a copy of the key?"

"It's possible," Jackson said. "The landlord told me he has the keys marked with 'do not duplicate,' but people ignore the marking all the time. Besides, some hardware stores have do-it-yourself key-making equipment. A person could copy any key on one of those self-service machines."

Looked like we couldn't entirely eliminate the possibility that the repairman who had fixed the items noted on Shelby and Greg's list had copied the key with the intent of later accessing the home. But what were the odds that a repairman would have known Greg handled cash deposits for a movie theater? Might he have seen Greg in uniform and inquired about his job? An alternative theory popped into my head, too. If a repairman had noticed the photographs of the couple in the house, maybe he'd assumed the Olsens would be out celebrating Valentine's Day. Maybe he'd recruited a buddy and planned to burglarize the place, but had been discovered when Greg came home. Or maybe I was grasping at straws. The theory seemed farfetched, to assume too many coincidences. Still, I ran it by Jackson.

"I've run background checks on both the repairman and the landlord," she said. "They're clean."

Of course we knew the lack of a criminal record didn't necessarily mean a person was innocent. It could mean they'd never been caught committing their dirty deeds, or that a particular incident was their first foray into the world of crime. But what the lack of record told us definitively was that we were better off for the time being keeping our focus on the task at hand—getting information from the bank.

The branch where Greg had made the deposit was housed in a small, one-story building situated in the front corner of a strip shopping center. Heads turned our way as we entered the lobby, customers exchanging nervous glances on seeing a uniformed cop and K-9 coming into the place.

A sixtyish man in a blue security guard uniform was stationed just inside the door. "Everything okay?"

Jackson raised her palms. "It's all good," she said, loud enough for everyone to hear. "We just need to get some information from the manager, that's all."

A teller picked up her phone and punched a couple of buttons, informing her unseen boss that police had arrived. A moment later, a fortyish Asian-American man in a business suit and stylish eyeglasses stepped up behind the counter. "Can I help you ladies?"

"We need to speak in private," Jackson said.

"Sure." The manager motioned for us to proceed to a door in a wall next to the teller counter. He punched a button to buzz us through. *Bzzzt.*

Shortly thereafter, Jackson and I were seated in front of his desk with Brigit lying at our feet. His oversized monitor perched on the far corner of his desktop, positioned at an angle to make the best use of the space. He offered us coffee, but we both declined.

While Brigit surreptitiously sniffed the toes of the man's shoes under his desk, Jackson told him why we were there. "We need information about one of your customers. A man by the name of Greg Olsen. He's a manager at Take Two Theaters, takes care of their business banking at this branch. He and his wife also have a joint checking account with the bank. Mr. Olsen disappeared last night. We suspect foul play."

The man's eyes widened and his lips parted, but he seemed unsure how to respond. Who could blame him? It was an uncomfortable and horrific situation, one he had clearly not been in before. With any luck, he'd never be in this position again.

Rather than wait for him to come up with a response, Jackson plowed ahead, pulling a folded piece of paper from the inside pocket of her jacket and laying it on his desk. She pushed the document toward him. "That's the court's authorization for you to put a hot watch on the Olsens' account. If anyone other than Shelby tries to make a withdrawal or order a new debit card, the bank should contact law enforcement immediately."

Setting up a hot watch was standard procedure in cases like this, a way to try to track the movement of a person or suspect via their financial trail. Criminals had been apprehended after using a stolen debit or credit card at a bank, hotel, gas station, or restaurant. In this case, however, the hot watch was likely to be a futile effort. Greg's credit and debit cards were still in his wallet in an evidence locker, along with his driver's license. Whoever had taken him away would have a hard time accessing the Olsens' accounts with the cards or an ID.

After the bank manager reviewed the document, he pulled up the Olsens' account on his computer screen, which was easily visible from my seat. Once again I noticed what seemed to be an inordinately large number of transactions at grocery stores, dollar stores, Walmart, and Target. They all fell within a general range, from slightly over $60 to slightly over $100. There'd been three transactions in the last week alone for $103.49, $82.78, and $64.36.

"Done," the manager said, after flagging the account and clicking a button to exit. The monitor returned to a home screen. "What else can I do for you?"

"We need to view your security camera footage. Mr. Olsen made a deposit for the theater late yesterday afternoon. We need to see whether someone might have followed him when he left the bank."

The man went rigid. "You think someone went after him because he handles cash for the business?"

"It's a theory we're working," Jackson said. "Olsen left the theater a little after four and returned shortly after five. He made the deposit at some point during that time period."

Putting his hands to his keyboard again, the man ran a search for Take Two's account number. He leaned in to take a closer look at the screen, quirking his nose to push his glasses back when they slid downward. "Looks like he made the deposit at four forty-five, shortly before the lobby closed for the day."

Having pinpointed the timeframe, he logged into the security camera feeds. He pushed the far edge of his monitor so that it now sat perpendicular, where we could all get a look at the screen. "We've got five cameras," he said, tapping a key to show us the current view from one that looked out onto the front of the bank. "The first is over the front doors, as you can see." He tapped his keyboard several times, taking us through each of the cameras. "The second is in the foyer over the ATM machines. Of course, the ATMs also have built-in cameras. The third device is over the teller's station." The backs of the two young women working the counter were visible. One helped a customer, while the other straightened a display of brochures. "The fourth camera shows the drive-through lane." The drive-through was currently in use, a harried mother in a minivan cupping her hand around her ear to hear the teller over the wails of her toddler in the backseat. "The last camera is over the emergency exit out back." There was nothing to see on that one except a small metal trash bin and the row of evergreen bushes that separated the bank property from the rest of the strip mall's parking lot.

"Show me the feed from the lobby first," Jackson said, "then we can take a look at the others. Start a couple of minutes before Mr. Olsen arrived."

The man maneuvered his mouse and clicked to start the feed. We watched as everyone on the screen moved about, performing their duties. There was a line of people waiting, last-minute customers trying to get their banking business done before the branch closed for the day. The last in line was a grungy-looking biker, helmet in hand. He wore dark boots, jeans, and a leather jacket, all of which had seen better days. He also sported leather motorcycle gloves, several day's stubble on his cheeks, and an irritated expression, clearly annoyed by the wait. A man walked in and took a place at the end of the line, behind the biker. It was Greg Olsen sans the sport coat. He must have left it in his car. A smart move. Wearing the signature jacket would have clued others in that the guy carrying the cash had come from the Take Two Theaters.

As Greg stepped into line, the biker glanced back at him. Greg offered a nod of acknowledgment that the biker didn't return. We watched as Greg wound his way through the line, demarcated with retractable nylon belts stretching between metal stanchions. The teller on the left summoned the biker to her station. A moment later, Greg proceeded to the teller to her right. The two men were separated by only three feet and a candy dish full of conversation hearts on the counter.

The biker retrieved a roll of crumbled bills and tossed it onto the counter in front of the teller serving him. Meanwhile, the teller tending to Greg took the zippered bank bag, opened it, and removed the stack of bills. After encircling the stack with her hands and tapping it on the counter to straighten it, she placed the stack into a bill-counting machine and pushed the button to activate it. The machine fanned the bills and the readout gave the total. The woman took a look at the readout and her mouth opened as she apparently confirmed the total with Greg. The biker cut a glance at Greg, his scowl deepening. The teller printed out a receipt, tucked it inside the pouch, and zipped it closed before handing it back to Greg. He gave the teller a smile, said something that appeared to be "thank you," and turned to go.

As Greg disappeared out the front door, Jackson asked the bank manager to change the feed. "Show me the one over the entrance now."

The manager changed the feed, and we watched as

Greg walked down the front sidewalk. He didn't stop at the ATM to withdraw any funds from his personal account. He climbed into his black VW. In the parking spot next to his car sat a blue Harley Davidson touring bike with mini ape handlebars.

Through his windshield, we saw Greg fasten his seatbelt, turn the ignition, and reach out to turn on the radio. He looked back, waiting as an SUV eased past behind him. Once the SUV was out of the way, Greg backed up, shifted gears, and drove out of sight. Just as Greg left the screen, the biker exited the branch, put on his helmet, and climbed onto his bike. He walked the motorcycle backward until he could proceed, and took off in the same direction Greg had gone. We continued to watch in case something else caught our eye, but nothing did.

Jackson made a circular motion with her hand. "Rewind that tape so we can see Mr. Olsen exiting again."

The manager did as she'd requested. Jackson whipped out her notepad and narrowed her eyes at the screen, taking in the motorcycle's license plate number and jotting it down. She had the manager play the footage of Greg arriving at the bank. The motorcycle was already parked in the lot when he arrived. We watched the other camera feeds at double time, but none seemed to yield any clues. Nobody else seemed to pay Greg any mind.

Jackson stood, pulled a business card from her pocket, and handed it to the manager. "Thanks for your time."

I stood and Brigit lumbered to a stand, too. We followed Detective Jackson back through the lobby, bidding goodbye to the security guard as we headed out. The instant our butts hit the seats of my squad car, Jackson logged into my dashboard-mounted laptop. "Let's see who owns that motorcycle, find out if he's got any priors."

Once again, I found myself eyeing a screen for information, glad to be working as a cop in a time when much of the information we needed was right at our fingertips rather than in a filing cabinet somewhere. The motor vehicle records showed the motorcycle belonged to a Duke Knapczyk. A search of the driver's license records produced a license photo that confirmed Duke Knapczyk was the man we'd seen in the bank. It also confirmed that the guy never smiled. He was scowling in his driver's license photo, as well. A review of the criminal database revealed Knapczyk had two priors, though the offenses were minor, nonviolent, and occurred over a decade ago. Possession of marijuana. Public intoxication. Still, just because the guy hadn't been violent in the past, and had seemingly been behaving himself in recent years, it didn't necessarily mean he hadn't rounded up a buddy and attacked Greg Olsen. It might just mean he'd been lucky enough not to get caught doing anything shady in the interim. Besides, his record noted that he'd been arrested three years ago on a theft by check charge, though the matter was later dropped. He'd once been suspected of stealing. Might he have made a botched attempt to steal from the theater last night?

"What do you think?" I asked the detective. "Do we go see Knapczyk? Or do we go to the movie theater?"

She tilted her head one way then the other as she thought it over. "Theater," she decided. "We'll see if Knapczyk shows up on the security cameras there. Besides, the blonde manager is on duty this morning. I want to see what she might tell us. But first, let's make a quick detour."

NINE
WEATHER OR NOT

Brigit

Brigit lifted her snout and flexed her nostrils as they walked to the patrol car. Her sensitive nose could smell moisture in the air. Ozone, too, though she had no idea that's what the chemical was called, or that it was a by-product of lightning and wind. She only knew that her instincts were telling her that bad weather was on its way and that she should seek shelter.

If it were up to her, she and Megan would return home and snuggle under the bedcovers, where it was safe and warm. But it wasn't up to Brigit. On the job, Megan called the shots. Brigit didn't think this was an entirely fair arrangement, what with her canine abilities being far superior to Megan's in many ways. But humans were a bossy species, and they liked to feel superior even when they were not. If Brigit wanted more belly rubs and liver treats—and she definitely did!—she'd have to be obedient and keep up her end of the bargain.

TEN
RUDE AWAKENINGS

The Slasher

He rubbed his eyes and looked at the bedside clock. How could it be 9:53 a.m.? Had he even slept? Sure didn't feel like it. He'd been too hopped up on adrenaline. Besides, whoever was currently occupying the unit upstairs seemed to have suffered a bad bout of insomnia last night, which they attempted to cure by pacing back and forth either wearing wooden shoes or riding on a pogo stick. All night long it had been *clunk-clunk-clunk-clunk*. He didn't dare complain to the management, though. He needed to lie as low as possible, make himself invisible.

Before checking into the hotel last night, he'd snagged a half gallon of milk, a box of cereal, two packages of hot dogs, and three cans of beans from the convenience store across the street. It wasn't much, but it should hold him a few days.

He shuffled into the kitchen and fixed himself a cold bowl of cornflakes. He pulled open the silverware drawer to find a cockroach looking up at him, taunting him with his antennae. The bug seemed to know that he couldn't call down to the front desk and complain. He grabbed a paper towel to crush the bug with, but by the time he returned his attention to the drawer, the roach had skittered off down the counter and now taunted him from beside the toaster.

"You're dead!" he hissed, diving for the bug. But the roach disappeared under the toaster. He snatched up the appliance only to find the cockroach had seemingly disappeared into thin air. Oh, well. He might not have been able to kill this pest, but he'd put an end to Greg Olsen last night.

ELEVEN
POP-POP

Megan

Detective Jackson's "quick detour" involved a trip to Fritz and Winkleman, the law firm where Shelby Olsen worked, to ply her coworkers for information. We parked in the garage, boarded the elevator, and rode it up to the ninth floor. We emerged to find an accounting firm to our right and the law firm to our left. I followed Jackson as she pulled open the heavy glass door that led into the law firm's foyer.

After the detective flashed her badge at the receptionist and told the woman the reason for our visit, the receptionist summoned Regina to the lobby. Regina was impeccably dressed in business attire, but her eyes drooped, her cheeks sagged, and her general expression was weary and wary. Was she merely fatigued from being kept up late by the prior evening's events, or was she suffering the aftereffects of violence, guilt, and secrecy?

"Has Greg been found?" Regina asked, her voice strained, her mouth wiggling in worry.

"Not yet." Jackson glanced around the space. "Is there somewhere we can speak in private?"

"The small conference room isn't being used right

now." She motioned for us to follow her down the hallway behind the reception desk.

As we made our way down the corridor, we passed a row of four fancy cubicles formed by wood and glass panels. Twenty something women occupied the first two cubicles. Both cast glances our way as we passed them. The third space was empty, but the nameplate attached to the outside panel told me it belonged to Regina. The fourth cubicle was Shelby's.

Jackson raised her palm. "Hold on a minute."

She stepped to the threshold and peered into the space. On the built-in desk sat a photo of Shelby and Greg posing on the Brooklyn Bridge with the Manhattan skyline in the background. A daily desktop calendar with tear-off pages still showed yesterday's date along with a picture of the Eiffel Tower and a caption declaring Paris the most romantic place on Earth. A good choice to feature for Valentine's Day. Jackson stepped forward and flipped through the calendar. Each page depicted a different European tourist destination, from the Trevi Fountain in Rome to the Matterhorn in Switzerland to the monolithic La Sagrada Familia in Barcelona. Not that I had much hope of making it to Europe on a cop's salary, but the calendar got me thinking. *Where should Seth and I go on our honeymoon?* We'd have to discuss the possibilities soon, along with many other wedding-related details. But this was not the time or place to ponder the matter.

The marked-up commercial-lease contract and pen sitting on the desktop, as well as the nearly full water bottle, said that Shelby had intended to return to work today. I wondered how long it would be before she could bring herself to leave her home and come to the office. Standard bereavement leave was two weeks, but did that same time frame apply when your spouse was missing and had not conclusively been proven dead? The thought gave me an icky, prickly feeling. Since becoming a cop, I'd been faced with a lot of uncomfortable questions. Why do people risk their lives taking dangerous drugs? Why do people intentionally hurt those they purportedly love? Why does everyone play dumb when I ask them if they know why I pulled them over? Just once, I'd like a motorist to say, *"Was it because I was doing thirty miles over the speed limit?"*

Having satisfied her curiosity, Jackson backed out of the cubicle and we continued on to the conference room. The exterior wall was solid glass and looked out on the skyscraper across the street. A credenza topped with a telephone and a potted purple orchid rested against the interior wall. An oval table surrounded by six chairs filled the center of the room. Two chairs sat on each side of the table, with one chair at each end. Jackson and I took seats on one side of the table. I was curious to see where Regina would sit, and wondered what, if anything, it might tell us. If she sat across from us, it might mean she considered us adversaries, and wanted to put some distance between us. Or it could merely mean that looking directly at each other was the best for conversation. She took a seat on the end of the table, next to Brigit and me.

Jackson and I swiveled in our chairs so we could better address Regina. Brigit sniffed along Regina's leg before resting her head on the woman's thigh. I took that as a sign in Regina's favor. Brigit was a good judge of character, not only because she was a smart dog but because she could scent the chemical signals people put out, which were important clues to their moods. My guess was Regina smelled sad and Brigit hoped to comfort her.

Regina's mouth spread in a soft smile. "Am I allowed to pet her?"

I gave her nod. "She'd love that."

Regina ran her hand over Brigit's head and neck as Jackson launched into a series of questions, starting with, "How well would you say you know Shelby Olsen?"

"Reasonably well, I guess." Regina raised her shoulders, uncommitted. "I mean, as well as you can know somebody you just work with."

"So you haven't had a lot of interaction outside the office?"

"I wouldn't call it a lot," Regina said. "We go out to lunch every once in a while. Usually one or two of the other assistants come with us. She's joined us for happy hour after work a few times when her husband had an evening shift at the theater, but most of the time when we invite her she turns us down. She likes to be home with her husband. They seem really close."

"Close in a positive way?" Jackson cocked her head.

"Yes."

"So you didn't get any hint of problems in their marriage? Any cheating? Maybe some flirtation going on? A crush?"

"Not that I was aware of."

"What about control issues? Verbal or physical intimidation or abuse? Anything like that?"

Regina went pale and her hand went still on Brigit's head. "Was Shelby being abused?"

Jackson raised her palms. "I'm just fishing here, trying to get a feel for who Shelby and her husband were as a couple."

"I'm not aware of any problems," Regina said. "They seem like a happy couple. Kind of mushy, really." She cringed facetiously. "He comes by to take her out to lunch sometimes on his days off, and he sends her flowers every few weeks for no reason at all. They're very romantic."

Jackson clarified. "So you haven't had much one-on-one time with Shelby?"

"No."

"Coworkers often confide in each other," Jackson said. "Has she ever confided in you or your other coworkers?"

"About what?"

Jackson was the uncommitted one now, lifting a shoulder. "Any personal matter."

Regina looked up in thought before her gaze returned to Jackson's face. "I can't really think of anything. She's talked about some of the trips they've taken and the places that are on her bucket list to visit. Paris is at the top of her list. I remember once when we were at lunch she said she'd like to see the catacombs. I hadn't heard of the catacombs until she mentioned it. There's a bunch of people buried down in some kind of tunnels under the city. The group of us had a discussion about whether it would be creepy or cool to visit there. I thought it sounded creepy, but some of the others thought it would be interesting."

I'd read about the catacombs in a book when I was a kid. The catacombs were an ossuary, a resting place for human bones. The skeletons of over a million Parisians filled the tunnels. While it was a popular tourist destination, my opinion aligned with Regina's. The place sounded creepy. I'd much rather stay among the living.

Jackson's final question for Regina was, "Do you have any reason to believe Shelby could be responsible in any way for her husband's disappearance?"

Regina's brows shot up. "Shelby? No. I can't imagine that. They seemed happy and Shelby seems . . . well . . . *normal*. I can't imagine her doing anything that would hurt her husband."

But that was precisely the problem, wasn't it? Human beings often had a hard time imagining the people they knew, or thought they knew, committing heinous crimes. They expected those who committed violence to be odd, isolated, or angry people. Many times, that was in fact the case. But, just as many times, it was not. People could be good at hiding their true selves, especially sociopaths. They were master manipulators. Even so, Shelby didn't strike me as a sociopath.

"Could you round up Shelby's boss for me?" Jackson asked. "And don't repeat any of what we've discussed in here. If your coworkers ask, tell them everything's fine but that I've asked you not to talk about it out of respect for Shelby's privacy."

"Okay." Regina left the conference room and returned a few minutes later with a slender, platinum-haired attorney wearing a stylish blue pantsuit. Regina introduced the woman as Nadine Winkleman, and slipped quietly out of the room, leaving us to our business.

Jackson and I retook our seats, and Ms. Winkleman slid into a chair across from us. Her face was tight in concern. She looked from me to the detective. "Regina called me last night and told me that Shelby's husband had gone missing. Still no contact from him?"

"No," Jackson said. "We're still trying to piece things together. As you can imagine, the first place we have to look when someone goes missing is to their spouse. The sooner we can rule out Shelby or someone associated with her as a suspect, the sooner we can focus our efforts elsewhere."

"Understood. I'll cut to the chase. I have no reason to suspect Shelby of any involvement in his disappearance. She appeared to be a devoted wife, and I never noticed her engaging in any inappropriate behavior, harmless or otherwise, with anyone here at the office."

Jackson offered the woman a smile. "You knew precisely what I'd ask."

Winkleman smiled back. "Spent eight months working as a prosecutor for the Tarrant County District Attorney's Office back in the late eighties. Figured out pretty quickly that criminal law and courtroom work were far less interesting and glamorous than they make it look on TV. Decided I'd rather sit in a comfy chair behind a desk and handle commercial transactional work."

"That's what you do here? Business law?"

"Yes. Contracts. Financial matters. Negotiations. The occasional employment matter. I'll admit I was a little hesitant to hire Shelby as my assistant given that her background was primarily in estate and probate, but she came highly recommended and caught on very quick. She's a natural."

"You've known her just three months, correct?"

The woman's eyes narrowed slightly and she looked up for a moment as she appeared to be mentally calculating. "That's correct. She started here in mid-November."

"Has Shelby had any visitors to the office?"

"Just her husband as far as I know. He takes her out to lunch quite often."

"Any unusual phone calls?"

"Not that I'm aware of. Like I said, there's been nothing to give me any reason to believe Shelby could be involved in anything untoward."

Jackson pushed back from the table and stood. I followed suit.

The detective fished a business card out of her pocket

and handed it to the woman. "If you happen to learn anything that might be of use, please give me a call."

"I certainly will."

The sky darkened as we aimed for the theater and the wind picked up, gusts carrying winter's dead leaves up in to the air and creating dirt devils along the shoulder. Tiny drops of rain left a misty coating on the cruiser's windshield, and I activated the wipers so we could see better.

The detective gave me some details and instructions as we drove. "I spoke to the other evening manager briefly last night. All I told him was that Greg seems to have disappeared after he left the theater. I asked if he knew anything about Greg's whereabouts and whether Greg might have had trouble with anyone. I didn't mention the blood in the kitchen. Keep that under wraps for now."

"Gotcha." It wasn't unusual to withhold information in situations like this, to see if someone close to the victim might inadvertently let something slip that they shouldn't know.

Soon, we were turning into the parking lot of the theater. Its normally cheery bright yellow sign seemed muted and in desperate denial under the graying skies. We parked and approached the ticket booth, moving quickly to avoid the rain, which had intensified from mere mist to scattered droplets. Brigit crouched as she hustled along, blinking her eyes against the drizzle. The twentyish young woman selling tickets was too immersed in her cell phone to notice us standing at the glass. Jackson reached out and tapped her knuckles on it. *Rap-rap.*

Startled, the girl jumped up, juggling her phone in her hands as she reflexively tossed it in the air but managed to catch it. "Sorry! I didn't see you there. Can I help you?"

"We need to speak to Beth Moyer." Jackson pointed to the short-range radio lying on the ticket counter. "Can you ask her to meet us in the lobby?"

"Okay." The girl picked up the device and summoned her boss as we moved to make our way inside. "Cool dog!" she called after me.

"Thanks!" I called back. Brigit wagged her tail as if in agreement. My K-9 partner seemed to understand far more than people might give her credit for.

Inside, we were met by the enticing smell and *pop-pop-pop* sound of popcorn popping. On a dreary weekday, few moviegoers had ventured out and the lobby was empty other than a stooped, gray-haired man who appeared to have come out of retirement to hawk Milk Duds and overpriced sodas. Brigit shook herself, sending up a light spray, fluffing up her damp fur, and releasing the scent of wet dog. A moment later, a fortyish blonde woman wearing black pants and a bright yellow blazer with the Take Two logo emerged from one of the long hallways. She spotted us and strode quickly over.

The woman's face was drawn in concern. "Hello, Detective Jackson."

After the detective introduced Brigit and me, Moyer held out an arm to indicate the door at the back of the lobby. "Let's talk in my office." As we made our way across the floor, Moyer addressed a young man wiping down the self-serve soda machine. "Did you restock the napkins yet?"

"All done," he said.

"Good job." She raised her hand and the two exchanged a congenial high five.

As the manager typed in the code on the door, Detective Jackson discreetly kissed her fingertips and reached over to apply the kiss to The Rock's lips. Brigit, on the other hand, shoved her nose into The Rock's cardboard groin. *Maybe this dog isn't as bright as I'd thought.* Brigit's snout lodged in the crotch of the cutout. She whipped her head side to side to free her nose and I had to grab the display and right it before she could knock it over. I glared down at her and sent her a mental message. *Bad girl!* She did an up-down wag of her tail, sending me a message, too. *I do what instinct tells me to. If you don't like it, you can bite me.*

Moyer led us into the hallway and unlocked the door to the left. Unlike the assistant managers' space, which was windowless, Moyer's office had a wide window in the top half of the wall that separated her office from the lobby. The glass was lined with reflective privacy film so that she could keep an eye on the lobby but nobody could see in. She'd hung her business degree from Texas State University on the wall to our right. Atop her bookshelves sat three photos. One included her with two children who looked to be in the late single digits, one boy and one girl. The other two photos were individual school portraits of the two children, both of them missing a tooth or two. *What a couple of cuties.* Were they Moyer's children? Or maybe a niece and nephew? There was no man in what was purportedly a family photo, and a quick glance at her left hand found it bare. No wedding ring.

"Cute kids," I said, fishing for information. "Are they yours?"

She beamed. "Yes. They keep me busy. We're always running off to a ballet lesson or baseball practice." She held out a hand to indicate the two theater-style recliners facing her desk. "Please have a seat." As Moyer circled around her desk and dropped into her desk chair, Brigit lowered her haunches to the floor.

Once we were all sitting, Jackson got right down to

business. "I assume you've been notified that Greg Olsen is missing."

"Yes. The evening manager called me after you spoke with him last night. I'm completely shocked." She shook her head slightly and seemingly involuntarily, as if refusing to accept facts. "Do you have any idea where Greg is?"

"Still trying to make that determination," Jackson said. "Did you have any contact with Greg after you left the theater at five thirty yesterday?"

"No," Moyer said. "He hasn't contacted me. I've tried calling and texting him, but he hasn't responded."

Of course he hadn't. His cell phone had been found in a puddle of blood on his kitchen floor and taken into evidence. But Beth Moyer didn't know that.

"Greg told his wife he thought he might have been followed from the theater to the bank when he made a deposit a couple of weeks ago. Were you aware of the situation?"

"Yes," she said. "He mentioned it to me to next day. He said he wasn't sure he'd been followed, but that a gray car had been behind him the entire drive. It was too far back for him to tell how many people were inside it or what they looked like. It could have been a coincidence, but I instituted some new safety protocols, just in case."

"What kind of protocols?" Jackson asked.

"Under the old system, the manager working the early shift would get the deposit out of the safe and take it to the bank before opening the theater for the day. That meant they would come into the empty theater alone, and they'd be alone when they went back out to their car with the deposit. Now, we vary the time of day that the deposit is made and we don't do it unless there's someone else on site to accompany the manager to their car. I instructed the managers not to get out of their cars and unlock the building in the morning until another staff member has arrived. I've also scheduled a staff member to remain on site with them until they lock up for the night."

"Safety in numbers," Jackson said. "Good practices."

"We've also been taking indirect routes to the bank," Moyer said. "Switching up which way we go."

Another good idea. If someone was lying in wait along the usual, direct route, they wouldn't spot the manager heading to the bank.

Jackson continued her inquiry. "After Greg Olsen first reported the car following him, did any of the managers spot it again when they made a subsequent deposit?"

"No one noticed it. That's not to say the car wasn't there, but if it was it wasn't obvious."

She asked the woman many of the same questions she'd asked Shelby the night before. "Are you aware of anyone Greg might have had trouble with? A coworker maybe, or a customer?"

"Nobody I know of," Moyer said. "Greg seems like a nice guy, gets along with everyone as far as I can tell. He's quiet, though, kind of introverted. I can't say I know him well. He hasn't worked here long, only since his transfer request came through right before Thanksgiving."

"Mr. Olsen requested the transfer?" I asked. After Jackson's interview with Shelby the night before, I'd come away with the impression that it had been the company's decision to move Greg down here from Oklahoma. Then again, it was possible I'd misunderstood Shelby or made an incorrect inference.

"Yes," Moyer said. "It was a lateral move, not a promotion. When I asked him what brought him down to Texas, he said he and his wife had nothing keeping them in Oklahoma and that they wanted a change of scenery."

Understandable, I supposed, though the scenery in Fort Worth and Oklahoma City were essentially the same. Mostly grassland, scrubby trees, and strip malls. Still, each place had its own charms and, even if they weren't the most scenic cities, both were nice places to call home with affordable housing, low taxes, and friendly people.

After Moyer answered my question, Jackson resumed her line of questioning. "Has there been any problem here recently? An unruly customer, maybe an argument among the staff?"

"Nothing out of the ordinary," Moyer said. "Greg mentioned a young couple with a fussy baby. He'd asked them to leave a movie after other customers complained, but he gave them a refund. He said they seemed frustrated, but they didn't make a big issue of it."

"When was that?"

"A week or so ago."

"Have they been back to the theater?"

Moyer shrugged. "I have no idea."

Having gotten nowhere with her questions so far, Jackson changed her tack. "Has anyone come to see him here at work?"

"His wife comes by two or three times a week," Moyer said. "Employees get free movie passes and she uses them to see chick flicks or rom-coms. The two of them come in together on his days off to see movies, too. He's a real film fan. Knows tons of movie trivia."

While it was nice of her to offer information about Greg, her telling us that he was a cinephile wasn't likely to help the investigation. Jackson seemed to feel the same way. She steered the conversation back to Greg's associates. "Anybody besides his wife come by to visit with him?"

"Not that I've noticed."

Jackson hesitated a moment before saying, "I need to explore all potential angles here, so I'm going to ask some awkward questions, okay?"

The woman's body went rigid, but her mouth said, "Okay."

Jackson leaned forward. "Do you think Greg could have been involved with someone other than his wife?"

Moyer's nose scrunched in skepticism. "Anything's possible, I suppose, but it would surprise me. He and his wife always look happy together. They even hold hands sometimes. It's sappy but cute. They're one of those couples that are joined at the hip."

Jackson watched the woman closely. "Do you have feelings for Greg?"

"Me?" The woman barked a laugh, but then had the class to look sheepish for doing so. "No, not at all. Don't get me wrong. I think he's a nice guy, but he's not my type."

"What do you mean?"

She cringed and bit her lip. "He's a little too . . ." She looked up, as if the right word might be found on the ceiling. When she looked down again, she said. "Nerdy, I guess. He's too nerdy for my taste."

"Uh-huh," Jackson said, gauging the woman with her gaze. "You touched him yesterday. On the shoulder." Jackson demonstrated by touching my shoulder the same way this woman had touched Greg. "We saw it on the video feed."

"I did?" Moyer looked from Jackson to me. I dipped my chin in agreement with Jackson. Moyer's lower jaw went slack. "If I touched him, it was innocent. I wasn't even aware of it."

"Are you married?" Jackson asked.

"Not any more," Moyer said. "My ex and I split up

when our youngest was two. We were a mismatch from the start, but realized it too late. We're civil, though."

The detective dug a little more. "Dating?"

"Some," Moyer said. "I'm on all the apps. But it's slim pickings. A lot of losers out there."

It was Jackson's turn to laugh now. "Tell us about it. Those losers keep us cops in business."

Jackson and I exchanged a glance and a silent assessment. Both of us sensed Moyer was being sincere. The high five she'd exchanged with her staff earlier told us that she was a relaxed manager not overly concerned about maintaining strict physical boundaries. When she'd patted Greg's shoulder, it was likely just a small sign of gratitude or a goodbye gesture.

The detective rose from her chair, pulled a business card from her breast pocket, and lay it on Moyer's desk. "If you happen to hear from Greg or think of anyone who might have wanted to harm him for any reason, call me immediately."

"I will." Moyer picked up the card and secured it in her pencil drawer. She stood and breathed a shuddering breath. When she spoke again, her voice was strained and squeaky, her eyes bright with alarm. "Is the theater staff in danger? Should I hire security?"

Jackson gave her a pointed look. "It certainly couldn't hurt."

Moyer led us out of her office. She'd just opened to door to the lobby when another *pop-pop-pop* sound met our ears. Only this time it wasn't the popcorn popper.

TWELVE
THE SKY IS FALLING

Brigit

Brigit pricked up her ears at the new sound coming from overhead. *Pop-pop-pop.* She recognized the sound and she didn't like it. It was the same sound she had heard another time, right before a swirling gust of wind had picked up the cruiser she and Megan were cowering in and flipped it over.

She knew she was expected to be a brave dog and, most times, she was. She knew she could take down any person, so she didn't fear humans. She also didn't fear the big dogs at the dog park. Most were all bark and no bite. But she was smart enough to know that even a well-trained dog like her was no match for Mother Nature. She pressed herself tight against Megan's leg and issued a soft whimper.

"Don't worry, girl," Megan said, reaching down to stroke her. "It'll be okay."

THIRTEEN
ICE, ICE, BABY

The Slasher

He stood at the window, watching the hail hammer the hotel and the cars in the parking lot. The *pop-pop-pop* of the hail hitting the building reminded him vaguely of popcorn popping, while the *tink-tink-tink* as it impacted the vehicles took him back to the gun range and the sound of spent cartridges hitting the concrete. He wondered whether the car he'd left in the park had been found yet, whether it, too, was being peppered with chunks of ice from the sky. He'd kept the television turned on all day, watched the early morning local news and paid attention to the teasers. There'd been only a brief blurb in the reports. The anchor asked viewers to keep an eye out for the black Jetta, noted the license plate number, and said the car's owner, Greg Olsen, might have been the victim of foul play.

Might have? Sounded like the police hadn't gotten very far in their investigation. They surely didn't work as quickly in real life as they did on TV and in the movies. He hoped they'd speed things up. The sooner they reached a dead end and the case went cold, the sooner he could get out of here.

FOURTEEN
RIDING OUT THE STORM

Megan

Although we wanted to keep the investigation moving along as quickly as possible, it would be dangerous to venture out in the hailstorm. Detective Jackson and I stood behind the double glass doors of the theater, watching helplessly as the hail fell. The accumulation on the ground showed that the hail was increasing in size, from dime to quarter. While the hail scale began with comparisons to coins—dimes, nickels, quarters—at a certain point, it switched to sports balls: golf balls, baseballs, softballs. With the rapid changes in climate, we might soon experience our first bowling ball–sized hailstone. *Heaven help us.*

Brigit whimpered again, the noise making her nervous. She could use a distraction. "Come with me, girl." I led her over to the snack bar where I ordered a large popcorn and two small drinks. "Throw in a box of Hot Tamales, too." *In for a penny, in for a pound.* I only hoped this mid-morning snack wouldn't pack the pounds onto my backside. I had wedding gown shopping to do. Then again, maybe I could get a design with lots of ruffles to cover my butt.

After paying for my order, I handed one of the cups to Jackson and held the tub of popcorn out to her. She grabbed a handful and shoved it into her mouth, moaning in bliss.

"This is your breakfast, isn't it?" I asked.

"And lunch." She shrugged. "I've had worse. I was on a stakeout at a drug house for a full week once. Survived on nothing but Diet Coke and Skittles."

So that's what I have to look forward to when I make detective. I tossed pieces of popcorn to Brigit, and she caught each of them expertly, snapping them out of the air like a frog catching flies. Meanwhile, outside, my cruiser was taking quite a beating. I could only hope the windshield wouldn't crack.

When the popcorn was gone, I pulled my baton from my belt and extended it with a *snap*, spinning the nightstick in my fingers with a *swish-swish-swish*. The repetitive motion and soft sound comforted me, like a mantra. I'd been a twirler in my high school marching band and could handle a baton with finesse and flair. My gun? Not so much. Shooting hadn't come naturally to me. I'd had to practice for hours on end to pass the marksman test.

Fortunately, the hail let up after several minutes and we were able to scramble through the rain back to my squad car. I inadvertently kicked a few hailstones as we ran, sending them skittering across the parking lot. Brigit snatched one up in her teeth and crunched down on it, like a frozen treat. My patrol car sported a fresh ding or two, but all of the glass was intact.

Jackson buckled her seatbelt and put a hand over her mouth to stifle a yawn. "Let's go talk to Knapczyk."

She gave me the address listed on his driver's license and in the DMV records for his motorcycle. I knew the street. It sat about halfway between the theater and the bank.

As we headed down a short stretch of highway, my eyes spotted no less than three roofing company trucks. Jackson pointed at one as we drove past it. "They didn't waste any time, did they?"

Any time there was a hailstorm, roofing companies engaged in a mad scramble immediately afterward, hoping to lock down homeowners before they could sign with another company. The noise of hammers would be heard throughout the city for the next few months as new shingles were installed.

We exited the freeway and turned onto Knapczyk's street. The biker lived in the left side of a rundown brick duplex that slumped on its lot. Hailstones gathered in the dented gutters and littered the muddy front lawn. The motorcycle was parked out of harm's way on the covered porch. A pack's worth of cigarette butts littered the area around the bike.

It took four times knocking and a full minute to bring Duke Knapczyk to the door, but he finally pulled it open. He held a lit cigarette and wore his signature scowl. His place smelled like corn chips, dirty laundry, and an unsuccessful pine-scented attempt to negate the other odors. When the man took in my uniform and the furry, fanged K-9 beside me, his face wriggled with a fresh mix of emotions, at least one of which was confusion. "What are y'all doing here?"

Jackson introduced herself, me, and Brigit, and motioned for the man to step out onto the porch. It would be safer to have him out here, where we had a chance of escape if he pulled out a hidden weapon. Knapczyk hesitated a moment, but stepped outside. My gaze dropped to his feet. He appeared to be wearing the same dark boots he'd had on in the video footage from the bank, a type with smooth soles. If he'd been in the Olsens' kitchen last night, it hadn't been in these boots. The soles on the men's shoes we'd seen last night had all been patterned rubber, typical of sneaker-type footwear.

Jackson didn't pussyfoot around. "Where were you yesterday evening?"

"Here." He waved his cigarette around like a kid waving a sparkler, using it to indicate the place.

"*All* evening?" Jackson clarified.

"Yeah."

"Was anyone with you?" Jackson asked.

"Jack Daniel and Jose Cuervo." He snorted in amusement. "Why?"

"We'll get to that, if necessary," Jackson said. "For now, I want to talk about the deposit you made at the bank yesterday."

He took a long drag on the cigarette, released the smoke out through his nostrils, and narrowed his eyes in challenge. "I didn't make a deposit."

"I've seen video footage that says otherwise."

"No, you haven't." His mouth spread in a smug grin. "What you saw was me paying NSF fees on an account they closed without my permission. Them banks are crooked. You screw up balancing your checkbook and they treat you like a criminal, charge you all kinds of penalties. It's not like I did it on purpose. I'm just not good at math. Never was. Back when I was in school they diagnosed me with that math dyslexia."

"Math dyslexia" was a common nickname and misnomer for dyscalculia, a learning disability that left those who suffered from it struggling to accurately perform basic math computations. As a child, I'd suffered from a stutter. Because many children who stutter have associated learning disabilities, I'd been tested for a slew of issues, despite the fact that I earned good grades and showed no other symptoms. I'd later learned the terms for the conditions. Dyslexia. Dyscalculia. Dysgraphia.

Knapczyk could have inadvertently overdrawn his account, or he could be up to his old theft-by-check tricks, intentionally bouncing checks like they were basketballs. His situation raised an interesting and complex issue for law enforcement, one my professors at Sam Houston State University had taught as part of my criminal justice curriculum. What crime a person should be charged with, or whether the person should be charged for a crime at all, was not necessarily determined by their actions and the results thereof, but was entirely dependent on their *mens rea* or mental state. For instance, a person who'd caused the death of another could be guilty of murder if the person had intended to cause the death, but they might only be guilty of manslaughter or assault if they intended to hurt the other person but not kill them.

Knapczyk's situation was even more complicated, straddling the divide between criminal and civil law. His mental state would determine whether a criminal act had been committed. If he'd intentionally written checks knowing there would be insufficient funds in the account to cover them, he could appropriately be charged with theft by check. If he'd simply made a math error and unintentionally bounced a check, the matter wouldn't be one for criminal law enforcement, but rather one for the civil courts to handle. Of course, the distinction could be a fine line, and it was often impossible to truly know what a person's intent was. I presumed the inability to prove intent might be the reason Knapczyk's earlier charge for theft by check had been dropped. But in the relevant case, even if Knapczyk had purposely issued bad checks, it didn't make him a killer.

Jackson stared at the man, assessing him. "What about the man at the teller next to you?"

Knapczyk's expression didn't change. "What about him?"

"You were eying the money he deposited. Hundreds of dollars in cash."

"What if I was?" He lifted a shoulder. "Can't blame me for wishing it was mine. Some guys get all the breaks. Then there's guys like me that life craps on over and over again."

Jackson and I exchanged looks. If this guy had attacked Greg Olsen in hopes of stealing the theater's money, it seemed he wouldn't be so open. Instead, he'd try to deflect his guilt by lying, saying he was checking out the conversation hearts in the candy dish or something like that.

He elaborated. "Anyways, the money wasn't why I was looking at him. The phone in his pocket wouldn't stop going off. It kept playing that 'Popcorn' song. Annoying as hell."

"Popcorn" seemed like an appropriate ringtone for a manager of a movie theater.

Jackson pointed down at Knapczyk's feet. "Could we see one of your boots?"

"What for?"

"Comparison."

It had been a vague answer at best, but nonetheless it seemed to satisfy him. He removed his left boot and handed it to the detective, standing like a flamingo with the leg crooked up behind him. A claw-like toenail in desperate need of a trim protruded through a hole in the end of his dingy sock. *Ew.*

Jackson turned the boot over, and the two of us took a look. The sole had worn evenly, no evidence of supination. When she turned the boot upright again, I tried not to gag at the musty food odor that emanated from it. She checked the tag sewn inside. "Size ten-and-a-half."

Unless Duke Knapcyk had been wearing someone else's ill-fitting shoes in the Olsens' kitchen last night, he wasn't one of the guys we were looking for.

Jackson dismissed him with "Stop bouncing checks." She turned and headed back to the cruiser.

"You going to at least tell me why you came by?" he hollered after her. When she didn't answer, he turned to me.

"Sorry," I said. "It's classified."

He muttered in irritation as Brigit and I returned to the cruiser.

As we rode back to the station, Jackson's cell phone rang. She pulled it from the pocket of her blazer and consulted the screen. "It's the lab." She tapped the screen and put the phone to her ear. "Got those results for me?" She listened intently, issuing one "Really?", a couple of "Mm-hms" and "All rights," and ending with "Thanks for turning this around so quickly." She slid the phone back into her pocket. "All of the blood in the kitchen was Greg Olsen's."

"Oh, no." My heart sank. "He has to be dead then, doesn't he?"

"The lab ran the math," the detective said. "There was three-quarters of a gallon of blood in the kitchen. No one can survive that kind of loss."

I knew from my forensics classes that the average adult body held between 1.2 to 1.5 gallons of blood. A person would feel fairly normal until they'd lost around thirty percent of their blood. Beyond thirty percent and they'd go into hemorrhagic shock, with their pulse rate and respiration rocketing to compensate as their blood pressure dropped. A person could not live if he or she lost more than forty percent of their blood or, on average, a little over half a gallon. Even assuming Greg's blood supply ran on the higher end at 1.5 gallons, he'd lost fifty percent of his blood. Facts were facts, and we had to face them. Greg Olsen was dead. *May he rest in peace.*

"What about fingerprints?" I asked. "Any luck there?"

"Most of them belong to Greg and Shelby. None of the others matched anyone in the system."

Darn. "What are you going to do now?"

"Review his computer and phone records. See what they tell me. I'll call businesses in the area, see if anybody caught the Jetta on their security cameras. I already canvassed the Olsen's immediate neighborhood. Quite a few of the houses are rentals, so there's no security cameras on them. Neither the landlords nor the tenants wanted to make that kind of investment. One of the neighbors has an inexpensive doorbell system, but it only shows their front porch and walkway."

I knew from experience that even if the Jetta showed up on camera footage, the video was unlikely to be helpful given that the car was dark and it was nighttime when it had taken off, presumably with Greg inside. The quality of the video on most security cameras wasn't very good, either. But even if the odds were stacked against us, we owed it to Shelby to perform a thorough investigation. We owed it to Greg, too. The dead deserve any justice we could provide.

"Before I look at Greg's phone and computer," Jackson said, "we need to pay a visit to Shelby, give her the news."

We? A lump of dread clogged my throat and I had to

gulp to force it down. I had to learn to face difficult tasks like this head on or I'd make a lousy detective.

I drove the cruiser to Shelby's house, half hoping we'd get into a fender bender along the way that would delay the heartbreaking task. But no sense putting off the inevitable. The crime scene tape had been removed from her yard, but a white van from the cleaning service sat in the driveway. The sides and back bore the biohazard symbol, a clear indication that something awful had happened here. Shelby's car had been moved into the garage, which stood open. Shelby sat on a folding lawn chair inside the space with Marseille on her lap. Both the woman and the dog were wrapped up in a blanket. The front door of the house was open, too. Through it, we could see workers in hazmat suits moving about.

Shelby stood when she saw my cruiser pull to the curb, but she didn't move forward. She seemed to sense we came bearing bad news.

Because we wouldn't be going into the house, I left Brigit in her enclosure in the back of the cruiser with the windows cracked. She stood at the glass, fogging it with her breath and watching as the detective and I walked into the garage. Shelby looked as exhausted as the detective. Her eyes were bloodshot and rimmed in dark pink. She smelled faintly of mentholated ointment. All that crying had probably caused her sinuses to become stuffy. I recognized the scent right away. Cops carried small jars of the stuff in their pockets or cruisers. Between the stench of rotting corpses, the odiferous squalor of flop houses, and the funk of evidence tossed into garbage dumpsters, police officers often found themselves in stinky situations.

"I'm afraid I've got some difficult news, Shelby," Jackson said, preparing the woman for the blow she was about to deliver. "We heard from the lab. All of the blood was Greg's."

"All of it?" Shelby's tone was high-pitched and incredulous. "None of the blood spatter came from anyone else?"

I noticed Shelby used the correct term, "spatter." Many civilians inadvertently used the wrong but more familiar "splatter." Perhaps she read crime novels or watched detective shows on television. Or maybe she'd learned it from one of the many movies in her husband's DVD collection.

"We're as surprised as you are," Jackson said. "I'd expected for the blood to have come from at least two sources, maybe three."

"Could he—" Shelby closed her eyes and shook her head, before forcing herself to ask the question. "Could he lose that much blood and still be alive?"

"Honestly?" Jackson said on a sigh. "It would be a miracle."

Shelby stood stock-still for a moment before dropping into the chair, her shoulders shaking. She buried her face in the blanket. Jackson and I took up positions on either side of her, putting supportive hands on her back.

"I'm so sorry, Shelby," Jackson said.

"Me too," I added.

We let her continue to cry for a minute or two, both of us dabbing at our eyes as well. The tough-cop cliché was just that, a cliché. Most cops cared about the people they served. Those who didn't rarely lasted long in law enforcement.

Finally, Shelby's sobs eased up. She wiped her eyes on the blanket before looking up at us. "Do you have any suspects?"

"Not yet," the detective told her. "We've reviewed the

security camera footage from the bank and spoken with another customer who was in the branch at the same time as your husband. He checked out."

"What about Greg's car?" Shelby asked. "Has anyone seen it?"

"No reports so far," Jackson said. "We've spread the word. If law enforcement spots it or pulls anyone over in it, they'll detain the occupants for questioning."

"So what now?" Shelby asked, her voice desperate. "I just wait?"

"That's really all you can do at this point," the detective said gently. "I'm heading back to the station now to look over Greg's phone and computer. I'll let you know if it generates any new leads." She eyed the woman. "Sure you don't want to go somewhere else? Or get someone over here to sit with you?"

Shelby wrapped her arms tighter around herself and Marseille and shook her head. "I can't face people right now. I want to stay here in case Greg comes home." She sniffled, blinked, and looked directly at the detective, her voice soft. "Miracles happen sometimes, don't they?"

Jackson didn't respond to the question. If she answered honestly, it would seem cruel. And if she agreed with Shelby, gave the woman false hope, it would be just as cruel. Besides, the question was likely rhetorical, and Jackson seemed to assume as much as well. She settled for saying, "I'll be in touch."

Her lip quivering, Shelby nodded.

As we drove off down the street, a news van from a local television station came around the corner. In the passenger seat sat Trish LeGrande, a brassy, bosomy reporter with hair the color of orange sherbet or circus peanuts. No doubt she'd come here in the hopes of interviewing Shelby Olsen about her husband's disappearance. She was like a buzzard, searching for carcasses on which to feast. But we had no legal right to stop her from approaching the grief-stricken woman we'd just left behind and, in fact, there were times the media could be a police department's best ally in identifying or tracking down suspects or people of interest. I only hoped her arrival wouldn't send Shelby over an emotional edge.

The heater whirred and warmed the car on our drive back to the station. Jackson's eyes drifted closed and her head bobbed a couple of times as she nodded off only to jerk awake again. She groaned and shook herself alert as the cruiser rolled to a stop at the curb in front of the station. "Thanks for your help, Megan."

"Any time."

With that, she climbed out of my cruiser, and my partner and I set out on our beat. I had quite a bit of autonomy while out on patrol, and I decided to use that discretion today to see if I could locate Greg's car. My guess was that Greg's killers wouldn't have risked traveling very far in his vehicle, especially once they realized they were transporting a dead body. They'd have likely ditched the Jetta, and Greg, too, within a short distance from the Olsens' home.

I drove to the more secluded areas of my beat to see if the Jetta had been abandoned in any of the out-of-the-way spots. The car wasn't in any of the parking lots at Forest Park. It wasn't hidden behind the bathhouse at the park's pool. It wasn't parked in the remote reaches of the TCU stadium's parking lot. It wasn't behind the dumpsters at a church or a shopping center. *Damn.*

I continued on and crossed the bridge over the Trinity River, which was brown with silt and moving swiftly with runoff from the morning's storm. I wondered if Greg Olsen and his car might be in the water below. It wouldn't be the first time someone had pushed a car into a body of water in an attempt to hide the evidence of their crime. Other times, criminals set cars on fire for the same reason. I supposed only time would tell what had happened to Greg and his Jetta. Then again, even time didn't always yield answers. Some cases went cold and remained unsolved for decades. But for now, I needed to issue a speeding ticket to the college kid in the sports car who'd just passed me doing 68 miles per hour in a 35 zone. I reached out to the dash, flipped on my lights and siren, and hooked a U-turn.

The following morning, as our shift began, Brigit and I headed directly to Detective Jackson's office for an update. On her desk sat Greg's computer and cell phone, the plastic evidence bags beside them. Both were plugged into a surge protector on the floor behind the detective's desk.

She looked up from her chair as we stepped into her doorway. Although her forehead was furrowed in concentration, she appeared better rested today. She motioned for my partner and me to come into her office. While I took a seat in one of the chairs, Brigit circled around the desk for one of Detective Jackson's ear rubs. Jackson reached down to grasp a furry, pointed ear in each hand and massage them. "How's the big girl this morning, huh? How's the big girl?"

Brigit wagged her tail to let the detective know the big girl was doing quite well this morning, thank you very much.

Jackson continued to stroke my partner while she filled me in. "There was nothing on Greg's computer or phone that gave any indication he's been having an affair or any type of problems with anyone. In fact, there was little on his phone or computer at all. What few personal e-mails there were in his inbox were mostly from Shelby or online stores he's ordered stuff from. His work e-mail account had nothing of interest, either. There were only a handful of contacts in his phone. His recent call history showed that the only numbers he'd called in recent weeks were Shelby's and his boss's number at the theater. He had the usual incoming calls from spammers and solicitors, but nothing from a private number other than Shelby's or his boss's."

"So he led a fairly insular life."

"Looks that way. He had a bunch of photos on his phone, but they were mostly of him and Shelby and their dog. He'd snapped a few pics of movie posters and a selfie of him with that cardboard cutout of The Rock from the theater's lobby, but that's it."

From what I'd heard, it wasn't unusual for a man who'd been married a while to lose touch with friends. Besides, I'd gleaned that the Olsens were one of those couples that did nearly everything together, functioned almost exclusively as a unit. Their unit didn't seem particularly extroverted, either. Nearly all of the photographs at the Olsens' house and on Shelby's social media showed the couple doing things by themselves, not with other people.

As the detective and I talked, the screen on Greg's phone lit up and the device blared the standard default ringtone. I looked at the screen. Although the phone faced the detective's side of the desk and I was reading upside down, I could tell the words on the screen warned SPAM RISK. There was no point in answering the call. *But wait a minute . . .* "Didn't Duke Knapczyk say that Greg's phone had played the 'Popcorn' song?"

Jackson sat up straighter, her brows moving up her

forehead. "He did." When the phone stopped ringing, she picked it up, typed in the password, and reviewed his ringtones before turning her gaze on me. "I don't see a 'Popcorn' ringtone on here."

"Think he deleted it yesterday after he left the bank? Maybe he got tired of it."

"Or maybe Knapczyk only thought the sound was coming from Greg. Maybe it was coming from someone else. There were quite a few people in line."

"If the sound was coming from someone else, it would explain why we didn't see Greg reach into his pocket to turn off the ringer." Besides, even though popcorn was generally associated with movie theaters, the song itself wasn't. "Or Greg could have had a burner phone on him and ignored the call."

"That's always a possibility." Jackson leaned back in her chair. "I'll run by the bank again, see if anyone heard the ringtone Knapcyk mentioned and whether they could tell where it had come from. In the meantime, I'll have the technical team take a closer look at Greg's computer and phone. They'll be able to recover any deleted files or browsing history, make sure I didn't miss anything. But unless they find something, this investigation could stall out."

"Nothing turned up on security cameras near the Olsen's house?"

"A convenience store picked up a glimpse of what might have been the Jetta heading north on Hemphill, but that's it."

With nothing left for the detective and I to discuss, I stood and patted my leg to round up my partner. "Call me if I can help."

She gave me an appreciative smile. "You know I will."

Brigit and I set out on patrol. As we cruised through

the well-established, exclusive Mistletoe Heights neighborhood, I spotted a white Chevy pickup with New Mexico license plates parked in front of one of the largest, fanciest homes. A sixtyish woman with olive skin and shiny black hair stood in the front yard next to a trim, silver-haired man wearing khaki pants, a white dress shirt with striped tie, and a heavy, fleece-lined shearling jacket. The two stared up at the gabled roof, the man pointing first to one spot, and then to another. Looked like the out-of-town roofing companies had set their sights on Fort Worth, too. Typical. Many contractors were mobile, taking their crews to disaster areas where skilled labor would be in short supply. Houston had become a contractors' mecca after Hurricane Harvey, pulling in construction workers from far and beyond to rebuild homes and businesses. Fortunately, the fact that contractors were willing to travel meant repairs could be made sooner and homeowners could get their lives back on track quicker than if everyone had to rely only on local construction crews. It was a win-win situation.

Brigit and I continued down the street and turned into Forest Park. My first murder case had originated in this very park, after a jogger found a corpse in the woods. The victim's face had been pulverized, and I'd lost my breakfast in front of a group of bystanders. I'd become more hardened since, but I doubted I'd ever get to a point where a violent crime scene didn't affect me. I might be a cop, but I was first a human being. It was impossible for those of us in law enforcement to completely set aside our emotions when working a traumatic case.

As a greenbelt that was dark at night, the park made a good place to dump a body. Although I'd driven around looking for Greg's car in the more isolated areas of my beat yesterday, I figured it couldn't hurt to make a more concentrated effort today on searching for his body. Greg might have been left here before his killers took off in his car. I decided to park and take Brigit on a walk down the trails, see if I spotted his body anywhere, or maybe a pile of loose dirt that marked a shallow grave.

I let Brigit out of the back of the cruiser and grabbed a tennis ball from her enclosure. We walked to an open area, where I threw the ball for her several times, letting her get some exercise and work out the kinks in her muscles from sitting in the car. I, too, worked out some kinks, performing some knee lifts and stretches. When I realized I was procrastinating out of fear that I might actually locate Greg's corpse in the woods, I called Brigit over, took a deep breath, and set out on the trails.

Enjoying her off-leash freedom, Brigit chased a squirrel up an oak, putting her paw up on the trunk as she barked up at the little beast. The squirrel clung to the bark, chirping down at Brigit, cursing her out in squirrel-speak. *Chit-chit-chit!*

Although the rain had moved on, yesterday's brief yet heavy storm had left quite a few puddles behind. Brigit stopped to lap at each one we came across, sampling each puddle as if she were a sommelier tasting a variety of vintages. *This puddle is mud-forward, with subtle hints of dry oak leaves and earthworm.*

As we made our way down the path, I peered carefully into the woods, looking for any clue that a body might be secreted among the trees and dead leaves. But all I seemed to see were squirrels making desperate searches for overlooked acorns, and twigs broken in the torrential storm. As we drew closer to the Trinity River that formed the northwest boundary of the park, my eyes landed on something bright yellow sticking out of a pile of leaves in the woods. *Could it be Greg Olsen's yellow theater uniform?*

It was a Schrödinger's cat situation. So long as I didn't verify what the yellow thing was, Greg Olsen wouldn't be confirmed dead. But if I determined that the yellow object was Greg's blazer—and found him dead still wearing it—there'd no longer be any hope at all. But there wasn't really even a glimmer of hope any more regardless, was there? Not with the lab confirming that all of the blood found in the kitchen belonged to him.

Ordering Brigit to stick close by my side, I ventured into the trees, the leaves crunching under my feet. I circled wide so as not to disturb any evidence that might be about. When I drew close, I squatted down and squinted at the object. *It's only a Lay's potato chip bag.* I released a long breath, equal parts relieved not to be facing a corpse and frustrated it wasn't the missing man. Brigit, on the other hand, stuffed her snout into the opening and licked the salty remnants from the crumpled bag.

My partner and I continued our trek through the trees. When we reached the river, Brigit traipsed down the bank and lapped at the water's edge, taking another drink. I, on the other hand, ran my gaze over the water and riverbank, looking for a body washed up on the shore or anything that might indicate a car sat under the surface or had been pushed down the slope. A pair of ducks floated past on the swiftly moving current, but nothing else caught my attention.

Where is Greg Olsen and where is his car? Normally, as we worked a case, I could sense us drawing closer and closer to the truth. In this case, though, it seemed that the truth was drifting farther away, much like the mallards floating on the Trinity.

FIFTEEN
BACK TO NATURE

Brigit

Brigit enjoyed being a pampered pooch, sleeping on Megan's bed and having her meals doled out from a can or bag rather than having to hunt down something herself for her dinner. But she also enjoyed taking breaks in Forest Park, where she could get in touch with the wild wolf deep inside her, chase the squirrels, feel the cool breeze ruffle her fur. She'd enjoyed the best of both worlds today. After Megan led her into the woods, Brigit hunted down a potato chip bag and licked the salty crumbs from it. She quenched her thirst afterward by drinking from the river and the puddles they came across.

After the break in the cold outdoor air, it felt good to be back in the warm cruiser, where she settled down on the fleece-covered cushion in her enclosure to take a nice little nap. Yep, while she'd enjoyed getting in touch with her inner wolf, she was also grateful to her ancestor who realized that buddying up with the two-legged creatures who could make fire might not be such a bad idea.

SIXTEEN
A PRISON OF HIS OWN MAKING

The Slasher

It was only his third day at the hotel, but already it felt as if the walls were closing in. It was like the COVID-19 lockdown all over again, except then he hadn't been alone. At least there was a sufficient supply of toilet paper this time. He was lonely and bored, his gloomy mood exacerbated by the dreary weather. He found himself humming the Eagles' "Hotel California," feeling, as the lyrics said, like a prisoner who could never leave. Ironic, since by hiding out here he was doing his best not to become an actual prisoner.

He'd shaved his head but not his face, doing what he could to begin transforming his appearance. According to the news reports, there'd been little advancement in the case. No suspects or even persons of interest had been identified. The car had not yet been found, either, though with the recent run of cold, wet weather that wasn't a surprise. Not many people wanted to venture out in frigid drizzle. Seemed the police hadn't determined a clear motive yet, either. Looked like they didn't know about the cash. *With any luck, they'll never find out about it.*

SEVENTEEN
THERE GOES THE BRIDE

Megan

Late Saturday morning, I stood in front of a three-way mirror in a bridal shop with four sets of eyes on me. One set belonged to my mother. The second set belonged to Gabby. The third belonged to Frankie. The final set belonged to Seth's mother, Lisa, who'd been thrilled to hear about our engagement. She'd never been married herself and would never have a daughter. She asked if she could be included when I went dress shopping, and I'd said, "Of course! The more the merrier."

Oh, how wrong I'd been. Had five women ever agreed on anything, much less a wedding dress? My mother preferred the old-fashioned styles with poofy sleeves and lots of ruffles. Gabby liked the excessively ornate models more suited for a princess than a police officer, while Frankie leaned toward the sexier, sleeker contemporary styles. Lisa liked the dresses in stark white, while I thought antique ivory better complemented my skin tone.

I wriggled into yet another overwrought model, with more shiny beads than a Mardi Gras parade. When I emerged from the dressing room, Gabby squealed, "It's so glamorous!"

"It is," I said. "But it feels too frou frou to me."

My mother rolled her eyes. "That's only because you're used to wearing epaulets and tool belts and holsters, not to mention those ugly metal-toed combat boots."

My tactical shoes were not combat boots, but there was no sense arguing the point. The only real difference between the two was the height of the shank. Neither was designed to be pretty.

I was a dozen dresses in, and going out of my mind, when Detective Jackson called and rescued me. "Greg's car has been located near Lake Worth. Want to head out there with me?"

Did I ever! "I'll be right there."

I begged off with profuse, if insincere, apologies to my family and friend, and to the sales clerk. "Sorry! Duty calls."

An hour later, Brigit, Detective Jackson, and I parked and approached a trailhead at Marion Sansom Park which flanked Lake Worth in the northwest part of the city. The Trinity River flowed through Texas for more than 700 miles, from its beginnings just south of the Red River that separated the Lone Star State from Oklahoma all the way down to Houston, where it emptied into the Gulf of Mexico. Dams formed a long series of lakes along the river's path, including Eagle Mountain Lake and Lake Worth, which were popular recreation areas.

A sign to the left of the path's entrance identified it as the Dam Drop trail. Cordon tape stretched from the sign to a tree on the other side, preventing anyone from coming this way. Jackson and I ducked under the tape and strode along a rough, rocky mountain-biking route that sat on a bluff above the dam. Brigit walked by my side, restrained by a short leash I'd wrapped tightly around my hand. The three of us moved as fast as we dared given the multiple tripping hazards posed by stones and roots along the way.

While the trail was wide enough in some places for two or three bikers to ride side by side, in others it was too narrow for a car to pass easily. Broken limbs on the scrubby branches along the way evidenced the damage caused when the driver forced Greg's car down the more constricted parts of the trail.

As we made our way, I inquired about Jackson's follow-up with the bank. "Did any of the employees hear the 'Popcorn' ringtone?"

"The tellers who served Greg Olsen and Duke Knapczyk both said they heard it, but they said it wasn't as loud as Knapczyk made it out to be. He was in a foul mood, so that might explain why it got on his nerves so bad. At any rate, since Greg didn't react when it went off, the teller he was dealing with assumed the sound was coming from someone else in line. Both tellers were in a rush to get all the customers handled before closing time, so they didn't pay it much attention."

In other words, the ringtone was another dead end. "What about Greg's phone and computer? Did the tech team discover anything that had been erased?"

"Nope. Greg doesn't appear to know a lot about technology. He had all sorts of cookies on his computer, and had never cleared his browsing history. Greg hadn't even emptied the trash on his computer since he bought it."

"So anything that was ever there is still there."

"Yes," she said. "And so far, none of it points to any personal reason for the attack. The theory that the attackers were after Greg to get access to the theater's safe is looking more viable."

The three of us strode around a bend, and there it was. The Jetta blocked the trail. In fact, the mountain biker who'd discovered the car this morning had barreled around the curve and slammed into the trunk, unable to stop in time. Luckily, the woman hadn't been seriously injured, though her front tire had popped and both the wheel and the frame of her bicycle had been bent. The athletic thirtyish woman and her bike sat off to the side. The woman was dressed head to toe in black Lycra and sported specialized biking shoes and gloves, as well as a helmet. A long auburn braid hung down her back.

An officer from the northwest beat guarded the scene, while a couple of the techs who'd worked the crime scene at the Olsens' house were also on-site, waiting to begin working this scene, too. Jackson had evidently told them to keep the scene intact until she arrived.

I eyed the Jetta. It sported no evidence of hail damage. The storm earlier in the week hadn't hit this area as hard as the central and southern parts of the city. Still, the damp ground told me this area had received some rain.

The detective held out her hand for a set of protective gear. As the tech handed it to her, she asked, "Is there a body inside?"

"Not in the cab," the female tech said.

She turned to the bicyclist. "Tell me what happened."

"I was coming down the trail pretty fast," the woman said. "It was my first trail of the day. I came around the curve, saw the car, and hit my brakes, but I couldn't stop in time. I plowed right into the back of the car."

"Did you touch anything?"

"I put my hands on the trunk to pull myself up after I crashed," she said. "I peeked in the windows, too, to see if anyone was inside. When I realized there was nobody in the car, I hollered to see if whoever had driven it back here was still around. I was really pissed, to be honest. I could've broken my neck, and I'm going to need a new wheel and tire and major repairs to my frame. This bike set me back nearly two grand. It's going to cost several hundred to fix it. Anyway, nobody responded when I called out. That's when I took a closer look through the window and saw what looks like blood smeared on the seats. I used my cell phone to call nine-one-one."

"So you haven't moved anything?" Jackson asked. "Picked anything up? Removed anything from the car or the vicinity?"

"No," the woman said. "I just waited here. This is the car that's been missing, isn't it? The one they've been talking about on the news?"

"It is."

The woman's face brightened and grew wary at the same time. She seemed excited she'd discovered critical evidence in a pending missing-person's case, but also wary to realize that violent activity might have taken place right here, where she had been mountain biking all alone this morning. My guess was the car had been ditched here shortly after Greg disappeared, but I could be wrong. It could have been dumped here as late as this morning.

"Mind if we get your prints?" Jackson asked the woman. "We need to be able to distinguish them from any others we might find."

"No problem."

The tech pulled a fingerprint card and ink pad out of his plastic tool kit and proceeded to take the woman's fingerprints, handing her a wet wipe when he was done so she could clean the ink off her fingers.

Jackson gave the woman a pointed look. "Have you told anyone else about finding the car?"

"Only my boyfriend. I called him after I called emergency services."

"Tell him to keep the information to himself and don't tell anyone else. Okay?" Jackson jotted down the woman's name and phone number, and told her she was free to leave. "I'll give you a call if I have any more questions."

The woman lifted her bicycle by the handlebars, keeping the flat front tire and bent frame off the ground and rolling the bike away on the back tire only.

After donning a pair of booties, gloves, and a disposable cap over her hair, Jackson approached the vehicle and waved the tech over. "Dust this door and handle for prints before I open it."

The tech did as he'd been told, applying dust along the edges of the door, paying special attention to the area just below the windowsill and along the outer door, where a person would have been most likely to touch it. He leaned down and looked closer. "Nothing's sticking. The door and handle have been wiped clean."

Jackson exhaled a huff of frustration. The attackers had kept their wits about them and covered their tracks. That told us they'd probably planned ahead.

Now that she knew she could pull on the handle without disturbing any prints, Jackson tried the door. It had been left unlocked and came open. At the detective's direction, the tech dusted for prints on the inside door handle, the lock, the steering wheel, and the gearshift. All had been wiped clean. So had the trunk release lever under the dashboard.

"Damn," Jackson muttered. "These guys were thorough."

Jackson cast a glance back at me before bending down next to the driver's seat to activate the trunk release. With a *pop*, the trunk latch let go and the top lifted an inch or two, not enough to give me a look inside the bay, but enough to make my heart race and my stomach turn a back flip like an extreme BMX biker coming off a ramp. Jackson gestured for the tech to check the trunk for prints.

He ran his powdery brush along the edge of the trunk and over it. "There's some prints on top," he said. "Two hands. Probably where the biker pulled herself up. But the edge has been wiped."

Jackson nodded and put her fingers under the lip, pausing just a second before lifting it. When a flash of bright yellow caught my eyes, I gasped and took a step back, my hand reflexively cupping my mouth. Jackson cut me some side-eye before waving me forward. "Buck up, Officer Luz. You want to be a detective? This is what a detective does."

Biting my lip, I stepped to the trunk and forced myself to look inside. Although Greg's bloodied yellow blazer lay balled up in the trunk, Greg himself did not. The gray carpet that lined the trunk was smeared with blood, though. Soaked in it, in fact. The blood formed a large, roughly rectangular shape, like a human torso. A sound came involuntarily from me, something that sounded a lot like Brigit's whimper.

Jackson glanced over at Brigit and me. "You two do your thing. See if you can figure out where the killers took Greg's body when they pulled it out of the trunk."

Though I knew my partner had a skilled snout, superior even to most of the other K-9s, it was asking a lot for her to be able to pick up a trail that was several days old, especially when it had rained in the interim. Still, if any dog could do it, it was my Brigit.

While the crime scene techs began a more detailed inspection of the vehicle, I led Brigit to the trunk and issued the order for her to trail. She sniffed around the space, leaving wet nose-prints on the cold metal of the car. She lowered her head, sniffing along the edge of the car and the brush along the trail. It took her much longer than usual to pick up a scent, and several times during the process she looked up at me as if to ask whether she could give up yet. I signaled her to keep trying. When she'd finally managed to lock on to some small scent remnant, she led us past the car and farther down the trail. Signs posted along the way warned bikers of the unprotected bluff and to stay on the path. Here and there along the way the detective and I spotted dried bloody smears the rain hadn't managed to completely wash away and areas where something heavy appeared to have been dragged. That something had likely been Greg Olsen's body.

Eventually, we reached a rocky outcropping that overlooked the lake and sat directly above the dam. The sound of rushing water came from below us.

Jackson issued a somber sigh as she pointed to another thick blood smear on the edge of the rock. "This must be where they pushed Greg's corpse over the edge."

Lest Brigit accidentally fall over, I order her to sit and stay while Jackson and I carefully eased forward to peer over the edge of the precipice. Below, water from the lake rushed over the dam's spillway. Over the days since Greg disappeared, the storm and subsequent runoff had filled Lake Worth to capacity and then some.

Jackson turned her head to stare off downriver and vertical lines of anxiety formed on the inside edge of each of her brows. I could virtually read her mind. Unless they were weighted down, dead bodies tended to float. The process of decomposition released gases inside the body that gave it buoyancy. With all the water pouring over the spillway, Greg's body could have been caught up in a current and carried over the dam and downstream. Or, if he'd floated off before the rains hit, he might have been caught in the flow that churned on the lake side of the dam. Then again, for all we knew, his body might have floated to shore somewhere or out to Goat Island, a small brushy land mass in the middle of the large lake. It was too bad he was no longer wearing his bright yellow jacket. The vivid cloth would have made him easier to spot.

Jackson gestured to Brigit. "See if she can tell us where they went after here."

Again, I issued Brigit the order to trail. She sniffed around for a few seconds before heading back the way we'd come. She didn't stop at the car, though. She kept on going back down the trail and into the parking lot. She seemed to lose the trail there, sniffing around in circles, unable to pick it back up. Of course, it was possible that whoever had ditched Greg's car here had been picked up in this parking lot by someone else, or had left a car here as part of a well-orchestrated escape plan. We couldn't know for certain at this point whether the attack on Greg had been premeditated and planned out, or was simply an impulsive crime of opportunity.

Jackson reached down and ruffled Brigit's ears. "Good job, girl. I know we've been asking a lot of you."

Brigit wagged her tail. I pulled a couple of liver treats from my pocket and fed them to her.

"I'm going to get some divers out here," Jackson said. "A bloodhound, too. With any luck, maybe they'll find some new evidence. You're free to go if you want."

I wanted to see how things played out here, and Brigit was enjoying being outdoors, keeping an eye on the squirrels and birds. "We'll stick around."

"I had a feeling you'd say that. You are nothing if not dedicated." But while she offered her support, she couldn't offer remuneration. "Our overtime budget's nearly used up," she said. "If you stay, it's on your own time."

"Understood."

We waited around for nearly an hour, chatting and talking in circles about the investigation, before two male divers arrived. One was African American and the other Caucasian. Both had short hair and the same swimmer's build as Seth, a lean body with muscular thighs and strong, broad shoulders. The detective showed them the spot where we presumed the attackers had tossed Greg's body off the cliff. She pointed to the water below. "There could be some evidence down there, too."

One of the divers eyed the other. "That water's moving fast."

"Don't take any chances," Jackson said. "If we need to wait, we can wait."

"We'll just need to take some precautions," he said. "Tie ourselves to a tree. Use some lights and DPVs." Noting the question on my face, he clarified. "Diver propulsion vehicles. They're like motors we can use to help us get around down there. DPVs allow us to stay down for a longer time, too. We use less oxygen than we would swimming on our own, so our tanks last longer."

Jackson tied a stretch of yellow cordon tape to a tree so the divers could us it as a point of reference. After consulting a trail map, they gathered up their gear and we followed them down the trail until we reached a lower point where they could enter the water with ease. Fortunately, the spot was on a small peninsula from which we could see the yellow tape fluttering up above to our left forty yards away.

Moving as quickly as they could to combat the cold weather, the men stripped down to form-fitting swimsuits before pulling on their wetsuits, diving gloves, and boots. They donned harnesses and air tanks, affixed sturdy cables to two trees approximately ten feet apart, and attached the ends to their harnesses. They put on their full-face masks, which included a communication system so they could speak to each other while down in the depths. After sliding into their flippers, they picked up their waterproof lights and torpedo-like DPVs, and duck-walked into the murky water, stirring up silt in their wake. They appeared to be melting as they disappeared into the lake, until they could be seen no more. Only the cable, the red-and-white flag-topped buoy marking their location, and a few bubbles rising to the surface provided proof they were there.

"Gotta say," Jackson said quietly, "those two didn't look too bad in those tiny bathing suits. The white guy could use some sun, but you can't really blame him for looking a little pale this time of year." She shot me a knowing glance. "Saw you checking them out, too."

Just because I was engaged didn't mean I'd gone blind. "Shame on us," I said, feeling no shame at all. "But, yeah, I totally agree. Not bad."

Brigit lapped at the water and sniffed around the bank while Detective Jackson and I stood in wait, rapt and anxious. A minute later, we saw the men's heads surface as they looked for the yellow tape to ensure they were searching in the right area. Their heads disappeared again as they dived.

The minutes ticked by, flowing far slower than the current. What were the men finding down there? Had they found any evidence the killers had thrown over the cliff? Had they located Greg's body, tied to heavy cinder blocks or kettle-bells?

Finding it impossible to stand still any longer, I paced back and forth along a twenty-foot stretch of muddy, rocky bank. Detective Jackson, on the other hand, improvised a seat on the trunk of a downed tree. Finally, the dive buoy moved in our direction and the water came to life, as if it were boiling. The two men rose from the water like sea creatures. One of them held a black garbage bag in his hand. The other held up a set of keys. *Yes!*

Jackson stood and the two of us met them onshore.

The diver handed the keys over to the detective. They were on a colorful souvenir keychain from Destin, Florida that was shaped like a sea turtle.

The diver with the garbage bag plunked it down in front of us. "This is all I found. Don't know what's in it. Could just be trash."

"So no body?" Jackson asked, looking from one of them to the other. "No weapon?"

"Not that we could see or feel. It's dark and cloudy down there right now. It's possible we missed something. It might be worth a second look once the lake level stabilizes and the silt settles."

"I appreciate you making the effort," the detective said, "especially in these conditions."

Jackson crouched down to untie the garbage bag. After ordering Brigit to sit and stay a few feet away, I crouched down beside the detective. The bottom of the bag bore remnants of lake-bottom muck and smelled like sewage. *Ick.*

While the men slipped out of their wet suits and back into warm, dry clothing, Jackson wrestled with the tight knot. Not easy to do with latex gloves on. When the knot finally came loose, she opened the bag and pushed the sides apart to reveal the contents. We bumped heads as we both leaned in to take a closer look.

"Sorry," I said, backing off a bit in deference.

Inside the bag was an assortment of clothing. Jackson pulled the garments out, piece by piece, and held them up. A man's extra-large zippered blue athletic jacket. A man's flannel shirt in red-and-black plaid, also in XL.

A man's medium gray sweatshirt bearing the blue Dallas Cowboys star logo. None of the items was especially unique or distinctive.

Jackson checked the front and back of each tag and inspected the collars closely. "I suppose it's too much to ask that the killers' names be written here in permanent laundry marker, huh?"

"It was worth a shot." After all, most criminals weren't the smartest people. They often acted on impulse and didn't think things through. Some had even committed crimes on their way to or from work while they were wearing uniforms or name badges.

The next items the detective pulled from the bag were two pairs of men's tennis shoes. She lifted the tongues and took a peek. "Twelve and nine-and-a-half."

The same sizes as the footprints left in the Olsen's kitchen. Jackson turned one of the larger shoes over so we could look at the sole. As she did, a steak knife slid out of the shoe and fell with a tinny *clink* to the rocky shore. Like the car on the cliff above us, the knife appeared to have been wiped clean. There was no evidence of blood or tissue residue on it.

I pointed to the sole. "Mild supination. Just like the footprints we saw in the kitchen." We might not have caught Greg Olsen's killers, but we had their shoes. That was a step in the right direction, no pun intended.

The bag had a few small holes where it had likely snagged on tree limbs as the killers carried it to the bluff to toss it over. Although the moving water in the lake had surely washed away some of the blood, light stains remained on the clothing and shoes.

Fully dressed now, the divers stepped over. "Anything useful in the trash bag?"

"Only the murder weapon and the clothing the attackers

wore during the incident." Detective Jackson gave them a broad, grateful smile and raised her hand for a high five. After palm slaps were exchanged, she said, "I can't thank you two enough. This gives us a new lead."

The only question now was, would this lead actually lead to anything?

EIGHTEEN
DO YOUR EARS HANG LOW?

Brigit

She heard a *jinglejangle* and looked down the trail to see a handler coming their way with a dog on a leash. It was a funny-looking dog. His ears hung down past his jowls rather than standing up tall and proud like Brigit's. How could the dog hear with its ear flaps dangling down like that? His skin was floppy, too. There were wrinkles all around his face.

When his handler held the bloody jacket to the dog's face and gave it an order, Brigit realized the dog had been trained to track a particular scent. Maybe those floppy ears and wrinkled skin helped trap the smells. Brigit had been trained to sniff out illegal drugs and to trail the disturbance left behind by a fleeing suspect, but she hadn't been trained to track a particular person by scent. She supposed it might be interesting to know how to do that, but she figured trailing a disturbance was more fun because it was more likely to lead to a chase.

As the dog walked past her, she gave a small tail wag in greeting and stepped back to give him room to work. *Respect, pal.*

NINETEEN
IS NO NEWS GOOD NEWS?

The Slasher

He glanced out the window for what had to be the hundredth time already that day. A Fort Worth police cruiser had rolled slowly by earlier, and he'd nearly wet himself. Luckily, the car had continued on, the cop at the wheel merely cruising his beat.

Being cooped up was making him paranoid. The lack of information only made things worse.

According to the saying, no news was supposed to be good news. But the lack of news regarding the murder investigation didn't feel good at all to him. Not knowing what was going on had twisted his stomach into a tight knot. Had the police found any leads? Was law enforcement on their trail? Could cops be closing in this very minute without his knowledge, maybe sneaking into the hotel through a back entrance?

Muffled voices sounded in the hall outside his door and every nerve ending in his body went on red alert. He rose reflexively from the armchair, his fight-or-flight instincts kicking in. He didn't want to fight, especially with armed cops, but how could he flee from this room? Besides the door, the window was the only way out. For safety reasons, the window didn't open. He'd have to smash it. But with what? The chair was too large to pick up, and the bedside lamp was bolted to the wall. It was at least a fifteen-foot drop to the hard pavement, too. If he were lucky, he'd only break an ankle. How would he flee then?

The muffled voices faded to silence. *Are they gone?*

He got his answer when the quiet was broken by the last sound he wanted to hear.

Knock-knock.

TWENTY
A CIVIL MATTER

Megan

Like Brigit, the bloodhound had done his darnedest to track Greg Olsen, but with limited results. The dog had led us to the parking lot for the park and through a wooded area past the YMCA camp and the Carswell Federal Medical Center, a former Air Force hospital that was repurposed into a minimum-security facility for female offenders suffering from health issues. As we trailed along behind the dog, the detective and I searched for more tell-tale smears of blood or flattened areas where something had been dragged, but we saw nothing.

When he reached River Oaks Boulevard, the bloodhound continued along on the side of the road, slowing down and stopping several times to sniff around and find the scent. Once the dog reached the Jacksboro Highway intersection, however, he trailed the smell to a sewer grate.

The handler looked up at us. "Either the remaining scent was washed down into the sewer by the rain, or the person we're looking for is down there."

Yikes.

Jackson lifted the manhole cover nearby and shined

her flashlight down into the concrete pipe. She stood, locked her gaze on me, and angled her head to indicate the hole. "Want to take a look down there?"

Visions of ten-foot alligators and swamp creatures and clowns with sharp teeth filled my head, and I spurted, "Why me?"

"Because I outrank you," Jackson said. "And you've got a better chance of getting in and out of that hole without pulling a muscle."

True. I didn't much like exercise, but I forced myself to work out on a regular basis to stay in shape. I faced all kinds of physically demanding situations on the job, and it paid to stay fit so that I could better handle them. The detective, on the other hand, spent a lot of time behind a desk.

I stepped over to the hole, sat down on the edge, and dangled my legs through. Fortunately, they nearly touched the bottom and no water was rushing through the drains. I eased myself down and reached up for the flashlight Jackson offered me. I had to hunch down and perform an improvised crab walk to make it down one side of the tunnel. I steeled myself with a deep breath in case I came upon a corpse. *You got this, Megan.* With another whimper, I shined the light into the darkness. Nothing down there but some waterlogged fast-food wrappers, small twigs, and now-dried worms that had been washed to their death.

I crawled back to the sewer grate. Jackson stared down through the open manhole. "Anything?"

"Not that I could see. I'll try the other side."

I ventured a dozen feet into the tunnel on the other side and shined the flashlight about again. *Nothing.* "Nothing on this side, either!" I called, my voice echoing eerily through the concrete tunnel. It was creepy and claustrophobic down here, probably not unlike the Paris Catacombs. Why anyone would want to venture into them was beyond me. My dream vacation involved sunbathing on a sunny beach with a margarita in my hand or hiking on a wooded mountain.

I returned to the hole. Both Jackson and the bloodhound's handler reached down to help pull me up.

As I wrangled the cover back into place, I looked up at Jackson. "Do you think the rain could have washed his body farther into the sewer?"

"I doubt it," she said, hedging her bets with a simultaneous shrug. "The river and lake are full because they collect runoff from the entire region, and there were major storms farther upstream. The rains here in Fort Worth were heavy, but they were short-lived. If Greg Olsen became submerged in this sewer, he might have floated away, but this system empties into the lake so he would've ended up there. I'm no water expert, though. I'll check with the public works department, speak to a water specialist, get an educated opinion."

A wise move. While common sense played a lot into detective work, sometimes an expert's input could be helpful.

In addition to the snacks the bloodhound's handler gave him, I offered him a couple of Brigit's liver treats, too. He'd been a *good boy*, and certainly earned them.

To ensure all bases were covered, cops from the beat began a ground search in the area between the sewer grate and the park. If Greg Olsen's body had been dumped in the woods or buried in a shallow grave and the bloodhound had somehow overlooked it, they'd find it. Of course it was possible the killers had dumped Greg in the lake, but had taken on some of his scent while they were handling his body. The bloodhound might have been tracking a secondhand scent, so to speak. *If only dogs and humans could communicate in more detail . . .*

Brigit and I begged off then. We had a double date planned with Seth and Blast, and the detective and local beat cops could wrap things up from there.

Jackson thanked me for coming out. "The department's lucky to have you, Officer Luz. You, too, Brigit." A proud blush warmed my face as she gave Brigit a scratch behind the ears. It was nice to be appreciated for a job well done.

Seth, Zach, and I leaped from our seats on the first row of bleachers, cheering as Frankie zipped past in the skating rink before us. As usual, Frankie was leading her roller derby team, the Fort Worth Whoop Ass, to a solid victory against their opponents, the Abilene Annihilators. The score would have been even more one-sided if the Whoop Ass hadn't been short two of their best team members, both of whom were out with the flu. The influenza virus had been going around the police and fire stations, too. So far, Seth, Frankie, and I had been lucky. None of us had caught the bug.

Blast and Brigit lay on the floor in front of us, snout to snout, panting softly, sharing a moment together. They'd been to enough of these roller derby bouts that they knew to ignore the noise and enthusiasm of the crowd. They only got excited when we made a trip to the snack bar to get them greasy hot dogs as a special treat. Even working dogs deserve a cheat day from their usual healthy diet.

As we watched the bout, I updated Seth on the latest developments in the Olsen case. "Detective Jackson plans to give the media photos of the shoes and clothing. We're hoping someone will recognize them and call in. There's nothing particularly distinctive about them, though, just typical stuff guys wear. There were no fingerprints on the car, the knife, or the keychain. The lab is going to run tests on the blood in the car and trunk to see if it all belongs to Greg Olsen, too, or whether some of it might belong to one of the attackers. Detective Jackson is going to canvass the area for video cameras to see if any of them picked up the Jetta."

"So the wife has been ruled out?"

"Nothing points to her," I said. "She's got an ironclad alibi for the night her husband disappeared, and there's no evidence that either of them was cheating or anything like that. In fact, everyone we've talked to says they seemed really happy together. They'd planned a trip to Fredericksburg. Detective Jackson found their hotel reservation confirmation in Shelby's e-mail inbox. She'd opted for a reduced prepaid rate that's non refundable. From everything we've seen, they seem to have expected to have a future together." At least as far as this weekend, anyway.

"I saw the wife on the news," Seth said. "She looked broken up."

I wondered if reporter Trish LeGrande would attempt to interview Shelby a second time once news broke about today's find at the lake. Over the past few days, she'd repeatedly played a clip of her earlier interview with Shelby, during which Shelby pleaded for anyone with information about her husband's disappearance to come forward. Trish would probably be thrilled to have some fresh fodder for her newscasts. Sex might sell, but so did violence.

We rose from our seats again as several players collided, fell, and slid across the floor, crashing into each other or the side of the rink.

I grimaced. "This sport is brutal."

Zach wagged his brows. "I know. That's what makes it so sexy to watch."

Brigit and I were scheduled to work swing shifts all week, from 1:00 to 9:00 p.m. It was my least favorite shift. There was little time to run personal errands before work, and if I tried I'd have to constantly watch the clock. We'd arrive home too late and too tired after the shift to tackle household tasks. But at least I'd get to address an item on my extensive wedding to-do list. Seth and I planned to meet at a local wedding venue on my dinner break, get a feel for the place.

My furry partner and I stopped by Detective Jackson's office Monday afternoon before heading out on patrol. "Any luck with the cameras near the lake?"

"We've got some footage, but I can't make anything of it." She waved for me to come around her desk.

Once I was standing behind her, she pulled up the clip. The video was a six-second segment recorded on a security camera mounted over a cell phone store. The clarity wasn't bad. Whoever installed the camera had opted for an expensive system. Problem was, the Jetta was too far away for the camera to provide a clear picture of the people inside.

After playing the video for me at actual speed, she replayed it for me at one-quarter time. The driver, who was on the far side of the camera, was merely a light-colored blur. The person in the front passenger seat wore Shelby's purple beanie pulled down tight over his head and had her scarf wrapped around his neck and the lower half of his face. All that was visible was the narrow stretch of face that included his eyes and the bridge of his nose, with some wild dark hair to each side. It was as if he were wearing the opposite of the usual superhero-type mask, which only covered the eyes and part of the nose. Instead, only those parts were visible. The fact that his head appeared to be nearly touching the ceiling of the car told me he was the guy who'd been wearing the XL jacket and plaid flannel shirt we'd found in the garbage bag.

"Sorry, Detective," I said. "I can't make much of it, either. Are you going to release it to the news stations?"

"Gonna have to," she said. "We need to get this investigation wrapped up. I'm falling behind on my other work." She gestured to a stack of manila file folders in her inbox.

"Any word from the lab or water department?"

"All the blood in the car was Greg Olsen's, even the blood on the seats. It must have transferred from the killers' clothes."

"Sheesh. They must have cut a major artery for him to have lost so much blood. Maybe more than one." If the attackers had turned Greg into a human Pez dispenser, as Derek had surmised, they could have cut through the carotid artery in the neck. The spray pattern on the Olsen's kitchen wall was consistent with the theory. Maybe they'd also cut the brachial artery near Greg's armpit, or one of the mesenteric arteries in his abdomen. The femoral artery in the inner thigh could leak a lot of blood if cut, too. I was beginning to feel lightheaded at the thought when Jackson thankfully turned the conversation from blood flow to water flow.

"The water department says it's unlikely there'd have been enough of a current in the storm sewer to carry a body, but they couldn't definitely rule out the possibility."

It was too bad this crime had taken place in the winter. If it were summer, more people would be out on the lake and about the river. There'd be a better chance of someone stumbling upon Olsen's body and, though that would undoubtedly be horrible for whoever did so, it would have been helpful to our case. "You going to send the divers down again?"

"This weekend," she said, "assuming we don't get more rain."

Texas weather could change on a dime. While there was no precipitation currently in the forecast, according to a quick consult with my weather app, there were no guarantees we might not be facing a monsoon by Saturday. "I'll keep my fingers crossed."

Brigit and I ventured out to our cruiser. A head topped with rusty hair bobbed among the cruisers. *Derek. Ugh.* We passed him on our way across the parking lot. He was just getting off the early swing shift.

He jutted his chin. "You find that dead guy yet? Figure out who killed him?"

"We're working on it."

"What's taking you so long, Luz-er? Looked like a cut-and-dried case to me. Well, cut and *wet*. Must've been gallons of blood in that kitchen." He cackled, the only one amused by his words.

Derek had once aspired to make detective, too, but had eventually realized he wasn't cut out for it. His most effective muscles were on his arms rather than inside his skull. Even so, that didn't prevent him from suffering a case of professional jealousy. I wasn't about to stoop to his level and throw shade his way, though. At least not at the moment. My mind was too busy mulling over the video clip to come up with a clever comeback.

I loaded Brigit into the back of the cruiser and we headed out. It was a pleasant day. Sunny skies. Temperature in the mid-sixties. I rolled the windows down a few inches so she could enjoy sniffing the breeze, feeling the wind in her fur. She lay on her cushion in the back, and a quick glimpse in my rearview showed her nose lifted to the wind, taking in the scents of our beat: the aroma of burgers and potatoes frying at the fast-food joints along University Drive, the odor of animals and the stench of their excrement as we cruised past the zoo, the smell of orange spice tea coming from the travel mug in my cup holder.

Of course our beat was filled with sounds, too, and Brigit's ears were perked to capture all of them. The white noise of traffic going by and the squeal of the brakes on city buses. The chatter of TCU students making their way to class. The *bang-bang-bang* of roofers installing new shingles on houses, a sound that filled the skies every two to five years.

Dispatch came across the radio. "Officer needed on a possible fraud call in Mistletoe Heights."

A fraud case sounded much more interesting than the typical car accident or noise complaint. I reached for my radio and pressed the button. "Officer Luz and Brigit responding."

Dispatch rattled off the address, and in minutes we were easing past roofing trucks to pull to the curb in front of a well-maintained two-story classic home fashioned from tan-colored brick. Chimneys rose from either side of the gabled roof, and the entry door sat at the back of an expansive covered porch furnished with padded wicker seating. White statuary featuring Greek gods and goddesses was positioned about the front flowerbed, enough to add character but no so many as to be tacky. Athena, the goddess of war, clutching a pointed spear. Dionysus, the god of wine, raising a chalice in one hand and a bunch of grapes in the other. Zeus, god of the sky, wielding a bolt of lightning.

Leaving the windows down for Brigit, I went up to the door and rang the bell. My partner watched from behind the safety mesh of her enclosure. A moment later, a sixty-ish woman with olive-tone skin and shiny ebony hair answered the door. I couldn't say for certain, but I was pretty sure she was the homeowner I'd seen speaking with the roofer from New Mexico a few days ago. I introduced myself and she did the same, giving her name as Althea Nomikos. She invited me in.

I gestured back to my cruiser. "I've got a K-9 in my squad car. Okay if we talk out here on the porch where I can keep an eye on her?"

"Of course," the woman said. She grabbed a thin document from a table inside the door and stepped outside. A skinny black cat darted out with her. She set the paperwork down on the wicker coffee table and scooped the cat up in her arms. "You're such a naughty boy, Morpheus."

"The god of dreams," I said. "Great name for a cat." After all, the creatures slept an average of fifteen hours a day.

She cradled her cat in one arm and held out her free hand to indicate one of the wicker chairs. She sat in the one across from it. Morpheus eyed me suspiciously.

I took a seat and pulled out my pen and note pad. "I understand you'd like to make a fraud complaint?"

"I suppose that's what you'd call it." Cradling her cat, she ran a hand over his head. "I signed an agreement with a roofing contractor last week after that hailstorm. Gave him a check for five hundred dollars. It's already cleared the bank. He said the crew chief would get a team started on my roof within two to three days." She pointed upward to indicate the roof. "As you can see, that hasn't happened." As if to add insult to injury, a *bang-bang-bang* came from the roofers nailing new shingles on the roof across the street. She looked across the way and frowned. "I should've hired those guys. They were out here within forty-eight hours."

"What's the name of the company and representative you dealt with?"

"Stormchaser. Their rep was Tommy Something-or-other."

She reached down to the coffee table and pushed the paperwork toward me. I picked it up and perused it. The document was a three-page contract for roofing services. Stapled to the top was a business card for Tommy Perkins, Homeowner Liaison for Stormchaser Roofing, Inc. The company's logo on the left side of the card featured a dark cloud with a tail of wind. The phone number on the card was local, prefaced with an 817 area code. A Yahoo e-mail account was also listed. I ran my eyes quickly over the handwritten information on the contract. Beside a typed line that read "Project start date," he had written 2/17. We were only three days past the 17th, but I could understand this woman's concern. Spring storms in North Texas could bring torrential rains and wind, along with significant water damage if a roof wasn't up to snuff.

I looked up at her. "I assume you've called Mr. Perkins?"

"A dozen times! He hasn't once returned my call. I've e-mailed him three times, too. He didn't respond to those messages, either."

I pulled out my police department cell phone. "Let me see if I have better luck." I dialed the number on the business card. The phone rang five times before going to voicemail. I frowned and shook my head, letting Althea know I hadn't reached him. A friendly voice proclaiming to be that of Tommy Perkins instructed me to leave a message and he'd gladly get back to me as soon as possible. I left a message advising him to give me a call right away. After ending the call, I turned my attention back to Althea. "Any chance you made a note of his license plate?"

"No," she said. "Didn't think I'd need to. I noticed they were from New Mexico, though. He told me he'd just relocated to Texas. He probably hasn't had time to get them switched out yet. At any rate, I didn't think much of it. He was an older guy, dressed nicely, looked trustworthy. He told me a neighbor down the street had sent him my way. To make matters worse, I got some of my other neighbors to sign up with Stormchaser, too. He said he'd knock fifty dollars off my final bill for each person I referred him to who signed with Stormchaser. I sent him next door and to my friend up the block. They're waiting for their work to start, too."

"Mind if I snap some pictures of your contract?" I asked.

"By all means," she said.

I took a close-up shot of the business card, and a full-size photo of each page of the contract before sliding my phone back into my pocket and returning the contract to her. "Could be he's running a scam," I told her. "Roofing is a notoriously fraud-ridden business. That said, it could just be that the company's swamped. Nearly everyone in this part of the city needs a new roof, and he might be scrambling to make the arrangements. But I'll keep trying to get in touch with him and let you know what I find out. In the meantime, you let me know if you or your neighbors hear from him, okay?" I held out my business card.

"So?" she demanded. "What do I do about my roof? Wait until it rains again and I get mold in my attic and water running down my stairs?"

"I certainly hope that won't happen," I said, attempting

to appease her. "I wish I could give you more definitive answers right now, but it's going to take some digging. In the meantime, it couldn't hurt to call a lawyer, see what they might suggest."

The woman huffed in frustration. "This guy steals from me, and the police won't help me? What has this world come to?"

Mustering up every last bit of my patience, I explained the difference between a civil case and criminal fraud. "It all comes down to the person's intent. If Tommy Perkins intended to rip you off, he could be guilty of criminal fraud. If he intended to replace your roof as agreed, but has suffered some type of unavoidable setback, this would be a civil matter that would have to be hammered out in court."

She finally took my card but scowled, clearly having expected more from me. But what could I do? I wasn't a miracle worker. I had no idea where the guy even was at the moment. But when Morpheus locked his golden eyes on mine and issued a low, rumbling growl that said, *You better make sure we've got a solid roof over our heads or I'll bring out my claws!*, I knew I had to find Tommy Perkins quick and get some answers.

TWENTY-ONE
THE BIG BANG

Brigit

The sound of all those hammers coming from the roofs had bugged Brigit. *Bang-bang-bang!* It had been a too-loud, unpleasant sound, and she didn't like that it kept her from being able to listen to other noises that might be important to hear.

At least it was behind them now. She and Blast walked along beside Megan and Seth as they looked around two mostly empty rooms and spoke with a woman. She wasn't sure what they were talking about, but her ears perked up when she heard some words she recognized. *Food. Park. Walk.* Whatever Megan and Seth were talking to the lady about, it made them happy. Brigit could smell their happiness. And when Megan was happy, Brigit was happy.

TWENTY-TWO
ANOTHER MAN'S SHOES

The Slasher

He'd gotten lucky. The couple who'd knocked on his door a few days ago had been mixed up, knocked on the door to the wrong room. He'd never been more relieved in all his life.

Tonight's evening news provided an update on the case, giving him even more relief. The Jetta had been found in Marion Sansom Park. While the report didn't mention that the clothing and shoes were found in a garbage bag at the bottom of Lake Worth, the newscast provided a photograph of them, asking viewers to call the police department if they recognized the articles and knew who they belonged to. Of course they'd had someone Photoshop the pics to get rid of the bloodstains on the clothes and footwear.

They're appealing to the public. That means they don't have any good leads.

Buying used shoes and clothing at a thrift shop had been a genius idea. He wished he could claim it as his own, but it was his partner who'd come up with it. He was tempted to dance a happy jig, but the last thing he needed was the guest in the room below calling the front desk to complain about him. He settled for pumping his fists in victory.

He woke the next morning in a foul mood. The wooden-shoe-wearing Dutch pogo-stick rider had been at it again last night, moving back and forth across the floor above, preventing the Slasher from getting a decent night's sleep. To make matters worse, the last of the food had run out at dinner yesterday. While he could stuff toilet paper in his ears to stifle the noise from his upstairs neighbor, he'd have no choice but to venture out of his room to get some sustenance lest he die of starvation. He was tempted to walk to the grocery store down the street, but he figured it was best if he stuck as close to his room as he could for the time being.

He waited until 8:55, just five minutes before the end of breakfast service, before sneaking downstairs. He took the stairs to avoid facing anyone who might be riding down on the elevator. Unfortunately, he'd have to pass the front desk to get to the breakfast room.

He peeked out from the stairwell. The clerk on duty this morning was the same one who'd checked him into the hotel days ago. *Damn.* If the guy recognized him, he might realize that the Slasher had taken pains to disguise his appearance. But he'd have to take that chance.

As the Slasher walked past the check-in desk, the clerk looked up from his place behind the counter and gave the Slasher a "Good morning." The Slasher said "'Mornin'" in return, summoning a deceptively husky voice. There'd been no flicker of recognition from the clerk. *Good.* Hell, he barely recognized himself when he looked in the mirror these days. Between his shaved head and the beard he'd dyed dark with the Just For Men Mustache and Beard dye, he looked like an entirely different person. As an added bonus, it was actually a versatile look. Add in the reading glasses he'd bought at the dollar store and he looked like a wise professor of English literature. Remove the glasses and add a bandana and leather jacket, and he could pass for a member of the Hells Angels.

As surreptitiously as possible, he slipped into the breakfast room, glad to see no other guests were lingering about. A full-figured attendant made her way among the tables, picking up trash other hotel guests had left behind. She wore blue latex gloves, the same kind he'd worn the night he'd put an end to Greg Olsen. She looked over at him, casting him a look of irritation. "Better hurry," she said. "I'll be putting everything away soon."

He grabbed a napkin and a disposable plate and bowl before considering the remaining options. It was slim pickings. A bruised banana. Half a bagel that looked as if it had been handled and tossed back into the bin. Oatmeal with a thick skin on top. But he supposed beggars couldn't be choosers. He filled the bowl with oatmeal, adding brown sugar and raisins. He bypassed the bagel and snagged a bran muffin. The early risers must have taken the more flavorful blueberry and banana nut muffins. He lifted an aluminum lid to find a single dried-up sausage patty lying in the warming pan. The patty looking about as appetizing as a hockey puck, but he took it anyway. He grabbed a couple of yogurts from the refrigerator, too.

With a smile and a duck of his head to the attendant, he scurried out of the breakfast area and returned to his room. He lay the meager meal out on the table and frowned. It was bad enough to be sleep deprived, but he'd be hangry, too, by the end of the day. *Tomorrow, I'll be the first person downstairs for breakfast.*

TWENTY-THREE
REASONS OR DECEPTIONS?

Megan

While I'd made no progress with regards to my wedding dress, Seth and I had chosen a venue and date for our wedding. We'd tie the knot on a Saturday evening in late September at the Historic 512, an elegant venue downtown that featured Georgian Revival décor. The ceremony would be held in the Great Room downstairs, with dinner, reception, and dancing upstairs in the Grand Ballroom. It was the first place we'd visited, but once we'd taken a look we saw no reason to spend time looking elsewhere. It simply felt right. The site was beautiful and had received resounding reviews from other couples who'd been married there.

The venue was affiliated with The Center for Transforming Lives, an organization that helped better the lives of homeless and poverty-stricken women and children, many of whom had suffered abuse. Clients received job training and financial-management instruction, while their young children attended preschool in the child-development centers. The women served by the organization put their skills to work as caterers for events held at the venue. We'd not only found a beautiful wedding spot, but we'd be supporting a wonderful cause as well.

We'd talked with the director about the food options, and verified the number of parking spots within walking distance. Brigit and Blast wagged their tails when they heard the words "food," "park," and "walk." I hoped they realized we were only gathering information, not trying to tease them.

It was Tuesday now, and Brigit and I had another dreaded swing shift ahead of us. I'd come into the station an hour early to see what, if anything, I could dig up on Tommy Perkins, who had yet to return my call. I took personal offense to that fact. It was disrespectful and only raised my suspicions that he might be up to some shenanigans.

I took a seat in my cubicle in the shared administrative area for beat cops and logged into the department's system. I had trouble identifying exactly who the relevant Tommy Perkins might be. In light of the fact that his truck was registered in New Mexico, I assumed he'd been issued a driver's license there, too. A search of the state's database coughed up several men by the name of Thomas Perkins, but having only gotten a glimpse of the silver-haired man as he stood in the yard in Mistletoe Heights a few days ago, I wasn't certain whether any were him.

Three appeared to be possibilities, their ages ranging from fifty-four to seventy-one. I printed out their photos and ran their names through the criminal database. I got a hit on one of the men. Thomas Donald Perkins, the 71-year-old. He had a misdemeanor theft charge for stealing three cartons of cigarettes in his hometown of Clovis a year back. I reached down to scratch Brigit behind the ears. "We should give him a call, shouldn't we?" She wagged her tail in agreement.

I found his home phone number online and gave it a try. He answered after the eighth ring.

"Hello, Mr. Perkins," I said. "This is Officer Megan Luz from the Fort Worth, Texas, police department. I'm calling because I see that you've got a conviction for stealing cigarettes and—"

"I had to take 'em! They're up to seventy bucks a carton. How's a person living on Social Security supposed to afford cigarettes at that price? It's highway robbery! Those tobacco companies got me addicted, and then the government raised the taxes on cigarettes. The government and big tobacco are in cahoots!"

No point in engaging in a debate on the price of tobacco products or the irony of his accusation given that robbery and shoplifting were both forms of theft, neither of which were relevant to my purpose for calling him. "You're retired?"

"Going on six years now."

"So you haven't come to Fort Worth recently to work for a roofing company?"

"Fort Worth? Roofing? I have no idea what in the Sam Hell you're talking about, honey."

Honey. More disrespect, likely due to the fact that I sported an innie between my legs rather than an outie, so to speak. He'd never have called a male cop *honey.* But it was pretty clear this Thomas Perkins was not the Tommy Perkins I was looking for. "Thanks for your time, sir. I believe I've called the wrong person." With that, I hung up.

I typed the search terms "Tommy Perkins" and "roofing" into my browser, but nothing pertinent popped up. I tried "Thomas Perkins" and just "Perkins" along with "roofing," but still got *nada.* I found no website for Stormchaser Roofing. The business didn't have a Facebook page, either. *Hmm.*

A search of the Texas Secretary of State's corporations database indicated that articles of incorporation for Stormchaser Roofing, Inc. had been filed only a month prior by a John Smith, no middle initial designated. An almost entirely useless and possibly false name. The filing date told me the company was new, the ink barely dry on its formative documents. Of course, the ink being barely dry was merely a manner of speech. Most corporate filings were submitted via the department's online electronic filing system, only the Internet, but no ink, required. The address Smith had provided was a PO Box in Austin, three hours to the south of Fort Worth. The designated agent for service of legal process was A-1 Corporate Agents, Inc., a third party corporation operated for the express purpose of accepting lawsuit petitions and other legal documents for its clients should they be sued. The arrangement was not unusual, especially for businesses such as roofing, contracting, or consulting that did not maintain a physical headquarters but instead performed their services at their clients' locations. Many of these types of business didn't need a bricks-and-mortar location because their workers operated out of their kitchens or vehicles. As a "Homeowner Liaison"—a fancy name for salesman—Tommy Perkins wouldn't need an office. He could handle any administrative work at his kitchen table. But just where was his kitchen table? Was it here in Fort Worth, or back in New Mexico? And which, if any, of the 248 John Smiths who held a Texas driver's license was the one who'd filed the corporate paperwork?

I was mulling over these questions when a ballpoint pen tapped me on the head. I spun around in my chair to find Detective Jackson with two laptops tucked under her arm.

"I need you to return these computers to Shelby Olsen," she said. "I called her to let her know we were done with them and that she could come pick them up, but she said she's in no condition to leave her house."

"Mind if I take a look at them first?"

"I've created a monster, haven't I?" The detective groaned and lay the computers down on the desk in front of me. "You're a big help, Officer Luz, but you can also be a pain in the butt. I told Shelby you'd be coming by soon. You've got one hour."

"Thanks, Detective."

"Shelby's password is the same as Greg's."

I recalled the password Shelby had given us on Valentine's Day. "The word 'always' in all caps, an ampersand, the number four and the word 'ever' in lower case."

"That's it." She tapped her watch to let me know my time was ticking away and headed back to her office.

I plugged in Greg's computer first, and entered the password. ALWAYS&4ever. He'd made things easy on us. He'd bookmarked the sites he visited most often and had saved the passwords so that they populated automatically. I pulled out my notepad and pen and jotted down the user IDs and passwords for his e-mail account, banking site, even his Netflix and Rotten Tomatoes accounts. Detective Jackson might have only given me an hour to look over the computers, but armed with his logins, I could spend as much time as I wanted reviewing his accounts later.

I plugged in Shelby's computer and discovered that she'd done the same thing—saved her passwords so that they auto-populated. Her user IDs and passwords went into my notebook, too. A search of her browser history showed mostly an obsession with dog toys and vacation sites. She'd run no search on "how to kill my husband," "hiring a hit man," or "top ten places to dump a corpse in Fort Worth."

With their credentials now safely in my possession, I

returned to Greg's computer. His browser history told me he spent an inordinate amount of time on the Rotten Tomatoes movie review site. I logged in and looked for reviews he'd written. "Holy guacamole," I murmured. The guy had reviewed nearly every movie released in the last fifteen years, as well as many of the classics. Some of the other posted reviews were short and not particularly insightful. *"Not enough boobs." "Too many boobs." "Chris Hemsworth makes my toes tingle, among other body parts." "My preschooler could write a better script than this!"*

Greg's reviews, on the other hand, were well thought out and very perceptive. He commented on dialogue, characterization, plot points, motifs, and symbolism. He seemed to appreciate a wide range of genres. He'd reviewed dramas, comedies, horror flicks, action-adventure movies, even children's animated features. His opinions and commentary were so discerning, he'd even been awarded the designation of "Super Reviewer" by the site. He'd reviewed a recent complex crime drama I'd seen with Seth, giving it a full five out of five stars. If criminals in real life were as smart as they were in the movies, law enforcement would have a much harder time. Luckily, clever criminals were few and far between in the real world off-screen.

A search in his documents files showed his multiple attempts to write a screenplay, though none were complete and only a few had been developed beyond the initial scene. A look at the document details showed that the last time he'd worked on one of the scripts was two years earlier. Looked like he'd given up on being the next Hollywood sensation and settled for being a modern-day Siskel and Ebert.

My mind turned and turned like a movie reel. I mulled over the thought I'd had earlier, that real-life criminals were rarely very smart. Lucky, maybe, but not clever. So how had Greg's killers kept us at bay?

A light went on in my mind, like a projector coming on in a dark movie theater. Could Greg Olsen's disappearance, like the movies, have been scripted? Was the crime scene just that, a scene? A setting in a theatrical production? If so, was Shelby in on the scheme, or was it a performance written and produced by Greg without her knowledge, aided and abetted by two co-stars? And, if so, why would he do it?

Faking one's death, or pseudocide, was not unheard of. But when someone wanted to erase their existence and assume a new one, there was normally a big reason for doing so. Maybe they wanted out of a marriage that was no longer working for them, but they didn't want to go through the pain and hassle of a divorce. Or maybe they wanted a clean break from family or other people or commitments in their lives. Or sometimes they hoped to avoid creditors and pull themselves out of overwhelming debt, get a fresh financial start. Or maybe I only hoped this scenario could be possible because it was less evil than the thought that two men could viciously shred another man with a steak knife in his own kitchen in front of his sweet little dog.

Of course, there was one big problem with this theory. One big, *bloody* problem. Nobody could lose the amount of blood found at the crime scene, as well as on the seats and in the trunk of Greg's car, and still be alive. Greg Olsen had to be dead. Was it possible the performance had gotten out of hand and not gone as planned? Had a mistake been made, with Greg accidentally being killed in the process?

My cell phone jiggled in my pocket and I pulled it out to find a text from Detective Jackson. *Time's up. Get going, girl.* I responded with a thumbs-up and gathered up the computers and my partner.

My stomach twisted and turned on the drive to the Olsens' house, and was still wrestling with itself as I carried the computers to the door. The broken windowpane had been replaced, any direct evidence of a murder having taken place here now gone. The death would forever taint the house, though. Few people felt comfortable living in a house where a violent crime had been committed, and the murder would impact the home's property value. The Olsens' landlord was liable to take a hit if he sold the house later down the road.

I knocked lightly. Shelby answered a moment later. She wore no makeup and her hair looked like it hadn't been combed since the night her husband disappeared. She'd been slender already, but now she appeared emaciated.

"Hi, Mrs. Olsen." I held out the laptops. "Detective Jackson asked me to bring these by."

Shelby reached out and took them from me, clutching them to her chest as if they were a lifeline to her missing husband. Marseille wriggled at Shelby's ankles and barked a friendly greeting up at me. *Yip-yip!*

I bent down to give her a scratch under the chin. "Hi, girl."

When I stood again, Shelby said, "This case has grown cold, hasn't it?"

I didn't want to quash any hope she might be holding on to, but I didn't want to lie to her either. "We're hoping some new evidence will surface"—I cringed at my inadvertent reference, knowing that if anything surfaced, it was likely to be Greg's body in Lake Worth or the Trinity River. "Comes up," I said quickly, then realized that phrasing wasn't any better. "Rises . . ." *Argh! Just stop talking, Megan!*

Shelby looked me directly in the eye. "Even if you

figure out who attacked Greg, he's never going to come back, is he? I need to face facts and move on with my life, don't I?"

I was in no position to give this woman advice, but I figured it couldn't hurt to agree with conclusions she'd already reached on her own. "That's probably for the best, Shelby."

She swallowed hard and closed her eyes for a moment before opening them again. She lifted her arms to indicate the computers she held in them. "Thanks for bringing these back, Officer Luz. And thanks for your honesty."

I wished I had more to offer her than my honesty, but I supposed it was better than nothing. "Take care, Shelby."

She closed the door behind me and I turned to return to my cruiser, feeling guilty to be relieved the interaction was over. While searching for evidence and deciphering clues was the fun and interesting part of investigative work, dealing with the victims and those affected by crime was the dark, depressing side.

Brigit and I were back out on our beat when I turned down a street in the Fairmount neighborhood and spotted a white Chevy pickup with New Mexico plates parked in front of a wood-frame bungalow-style home. *Bingo! Thought you could avoid me, did you, Tommy Perkins?*

I slowed and eased past. Nobody was in the truck. A scan of the area showed nobody standing in their yard or on a porch. Perkins must be inside the bungalow or another residence in close vicinity. I pulled my cruiser to the curb in front of his truck, backing up until there were only a few inches between my back bumper and the truck's grill so he wouldn't get any dumb ideas like trying to speed off.

I waited for a few minutes, keeping an eye on the

front door of the house, as well as my side and rearview mirrors in case he came up the street from another direction. Brigit stood in the back and wagged her tail, alerting me to the activity as the door came open on the house. The silver-haired man stepped out sideways, his head turned to look into the residence as he bade goodbye to a thirtyish woman in the front foyer. He wore dark slacks with a white dress shirt and red tie, but had paired them with no-nonsense work boots and the same warm yet stylish shearling jacket I'd seen him wearing before. I climbed out of my squad car and circled around to lean against the passenger side, my arms crossed over my chest.

Perkins told the woman, "We'll have that crew out here ASAP." With that he turned and took two steps forward before spotting me at the curb and faltering in his step.

The female homeowner spotted me, too, and stepped into the doorway with a concerned expression drawing her features inward.

Perkins smoothed his tie, smiled, and came forward. "Good afternoon, ma'am. Something I can do for you?"

"For starters, you could've returned my phone call."

"You must be Officer Luz." He stepped closer, maybe too close, as if trying to keep our conversation from being overheard. At this proximity, I could see he had bluish-gray eyes that nicely complemented his silver-white hair. He resembled Paul Newman. He dipped his chin in greeting. "I'm Tommy Perkins. Nice to meet you."

I cocked my head, letting him know I was still waiting for an explanation.

"My apologies, officer. I've been planning to call you, but I've spent the last twenty-four hours putting out fires, so to speak." He motioned at the houses around us. "As you know, that hailstorm did a number on these homes."

"It sure did. Are you now doing a number on these homeowners?"

His brow furrowed, the deep lines reminding me of the wrinkly Shar-Pei Brigit had befriended at the dog park. "What in the world would make you think that?"

"You told Althea Nomikos that your company would get started on her roof right away. It's been a week, and she says you haven't returned her calls."

By then, the woman in the doorway had walked out to the sidewalk. "May I ask what's going on, officer?"

"That's what I'm trying to figure out," I told her.

Perkins looked from me, to the woman, and back again. "I stopped by Mrs. Nomikos's house twice to give her an update. I figured a personal visit would be better than a phone call. She wasn't home either time. As a matter of fact, I left my card in her door with a note yesterday evening. I assumed she'd let you know. The crew chief told me there's been a run on shingles and every building supply store within a hundred miles is out of them. The good news is that we're expecting shipments in another day or two."

The woman's eyes narrowed slightly as she eyed Perkins. "You didn't mention a shingle shortage."

"Like I said," he repeated, "we're expecting shingles to be available in just a day or so. It shouldn't delay the work on your place. Besides, every other roofing outfit will have the same problem. No one else can get a new roof on your house any faster than Stormchaser can."

He might have a point. Then again, he could be full of crapola. But maybe I was taking things too personally, finding offense where none had been intended. After all, it wasn't unreasonable for him to expect Mrs. Nomikos to follow up with me if he'd stopped by her place and left a message. This woman appeared appeased, at least. Her frown and posture relaxed.

His customer seemingly satisfied, Perkins returned his attention to me. "I've been trying to keep all the customers updated. I'm at the mercy of the crew chief, though. He's the one who schedules the jobs. But I'm busting my hump to help people get their roofs fixed before more rain sets in. You've got my word on that."

Question was, was this guy's word any good? Or was it just lip service?

Seeming to realize I had yet to be fully convinced, he said, "We've complied with the terms of our contract." Perkins riffled through his clipboard until he found a blank copy of the triplicate roofing agreement. "See here?" He held out the document, pointing to Section 9. "That part says that Stormchaser will make all reasonable efforts to begin work by the date noted. We've done that. It also says that start dates might be delayed due to unavailability of skilled roofers or necessary materials. There's nothing more we could have done. Wish there were. I hate to see folks upset."

Before I could respond, dispatch came over my shoulder-mounted radio. "K-9 unit requested at Magnolia and Washington."

I squeezed the button. "Officer Luz and Brigit responding." I turned back to Perkins. "Let me take a look at your driver's license real quick."

"Of course."

He pulled his wallet out of his pants pocket. He held it in his left hand as he removed his license. A shiny silver band encircled his left ring finger, telling me there was a Mrs. Perkins back home waiting for him, while his silver and turquoise watchband told me he appreciated

Native American artistry. He handed his license to me. As expected, it was a New Mexico license. The name on it was James Thomas Perkins. *No wonder I didn't find him in the drivers' license database.* I hadn't realized he was going by his middle name, and a nickname at that. I whipped out a pen and quickly jotted down the license number before returning it to him. "Have you moved to Texas?"

"Not permanently, ma'am. I work on a seasonal basis. I got this gig with Stormchaser to help them out during the busy spring storm season. I'll be heading back to Las Cruces once things slow down."

"Where are you staying here locally? A hotel?"

"No, ma'am. I got a long-term rental through Airbnb. Nice little house not too far from here."

"What's the address?"

He provided an address on West Gambrell Street in the South Hills neighborhood. I jotted that down, too.

After returning my pen and notepad to my pocket, I said, "Keep things moving along as quick as you can. And return phone calls from now on." After all, we could've avoided this exchange had he taken a minute to call me. With a pointed look I circled back around my cruiser and climbed in.

He raised a hand goodbye. "Have a nice afternoon, Officer Luz!"

In minutes, Brigit and I pulled up to the scene of a traffic incident. Derek's cruiser sat in the right lane, its lights flashing. Just ahead was a vintage convertible Ford Mustang in deep green with a tan ragtop. *Nice ride.* Both the driver and passenger doors were open, the seats empty. Derek paced back and forth on the curb, his face flaming as red as his hair.

I slowed as I passed the two cars and pulled to the

side in front of the Mustang, turning my lights on, too. I climbed out of my car and opened Brigit's enclosure to attach her leash. As she hopped down to the asphalt, I noticed the registration sticker in the Mustang's front window was a month out of date. It didn't take a detective to figure out what had happened here. "Let me guess," I said to my former partner who looked ready to explode. "You pulled the 'Stang over for expired registration, and it turned out it was stolen?"

Derek glared at me, as if it was my fault he'd been made a fool of. "The driver took off in one direction, and the passenger took off in the other." He tossed one hand to the right and his other to the left.

"You could've tried to chase one of them."

"Not after eating three bean burritos for lunch!"

Sheesh. "Duty before self, Derek. Ever heard that phrase?"

He scowled and spit out a comeback, complete with air quotes. "It's not 'duty before burritos.'"

"The burritos are implied." *Idiot.* "What did the guys look like?"

Derek shrugged. "One was white. The other was brown. Both are wearing dark hoodies."

I led Brigit over the driver's door of the Mustang and instructed her to trail the disturbance left by the fleeing subject. She trotted off through the parking lot of a microbrewery and pizza joint with me jogging behind her. We continued on for a quarter mile before she hooked a right into a residential area. We jogged on for a block or two, then turned down a side street where I spotted two navy blue hoodies that had been tossed into the bushes. After running off, they must have gotten in touch via their cell phones, hooked back up here, and ditched their jackets to be less recognizable. They should have made some attempt to hide the clothing. These criminals were typical, not the sharpest tools in the shed, leaving a proverbial trail of bread crumbs for my partner and me to follow.

De Zavala Elementary School sat just ahead. Several small groups of mothers wearing puffy coats and scarves stood huddled about, chatting amiably as they waited for school to let out for the day. The few fathers formed a faction, too, though they stayed close to their cars in the pickup line. Two twentyish young men hovered near the dads. One of the young men was white, while the other had light-brown skin. Though the two men did their best to blend in, the fact that they shifted nervously from foot to foot and wore only short-sleeve T-shirts despite the frigid temperatures told me we'd found our car thieves.

I ducked behind the school sign and activated my shoulder radio. "Suspects located at De Zavala Elementary. Transport needed."

I led Brigit out from behind the sign and instructed her to continue to trail. The two men looked our way as we approached. The white guy put a hand to his mouth so I couldn't read his lips as he spoke to his buddy, but my guess was he whispered something along the lines of "Be cool, bro."

Brigit led me right up to the two men and sat, giving me a passive alert that said *The trail stops right here.*

"Hi, there," I said. "You two here to pick up your kids up from school?"

They exchanged a glance before the white guy said, "Getting my little sister."

The other said, "I'm just with him."

My gaze shifted back to the white guy. "What's your sister's name?"

He hesitated a moment before coming up with "Grace."

"What grade is she in?"

"Second."

"I see. So y'all wouldn't know anything about the Mustang that was ditched on Magnolia Avenue, then?"

BZZZZZZZT. The school bell rang, telling me I'd better get this wrapped up quick before any children were put at risk.

The mouth of the Latino went slack as he tried to summon a response that refused to come. The white guy, on the other hand, bolted off across the school's front lawn. I gave my partner her orders. He made it only a dozen steps before Brigit sailed through the air, landed on his back, and brought him down face-first in the dried grass and dirt. He cried out and spewed a string of expletives that turned the head of every parent in the vicinity.

"Don't move!" I hollered. "Or she'll bite!" I turned to the guy still standing in front of me. "You gonna do something stupid like that, too, or do you want to just turn around and let me cuff you?"

He snorted. "I ain't stupid." He turned around and put his wrists together behind him, as if he knew the drill.

"You seem like an old pro at this," I said as I slapped the cuffs on him.

"This ain't my first rodeo."

"Maybe you should think about making it your last."

By then, children were streaming out of the school, some shouting and running, excited to be done for the day. Derek pulled his cruiser to the curb, lights flashing. After he took the shackled suspect off my hands, I walked over to the prone man on the ground. "I'm going to call off my dog and take your arms. No funny business. Hear me?"

"Loud and clear."

I signaled Brigit to climb off his back. She stood nearby while I cuffed the guy, hauled him to his feet, and handed him over to Derek, too. My former partner didn't bother to thank me or Brigit for our assistance.

"Hey, lady!" a little boy called. "Can I pet your dog?"

"Thank you for asking first," I told him. "She'd love for you to pet her."

Before I knew it, six or seven children had surrounded my partner and were petting her from head to tail. She flopped over on her back so they could scratch her chest and belly. They giggled and knelt down beside her. Pretty soon, so many children had gathered around wanting a turn that I had to make them form a line and limit each of them to a five-second interaction lest we be stuck here the rest of the day. *It's not easy managing a star.*

TWENTY-FOUR
I SMELL BULLSHIT

Brigit

Usually when people showed their teeth, it meant they were happy. Brigit had been smart enough to figure that out over the years. But the guy at that house earlier had shown his teeth even though he wasn't happy. Brigit could smell the adrenaline on him. He was nervous for some reason. Megan didn't seem to notice the scent, though. Poor humans and their inferior senses. If only they could smell better, they could determine who was a threat and who wasn't just by their odor.

The guy she'd tackled at the school had been a threat, too. He had given off all kinds of smells. So had the other guy who'd been with him. At least Megan had realized they were bad guys and taken them away from the children. Megan had fed her a liver treat after, but the scratches and belly rubs from those kids had been an even better reward. She wondered if maybe someday Megan would get a kid for Brigit to cuddle and play with. It sure would be fun.

TWENTY-FIVE
EARLY TO RISE

The Slasher

This place might as well be called Hotel Hell. He'd spent the better part of yesterday fighting a fever and nausea. Law enforcement might not have caught up with him, but the influenza virus had. What's more, a family had checked into the room next door to him at midnight and had banged around for a full hour before finally settling down. He'd just fallen asleep again when their baby woke at two o'clock and screamed for three straight minutes at the top of its lungs. The infant performed an encore performance at five o'clock. He'd barely closed his eyes again when his alarm went off at five forty-five, just in time for him to dress and be the first guest down to breakfast.

He relieved himself, splashed some water on his face, and slid into his jeans and a long-sleeved T-shirt. After more than a week in these same clothes, they could use a wash, but he had nothing else to wear while he ran a load of laundry. At least he'd been able to wash his underwear in the bathroom sink and let them dry while he slept commando. There was a Dollar General store only a mile from the hotel. Maybe he'd walk there and grab a few things, some clean socks and underwear, a shirt or two.

He was tired of feeling trapped in this place. He could use some fresh air and sunshine, too.

He took the stairs down to breakfast again, surprised to find two other early risers already digging into the spread. Neither of them paid him much mind, more interested in filling their plates. He followed suit, loading a plate with scrambled eggs and toast and two raspberry Danish. Thank goodness that bug he'd suffered yesterday had passed quickly. His appetite was back.

As he returned to his room, he wondered how his partner in crime was faring. He'd waited to reach out, not wanting to do anything that might lead the police to him. But the police investigation didn't seem to be leading anywhere, as far as he could tell. Soon, it should be safe to make a connection.

TWENTY-SIX
CASHING OUT

Megan

Frankie wandered into the kitchen Wednesday morning to find me sitting at the table with my laptop in front of me and a mug of steaming coffee in my hand. "What are you working on?"

"That murder case," I said. "I'm beginning to wonder if it's really a murder case, or at least I'm wondering if that's what it started out to be."

Her face screwed. "Sounds complicated. Let me get some coffee before you blow my mind." She reached for the pot, poured herself a cup, and plopped into the chair across from me. She slugged back a hot mouthful, leaned forward intently, and said, "Okay. I'm ready now. What the heck are you talking about?"

"I'm wondering if Greg Olsen might have meant to fake his death, but then went too far and accidentally got killed in the process."

"Why would a person fake their own death?"

I offered her the same reasons I'd heard. Bad marriage. Financial problems. Other relationships or commitments he might want to get out of. Evading outstanding arrest warrants.

She held her mug to her lips and blew on the hot brew. "Is there evidence to support any of those motives?"

"No," I said. "That's where the theory falls apart. By all accounts, his marriage was good. He and his wife were exceptionally close. He has no criminal record, and he seemed to like his job. He's been with Take Two Theaters for years. Detective Jackson ran credit reports for both Greg and his wife, and they've both got stellar scores. They recently sold their house in Oklahoma for a profit. There's plenty of money in their checking account." I turned my screen to show Frankie the balance in the Olsens' account before turning it back my way. "Still, something just doesn't feel right to me. Greg is really into movies, and something about this whole thing feels scripted." What's more, I didn't like being unwittingly cast in the role of bumbling cop.

"I suppose any premeditated crime is scripted, in a sense," she said. "But you've got good instincts. Detective Jackson and Detective Bustamente are always telling you that."

"Even so, I need something concrete before I can take this theory to Jackson or she'll think I'm nuts. I don't want to lose credibility with her." I eyed the checking account data again. "Their account shows several transactions on Greg's debit card for just over one-hundred dollars in the past few months. There's a bunch for just over eighty dollars and just over sixty dollars, too. It's odd, isn't it?"

"What kind of transactions?"

"Purchases at grocery stores. Dollar stores. Target. Walmart."

"Maybe he was getting cash back," Frankie said. She mentioned that when she'd worked as a night stocker at the Kroger grocery store before joining the fire department, she'd help out on the cash registers when the lines grew long or a cashier needed to take a break. "Customers would sometimes get cash back on their debit cards when they bought groceries. It saves them a separate trip to an ATM."

"So Greg might have been using these stores like a clandestine bank, withdrawing cash from his account along with small purchases." My body began to buzz. "You may be on to something, Frankie."

"Do you have his debit card number?"

"No, but his card's in the evidence locker at the station." I stood, circled the table, and gave my roommate a hug. "What would I do without you?"

"I feel the same way about you." She looked up at me, her blue eyes misty. "I suppose we'll find out soon enough."

Tears pricked at my eyes, too, and I fanned my hands in front of them in a vain attempt to dry them. "Just because we won't be living together anymore doesn't mean we'll be out of each other's lives. We'll still have our girls' nights, and you know I'll make every Whoop Ass game I can."

Zoe sauntered sassily into the kitchen, took one look at my fuzzy slippers, and pounced, her claws digging into my right foot as she rabbit-kicked my footwear. "Ouch!" I lifted my foot, cat and all, and glared down at the ferocious feline. "I'm not going to miss you one bit, Zoe."

"Sure you will," Frankie said as she extracted her cat from my flesh. "You love her almost as much as I do."

I reached out and ruffled the calico's ears. "Dammit, you're right."

Once again I arrived at the station early for my shift. I went to the evidence locker and asked to see Greg Olsen's wallet. "I don't need to check the evidence out," I told the clerk. "I just need to get his debit card number."

The woman consulted her computer to determine where the evidence was stashed and went to the appropriately numbered locker. She removed the plastic bag that contained the wallet and brought it to me. I opened the wallet, slid the debit card out of the slot, and set it on the counter so I could snap a photo with my phone. I returned the card to the wallet and thanked the clerk.

As Brigit and I patrolled our beat, I turned into one of the grocery store parking lots and led Brigit inside to the customer service booth. "I need some information about purchases made with a particular debit card. Is that something you can help me with?"

The attendant said, "I'll need to get the manager's okay first."

"No problem."

She picked up her phone and punched in two digits. "There's a police officer here who wants some information." She paused for a beat. "I'll tell her." She hung up the phone and turned her attention back to me. "He'll be right down."

Shortly thereafter, a door opened at the back of the booth and a fiftyish man with salt-and-pepper hair and a thick seventies-style mustache emerged. He stepped over to the counter. "Hello, officer. What can I help you with?"

I told him the reason for my visit. "I need information about transactions on a certain debit card made here in the store."

"No problem." He waved me over to a computerized cash register at the end of the counter that wasn't in use. After logging into the system, he asked, "Got the card number for me?"

No sense tipping my hand and risking information getting out, especially when I might be totally off base with my theory. Rather than show him the photo of the debit card, which revealed Greg Olsen's name printed across the bottom, I called the number out instead.

The man typed the number in as I read it off, repeating each set of four digits out loud to ensure we were in sync. When he was done, he hit ENTER and consulted the screen. "There've been twenty-two transactions on that card here in the store. The first was back in November and the last one was a little over a week ago. Would you like me to print copies of the receipts?"

"That would be great."

As the paper tape churned out of the top of the machine, he cut a curious look my way. "Stolen card? Fraud?"

"Something like that," I said.

He frowned. "I wish people would keep their PIN numbers secure. Grocery margins are small to being with, and we lose quite a bit of income to debit and credit card fraud."

"I feel your pain. Stolen cards take up a lot of the department's time, too."

When the tape finally stopped printing, it was nearly as long as I was tall. The man tore it from the machine and folded it over neatly, securing it with a paper clip. I thanked him and headed for the door, but Brigit had other ideas. She tugged on her lead and tossed her head, telling me she wanted to make a trip to the pet care aisle. I was dying to review the tape, but when she batted her big brown eyes at me, how could I tell her no?

"All right, girl. You win."

Brigit wagged her tail and let her nose lead us to the shelves of toys and treats. She sniffed the bags and boxes until deciding that a box of peanut-butter-flavored canine cookies smelled good. She put her paw on the box and looked up at me, batting her big brown eyes again. *That darn dog has me wrapped around her paw.*

I grabbed the box and tucked it under my arm. "Anything else, you spoiled mutt?"

She looked around, sniffed at the toys hanging from the pegs, and nudged a bone-shaped chew toy. I pulled it off the peg and we made our way to the self-checkout, where I rang up the toys and paid for them.

Back at the cruiser, I loaded Brigit into her enclosure. She wagged her tail and watched intently as I removed the chew toy from its packaging. I held it out and she grabbed it in her teeth, circling twice before plopping down on her cushion. I stashed the box of dog cookies in the front floorboard, removed the paperclip from the register tape, and reviewed the receipts. Sure enough, nearly all of the transactions on Greg Olsen's card involved a small purchase along with a cash back. A single bag of ground coffee. A loaf of whole wheat bread. A box of the same peanut-butter dog cookies Brigit had just chosen. Armed with this new, potentially incriminating information and a renewed sense of hope that we might actually make some progress in the case, I set off again.

In between dealing with traffic matters and a vandalism report involving garden gnomes posed in compromising and scandalous positions, I stopped at the various stores where Greg Olsen had used his debit card. While he sometimes used the card to buy a variety of groceries or other items, in the vast majority of the cases he purchased one or two items and received cash back in the amount of sixty, eighty, or a hundred dollars. There was nothing unusual about someone carrying around some cash for small purchases or incidentals, but it was rare for someone to carry large amounts of cash these days. Not only was it unnecessary with plastic being accepted almost everywhere, it was also risky. Wallets could be lost or stolen. While a credit or debit card could be deactivated and replaced, cash money couldn't. It was clear that Greg Olsen had been stockpiling cash. But what had Greg Olsen done with that cash? Had he spent it? If so, what had he spent it on?

Playing devil's advocate with myself, I racked my brain for a reasonable explanation. Restaurants were notorious hotbeds for theft of debit and credit card numbers. After all, the servers generally carried the card away to process it, giving them an opportunity to snap cell phone pics of the front and back of the card, including the three-digit security code and the card-holder's signature. Maybe the Olsens had heard that restaurants were risky places to use a card, and had used the cash at restaurants.

To determine whether this might be the case, I logged back into the Olsens' bank account. *Nope.* Their transaction history showed that they'd eaten out plenty and used their debit cards to pay for their meals. The account showed at least one restaurant charge each weekend, sometimes two. The couple seemed to gravitate toward upscale restaurants serving Asian or European cuisine. Charges appeared at several sushi and hibachi restaurants, as well as Thai, French, and German eateries across the Dallas-Fort Worth metroplex.

What about gas? Gas pumps were notorious places for unscrupulous card counterfeiters to install "skimmers" that read and stole card numbers. But no, that wasn't the case here, either. The Olsens had used their debit cards rather than cash to pay for gas, as evidenced by regular charges at a Texaco station near their home.

Could they have used the cash for parking? Again, nope. The bank records showed a repeated charge in the same amount for monthly contract parking at the building where Shelby worked. Greg parked for free in the theater's lot.

The only other ideas I could come up with involved some type of illegal activity, such as drugs or gambling, but neither seemed plausible in this case. Greg held a steady job, and there'd been no illegal drugs found in his car or the Olsens' home. None of his phone records showed calls to or from a known drug dealer or bookie. Then again, he could have used a burner phone to make those calls, a burner phone with a ringtone that played "Popcorn." *Maybe Duke Knapczyk had been right, after all.*

If Greg had withdrawn a large amount of cash directly from their account to pay a drug dealer or a bookie, Shelby would likely have noticed. But she was far less likely to discern that he might have taken cash back with his purchases to finance a drug or gambling habit. During the interview at her home on Valentine's Day, she'd said that neither she nor her husband used drugs or gambled. But my police work had taught me that people often didn't know their family members or friends nearly as well as they thought they did, or had blind spots or were in active denial about their loved one's shady activities.

But ugh. I realized that my thought process had taken me in a circle. I'd started out thinking Greg might have stockpiled cash to make his own escape, but then come around to thinking he might have been offed by a drug dealer or bookie he owed money to. Of course, he could have attempted to fake his death to get out of a debt owed to the dealer or bookie. But if that was the case, then who were the two people who helped him make the attempt that had evidently gone awry? He appeared to have no friends in the city. Might he have rounded up some unsavory types at a sleazy bar? My mind spun, unsure which theory to land on.

I drove to the station when my dinner break started at 5:00, and was lucky enough to catch Detective Jackson on her way out. I tooted my horn to get her attention, lowered my window, and raised a hand to stop her.

"Uh-oh," she said as I pulled to the curb in front of the station. "You've got that I-might-be-on-to-something look in your eyes."

"Only I'm not sure what it is I might be on to." I handed her the stack of receipts I'd collected and told her my theories.

She quickly perused the receipts and raised a brow before turning back to me. "I hate to burst your bubble, and I admire both your imagination and the thought you've put into this case, but I'm not on board with your 'faked death gone wrong' theory. It's too Hollywood. Greg Olsen has never been arrested, his credit score is good, and I confirmed what Shelby told us—that they had no outstanding loans." She held up the receipt. "But you did good getting these receipts, Megan. These prove Greg was either hoarding cash for some reason or spending the cash on something or someone his wife didn't know about."

"A mistress, you mean?"

"Exactly. Or drugs or gambling, like you guessed."

I posed another possibility to the detective. "You think Greg could have been spending the cash at stripper bars?" A guy could run through funds fairly fast at those places, especially if he were inclined toward lap dances. What's more, topless bars tended to attract a somewhat seedy clientele. If Greg had flashed some cash at a pole dancer or tucked a nice tip into a dancer's G-string, another man in the audience might have noticed and followed Greg home. Maybe one of the dancers worked in cahoots with two men, targeting customers who seemed to carry an excessive amount of cash. With Greg's irregular work schedule and overtime, he could have easily convinced Shelby he was working late when he'd actually been going to strip clubs.

Jackson lifted a weary shoulder. "Who knows? He might have even spent the cash on prostitutes. This clue could lead us to a motive, though. I'll call the lab and have them test a blood sample for illegal drugs so we can either pursue that theory or rule it out. But for now, let's go talk to Shelby." She circled around the front of my cruiser, climbed into the passenger seat, and off we went.

Minutes later, Brigit and Marseille were exchanging friendly sniffs on the rug while Detective Jackson and I sat on Shelby's sofa. Jackson eyed me and raised her hand, inviting me to discuss the matter with Shelby. I was proud she trusted me to take the lead.

"I came across something today," I said, handing the receipts over to Shelby and watching her closely to gauge her reaction. "It turns out your husband made a number of small purchases at various stores around town and obtained cash back. Around five thousand dollars in all since you've moved to Fort Worth."

"He did?" She ran her eyes over the receipts. "I wonder what he did that for."

"You weren't aware of the cash-back transactions?"

"No," she said. "I had no idea."

"This type of behavior can be indicative of illegal activity," I said, "such as drug use or gambling."

Shelby sighed. "I told you all before. Greg didn't do drugs or gamble. I would've known."

Maybe. Maybe not. But there was no point in arguing with her. "Another possibility is that he frequented strip clubs, or that he had a mistress and used the cash when taking her out on dates or buying things for her so that you wouldn't find out."

"No! Absolutely not!" Shelby shook her head so emphatically it was a wonder she didn't give herself a concussion. Once she stopped shaking her head, she pinned me with a pointed look. "I'm not one of those women who's in denial. I hope you know that. Greg and I were close and very much in love. He wasn't perfect, but he wasn't into cheap titillation and he would never *ever* have cheated on me. Even if he'd wanted to, when would he have had the time? When he wasn't at the theater, he was either at home or with me."

"Not on weekdays when he worked the later shift," I pointed out. "He would have been home alone in the mornings."

"Who has affairs at nine a.m.?" she snapped.

Jackson joined in. "Maybe Greg wasn't always at the theater when he said he was."

Shelby closed her eyes and drew a deep breath to calm herself. "Look, I know you two are only doing your job and, like you said before, you don't really know me or my husband so you've got to look at things from every possible angle. But here's an angle you haven't considered. What if Greg was taking out the cash bit by bit to surprise me with something? It's been my lifelong dream to go to France. He could have been secretly setting money aside to surprise me with a trip."

"But you have enough money in your checking account to visit France already," I said. "The money from the sale of your house in Oklahoma."

"That's true," Shelby said, "but Greg and I agreed that we were going to invest the profits into a new house here once we had a chance to look around. I didn't think it would be smart to spend the profits on a vacation. I wanted to invest the savings we'd accumulated since we moved here into a new house, too. We were planning to start a family, and I wasn't sure whether I would continue working if we had a baby. I felt that we had to be careful with our money. Greg agreed to the plan, but I could tell he thought I was being overly stringent. Maybe he figured he could set aside a few hundred dollars at a time and show me that we could afford both a new house and the trip."

Everything Shelby was saying made sense, but one question remained. "If he was stockpiling cash, do you have any idea where he might have hidden it?"

"None," she said. "I haven't come across any in the house." A moment later, her eyes went wide. "Do you think that money was why he was killed? Could someone have known he had a large amount of cash on hand?"

I looked from Shelby to Detective Jackson. "Greg didn't stop to get cash on his way home from the theater the night he disappeared. But it's possible one of the store clerks obtained Greg's name from his debit card or shopper's card and used it to figure out where he lived."

Jackson raised a shoulder. "Or another customer could have seen him get cash back on an earlier date, followed him home to see where he lived, and then come back and lay in wait the night of Valentine's."

While these new theories could explain why Greg Olsen had been killed, they gave us an enormous field of potential suspects to sift through. *Ugh*.

We thanked Shelby for being forthcoming with us, and told her we'd be back in touch if this new information led anywhere. The cash-back lead seemed to be taking us in several possible directions. But was it taking us closer to the truth?

TWENTY-SEVEN
PUPPER PLAYTIME

Brigit

While Megan and the detective had talked to the woman at the house, Brigit had been having fun with the dog with the smushed-in face. She'd been afraid at first that Megan might get angry with her for playing around on duty, but Megan was so focused on talking to the other women that she wasn't paying any attention to Brigit. She and the other dog had each taken an end of a rope toy in their teeth and engaged in a game of tug-of-war. Brigit thought she'd easily best the little beast, but the dog was surprisingly heavy for her small size. She got a good grip on the rope, too. She proved to be a much more formidable opponent than Brigit had expected.

In the end, Brigit had dragged the other dog across the floor and claimed victory. Luckily, the dog wasn't a sore loser. She'd wagged her tail, grabbed the rope, and run across the room with it, challenging Brigit to a second game. Brigit was just about to pick the rope up in her teeth again when Megan told her it was time to go. Brigit glanced back at the little dog from the front doorway and wagged her tail goodbye. *See you later!*

TWENTY-EIGHT
THE SMELL OF FREEDOM

The Slasher

On Wednesday evening, he ventured out of the hotel for the first time. He stopped in the parking lot, closed his eyes, and raised his head, inhaling deeply. Damn it felt good to breathe outdoor air again, even if that air was tainted with automobile exhaust from the nearby freeway.

He'd debated whether to leave the cash in the room. It didn't seem entirely safe to leave a big stash of bills in the room with the hotel management and housekeeping crew having access to the space, but it seemed even less safe to carry so much with him. He'd settled for tucking a hundred bucks into his wallet and hiding the rest of the roll under an inverted coffee mug in the kitchen cabinet while he was gone. If anyone entered the room with the intent of stealing from him, under the mug would hopefully be one of the last places they'd look for hidden valuables.

He walked down to the dollar store, where he grabbed a couple of shirts, underwear, and socks, along with a small box of laundry detergent and some canned food items. He was careful to keep his head down and not look directly at any of the security cameras. He was in and out in mere minutes. Though he'd felt entirely conspicuous, neither the clerk who rang him up nor any of the other customers in the store had given him so much as a second glance. Before he knew it, he was back in his room at the hotel. After checking on the cash and moving it back to his backpack, he used a steak knife to cut the price tags off his new clothing. He chuckled to himself. *I've become quite handy with knives.*

TWENTY-NINE
ROOF OR SPOOF?

Megan

I swung by to check on Mrs. Nomikos Thursday afternoon. Tommy Perkins had delivered some shingles to her home that morning and told her the crew chief had confirmed that her crew should be out the following day to begin installing her new roof.

I eyed the short plastic-wrapped stack of shingles on her porch. "That doesn't look like nearly enough shingles to cover your roof."

"I said the same thing. Mr. Perkins told me he'd run out of space on his truck and the crew would bring the rest of the materials with them when they come out tomorrow."

I stopped by to visit the other neighbors who had signed with Stormchaser Roofing. One wasn't home, but a similarly small supply of shingles sat on the front stoop. The other said Perkins had given him the same story, that there hadn't been room on his truck to carry all the shingles, but that the remaining shingles would arrive along with the crew in another couple of days. I hoped Perkins had delivered the supplies in good faith, and that this wasn't merely a stalling tactic.

* * *

Jackson called me into the station late in the afternoon. The lab hadn't yet completed their screen of Greg's blood, so we didn't yet know if he had illegal drugs in his system. But, since we'd spoken with Shelby the evening before, the detective had obtained lists of employees from the stores where Greg Olsen had completed his cash-back transactions. Considering that Greg had received cash back in over a hundred transactions at more than a dozen stores, it would be a nearly insurmountable task to attempt to identify another shopper who might have followed Greg home. It would take an immense amount of time to review both the indoor and outdoor security camera footage for each transaction. We simply didn't have the time and manpower for what could very likely be a futile task.

Jackson noted that she'd asked the store managers whether they were aware of any recent incidents in which any of their customers had been followed home from the store or mugged in the parking lot. "There was a single incident at one of the grocery stores. A man attempted to grab a disabled woman's purse from her scooter basket as she was loading her bags in her car." She went on to tell me that, while the two wrangled with her handbag, the woman drove her scooter back and forth over the would-be thief's foot until he finally gave up. The police nabbed him three blocks away, limping along the sidewalk. The suspect had a lengthy record and was still being held the night Greg Olsen had been attacked. "The mugger had skipped out once before, and no bondsman would post bail for him." Because he'd been in jail on Valentine's Day, he wasn't a viable suspect.

Given the difficulty of identifying shoppers, we focused our efforts on the stores' staff. I spent some time helping Jackson run background checks on them. The vast majority were clean. Though we found a couple of employees who'd been caught with small amounts of recreational drugs and several who'd been charged with driving under the influence, we found none with theft charges or a violent record. Stores tended to shy away from hiring anyone with a theft conviction or violent charge, and they'd generally fire someone who committed a theft or violent offense after being hired—assuming they learned of the arrest. Of course, it was still possible that an employee of one of the stores was, in fact, one of the people who'd killed Greg Olsen and that they'd brought a fellow employee or someone else along with them. But if that was the case then it was either their first violent incident or they'd skirted the law on any previous acts of violence. Once again, the lead had petered out.

When the detective had run her last report, she pushed away from her desk. Leaning her head back and closing her eyes, she groaned. "I'm getting damn tired of spinning our wheels on this case."

She wasn't the only one. The investigation had been an exercise in futility and frustration. "Maybe the guys who killed Greg will screw up," I said, "let something slip to a friend or family member who will turn them in."

She frowned at me. "Your optimism is annoying."

"It's also false," I admitted. "Honestly, I feel like kicking the wall."

"So do I," the detective said. She grabbed her coat and stood. "I'm going to blow off some steam at the firing range, then I'm heading home to indulge in a glass of wine and a romance novel. Those stories always end happily, and the girl always gets her man."

"We'll get ours, too."

"Dammit, Megan, I hope so."

We walked out to our cars together and bade each other goodbye in the parking lot. While she headed home, I headed back out on patrol, glad to have only one more night on the swing shift.

Late Friday afternoon, Jackson phoned me. "Got the latest lab results. There were no illegal drugs in Greg's blood."

"So we can rule out the possibility that he might have been killed by a drug dealer?"

"Not necessarily. Meth, heroin, cocaine, and MDMA stay in the system for only two to four days. Marijuana shows up for about a week. The only thing we know with full certainty is that he didn't take illegal drugs in the days immediately before he died. He doesn't appear to have been an addict, but he still could have been an occasional user. All this said, though, the probability that Greg Olsen was killed by a drug dealer seems remote. If he wasn't a regular user, he was unlikely to rack up a large debt that went unpaid. Besides, if he had racked up a debt and thought he might be killed for it, my guess is he'd have withdrawn money from the checking account to cover it and risked Shelby's wrath rather than his life."

We were left with the more viable theories that Greg had been targeted for the theater's cash, his own stockpile of cash, or because he was having an affair. But there was no evidence of infidelity other than the unexplained cash-back transactions. Would we ever get answers?

After leaving the station, I swung by Mrs. Nomikos's house. To my dismay, the single package of shingles still sat unopened on her porch and no crew from Stormchaser was on site. I rang her bell. When she came to the door, I said, "Still waiting on your roof?"

"I am." She issued a derisive yet delicate snort. "Today's excuse is that the crew that was supposed to work on my house ran into some trouble on their current job. Something about damaged decking that had to be replaced."

A reasonable explanation. But was it true, or was it another delaying tactic? "Did Mr. Perkins tell you when the crew would be coming here?"

"'As soon as they finish up at the other house' he said. Whatever that means." She rolled her eyes.

I chewed my lip as I mulled over the situation. Was Tommy Perkins on the up-and-up? Or was he simply stringing these folks along while he signed more customers up for roofs that might not ever be installed? It could go either way. He seemed like a nice enough guy, and police work could make anyone cynical. Maybe I was being overly suspicious. Even so, Perkins had made repeated promises he hadn't kept. I couldn't simply let that go. "I'll check back by next time I'm on duty."

"Why bother?" The woman crossed her arms over her chest and skewered me with a pointed look. "Doesn't seem like you plan to do anything about the situation."

My face flamed. I couldn't blame her for being frustrated, but I didn't appreciate being badgered when I was trying to help. "Tell you what. I'll make a stop by his place, see if he's there, and let him know I'm keeping an eye on him. How's that sound?"

"I suppose it's better than nothing."

"Better than nothing." Talk about a thankless job.

Before heading to the Airbnb where Perkins was staying, I stopped by the station to discuss the roofing issue with Captain Leone. The captain was a fortyish guy with springy dark hair and wiry eyebrows that would be right at home on a terrier.

I rapped on his doorframe. "Got a second?"

"No," he said. "But for you, Megan, I'll make one. Come on in."

I didn't bother to sit, but rather launched right into the reason for my visit. "I'm not sure if this guy named Tommy Perkins is engaging in criminal activity or not." I gave the captain the facts I'd gathered so far about Storm-chaser Roofing and Mr. Perkins.

"Could be a criminal, but seems more likely he's just an experienced salesman who overpromises to land the deal. Sounds like a matter for the courts, not the cops. There's not enough proof to bring him in. But keep an eye on him."

"Will do. Thanks, Captain."

I felt vindicated that the captain, who had far more years of policing under his belt, had reached the same conclusions I had. I climbed back into my cruiser and swung by the address Perkins had given me for his rental. The house sat a mile or so beyond the perimeter of my beat, but close enough that I could get back to my district quickly if needed. His truck sat in the driveway of the small wood-frame house. The place was painted dark blue with crisp white trim. Potted orange pansies flanked each side of the front door, providing a nice splash of color.

I let Brigit out of her enclosure for a potty break and, after she'd completed her business in the dried grass and sniffed around a little, I led her to the front door. From inside came the sounds of a basketball game—the Dallas Mavericks versus the Phoenix Suns. With Frankie and me both on duty tonight, Seth and Zach had decided to have a guys' night and had driven over to nearby Dallas to watch the game live. With Tommy Perkins's permanent address being in New Mexico, which sat right between Texas and Arizona, I wondered which team he was rooting for. *Rap-rap-rap.*

Perkins answered the door a moment later, opening it

wide and treating me to a wide smile, too. "Hello, Officer Luz." He looked down at my partner. "Hello to you, too, fluffy."

While Brigit often appreciated attention from people, she didn't wag her tail tonight. She merely stood stiffly, staring up at him. It was as if she knew something I didn't. *Wouldn't be the first time.* She was a smart, intuitive dog. If not for her lack of opposable thumbs and English language capabilities, I'd be taking orders from her instead of the other way around. I wondered what kind of treats she'd give me when I did good. Tootsie Rolls? Jelly beans? Lollipops?

"I stopped by to see Althea Nomikos, saw there was no progress on her roof."

Perkins sighed. "I'm as upset about that as you are," he said. "Trust me."

"I'd like to," I said, though when people told me to trust them I often found myself feeling doubly doubtful. Trust was something that was earned, not demanded. "What's the holdup?" I didn't tell him what Mrs. Nomikos had told me. I wanted to see if he'd remember his excuse, and offer the same one again.

"The crew chief told me that the guys who were supposed to start on her house today discovered a big patch of rotten wood at the house they're currently working on. You can't tell if the decking's bad until you remove the shingles. It was a bad surprise for both the crew and the homeowner. The insulation underneath was damaged, too. Anyway, the crew had to go round up some plywood so they could replace the decking. It'll add another day or two to the project, unfortunately."

"Where's this house with the bad decking?" If it was in the vicinity, I'd head over to speak to the homeowner, verify what Perkins was telling me.

"Up in Keller," he said, naming a town that was approximately 45 minutes north of our current location and too far away for me to make a convenient drive-by. Before I could ask for more details, he apologized. "Can't tell you how sorry I am about all of these delays. It makes the company look bad and it makes me look bad, too. I try to be a man of my word but sometimes it simply can't be helped."

"How about you give me the crew chief's number so I can call him directly?"

"I'd be happy to," he said. He retrieved his phone and pulled up a name and number in his contacts list. He held up his phone so that I could enter the information in mine.

When I finished, he leaned toward me, as if to share a secret. "Don't tell Mrs. Nomikos this because I haven't heard back yet, but I've e-mailed the boss to see if I can knock a few hundred dollars off her bill or upgrade her at no charge to those special gutters that keep the leaves out. I figure it's the least we can do under the circumstances."

Hmm. The situation wasn't under his control, and the guy seemed to be trying to make things right. Police work often took longer than victims or suspects would like, too. I supposed I should cut him some slack. "All right," I said. "I'll hope to see a crew at her house very soon. For now, I'll let you get back to the game. By the way, who are you rooting for?"

He offered me a grin. "The Mavericks, of course."

I gave him a grin in return. "Right answer." With a hand lifted in goodbye, I backed away from the door.

Saturday was my day off. I'd decided to go wedding dress shopping on my own this time. Well, on my own other than Brigit. She wouldn't be much help picking a dress, but I liked having her around. Lest the bridal shops balk at letting Brigit inside, I wore a long-sleeved T-shirt with the Fort Worth PD logo on it. People tended not to challenge police officers when it came to their K-9s.

I felt like Goldilocks trying on the dresses. Each one was too something. Too gaudy. Too tight. Too hard to walk in. Too shapeless. But unlike Goldilocks, I never found one that felt just right.

When nothing struck my fancy, I pulled out my phone and called Beverly Rubinstein, a seamstress I'd met in an earlier investigation. If the right dress didn't exist, maybe she could conjure it up for me. A custom design would likely cost far more than something off the rack, but you only get married once, right? Or at least that's supposed to be the plan.

"I've been hoping you would call!" Beverly said. "Ollie told me Seth proposed on Valentine's Day. I'm so happy for you two!"

Ollie was Seth's grandfather. We'd introduced Ollie and Beverly a while back, and they'd been keeping regular company since. Beverly had been widowed quite some time, and Seth's grandmother had been gone since Seth was young. It had been high time the two of them enjoyed the company of the opposite sex again.

"I need your help," I said. "I can't find a wedding dress that feels right."

She tsked. "You should've come to me first."

Though I hated to talk about money, I wanted to be honest. "I wasn't sure a custom design would be doable on a cop's budget."

"Don't be silly!" she said. "The dress is on the house. Consider it your wedding gift."

"Wow! That's incredibly generous of you."

She tsked again. "You saved me from being robbed, Megan. Maybe even worse. I would never have felt safe in my home again if those young men had gotten inside. You can't put a value on security."

It was true I had helped her out on a case a while back, but still, I didn't want to take advantage. "How about I cover the cost of the materials?"

"If you insist," she said. "Come right on over. I'll gather up some fabric samples and designs to show you."

I pulled up to Beverly's house shortly thereafter. She invited Brigit and me inside, and offered me a cup of chamomile tea. My partner, meanwhile, helped herself to the contents of Beverly's Chihuahua's food bowl.

"Brigit!" I snapped. "Bad girl."

Beverly waved a hand. "She might as well enjoy it. Pumpernickel is persnickety. Sometimes he'll eat that food, other times he turns up his nose at it."

The persnickety, plump pup lay sleeping on his bed in the corner, his aged ears no longer picking up much sound. At this point, he was more doorstop than dog.

The kettle whistled and Beverly poured me a cup of tea in a dainty china cup before pouring one for herself, too. Tea in hand, she led me through a set of French doors into a study that had been turned into her sewing room. Garment racks filled with dance and theater costumes, matching bridesmaid dresses, and wedding gowns lined the walls. A sewing machine sat in the back. Spread across a central work-table were a number of bridal magazines, along with binders filled with patterns and photos of dresses Beverly had designed and produced.

She pulled out a chair for me and perched on the one next to it. "Now. Tell me your thoughts about your dress."

"That's the problem." I raised my palms. "I have no idea what I want."

"Well, then," she said, undeterred, "we'll just have to figure that out, won't we?" She pulled a small pad of paper and a yellow number-two pencil toward her and launched into an interrogation not unlike a police inquiry. "When's the wedding?"

"Late September."

"Indoor or outdoor?"

"Indoor."

She jotted a note or two and held her pencil aloft. "Afternoon or evening affair?"

"Evening."

"Dancing?"

"Heck, yeah."

She asked me a dozen other questions before telling me to stand so she could take my measurements.

I raised my arms over my head so she could measure my bust. "Do you have any ideas yet?" I asked as she wrapped the yellow tape around my back.

"I do." She jotted my bust size down and moved her hands down to measure my waist. "I'm thinking ivory crepe, taffeta, or satin with a train. Nothing long that'll be cumbersome, but just enough to be elegant. I'll add a bustle so you'll be able to dance without having to worry about tripping over the train. You're not overly busty, so that gives us more options as far as the neckline. A soft cowl neck could be pretty. Or we could go with a sweetheart neckline or a halter style." She made another note on the page before moving down to my hips. "You know what would look fabulous? Sheer bell sleeves with tiny polka dots in the fabric. Maybe in a champagne color? It would be feminine but fun, too, add a touch of whimsy. I could make the train and veil out of the same fabric."

"It sounds beautiful."

She smiled. "It will be. Especially with you in it."

Her measuring done, she sat back down at the table and opened a sketchbook to a blank page. In minutes, she'd doodled simple mockups with the three different necklines. I knew the instant she finished that she'd designed the perfect dress for me.

"That's the one." I pointed to the design with the halter-style bodice. It was unique, unlike anything I'd seen in the stores, and it was the perfect combination of elegance and sensibility. It wouldn't take a crew to get me in or out of the dress, and I'd be able to enjoy my big day in relative comfort without sacrificing style. I reached over and pulled her to me in a sideways hug. "You're the best, Beverly."

She beamed. "I'm thrilled to be part of your big event, Megan. You work so hard for the rest of us. You deserve every happiness."

Once again I found myself fanning my eyes to dry the mist that had formed in them.

"Give me two months to get the bodice and skirt ready for fitting," she said. "Then you can come try it on before I add the sleeves."

The dress designed, we enjoyed a second cup of tea while Beverly updated me on her grandchildren's activities and other sewing projects. When we finished, I gave her another hug and bade her goodbye.

I flitted down her steps, my load lightened by having crossed another major item off my wedding to-do list.

Since seeing the debit card payments at Thai restaurants on Greg and Shelby's account earlier in the week, I'd been craving pad Thai. Seth obliged my need for noodles, and we had a nice, quiet dinner Saturday evening at a lovely Asian restaurant in the Cultural District.

Over a glass of white wine for me and a Singha beer for Seth, I told him that Beverly would be making my dress. "She came up with the perfect design."

He raised his hands. "Say no more. We don't want to jinx things. Just tell me what color tie and cummerbund I should get."

"Champagne," I said. The color would be a nice complement to both my dress and his blond hair.

He nodded and took a sip of his beer. "I had an idea for the honeymoon."

Leave it to the groom to be more focused on the honeymoon than the wedding ceremony. "Oh, yeah? What are you thinking?"

"Utah. They've got several parks with great scenery and hiking. Zion. Bryce Canyon. Arches. They've even got the spot where the golden spike was driven in to commemorate the joining of the eastern and western sections of railroad."

Two things joining seemed symbolic, perfect for a post-wedding vacation. Besides, long hikes together in remote wilderness would be both adventurous and romantic. "I'm game."

"Great! September will be the perfect time to go. The weather will be good. Not too hot, not too cold. I know you've got your hands full right now with that murder case. I'll take care of all the details."

One less thing to stress about? Woo-hoo! "I could kiss you!"

"Oh, yeah?" He leaned over and puckered up. "Put your mouth where your mouth is."

THIRTY
HAVING A BLAST WITH BLAST

Brigit

Megan and Seth had left Brigit and Blast behind at Megan's house. That meant only one thing. *Time to go wild!*

Without Megan and Seth here to scold them for messing up the bed covers or stealing snacks from the kitchen cupboards, Brigit figured anything was fair game. First, she challenged Blast to a game of chase. She zoomed from the living room to the bedroom, leaping onto the bed and down the other side, with Blast hot on her heels. She zipped back to the living room and grabbed the corner of a throw pillow in her teeth, tossing it into the air before hopping down and running into the kitchen to circle the dinette. Zoe, who'd been lying on the rug in front of the sink, hissed and scampered away. *'Fraidy cat!*

After three trips around the dinette, Brigit let Blast catch her. He licked at her mouth. *What a romantic.*

All that exercise had worked up her appetite. She ambled over to the cabinet where Megan kept her dog treats and crunchy human snacks. She put her nose to the door to nudge it open. It budged only an inch. *What the—?*

Blast cocked his head and looked at her.

Brigit tried again. Still the cabinet door didn't open. *Hmm.* She tried one more time. Her nose detected the scent of plastic, and her eyes spotted some type of latch on the inside of the cabinet that hadn't been there before. Looked like Seth and Megan had wanted to turn the dogs' pantry raids into a game. Well, Brigit was up for it.

She backed away and this time put her paw to the door. When it opened the little bit, she pawed at the space until her claws connected with the white plastic piece that was holding the door shut. She pulled first and, when that didn't work, pushed on it instead. The door came loose and she could nudge it open now. *What an easy game.* She hadn't been first in her K-9 training class for nothing.

Once the door was open, she sat down and looked over at Blast, inviting him to choose their snack. He stepped over and sniffed the boxes and bags. He decided on a box of crackers, taking the box in his mouth and removing it from the cabinet.

Good choice. Megan had tossed a couple of the crackers to Brigit the last time she'd eaten some. They'd been quite yummy.

The two dogs returned to the couch and tore into the box together. *We make a good team.*

THIRTY-ONE
SECRET MESSAGE

The Slasher

On Sunday evening, he watched the television news and checked online. There were no reports of any new evidence in the murder case. With waters having calmed, divers had searched Lake Worth a second time this weekend, but found nothing. Footage showed two men in wetsuits climbing out of the lake empty handed. The investigation seemed to be at a standstill. But he knew not to take the news reports at face value. Sometimes the police held their cards close to their vest and didn't reveal all of the evidence to the media. Were they on to him and his partner in crime? He couldn't be certain, but he had to touch base. Late Wednesday evening would be a good time to meet up.

He opened his laptop, logged into the new e-mail account he'd set up, and sent a quick, cryptic message.

THIRTY-TWO
COURTING TROUBLE

Megan

The weekend had been two steps forward, one step back. I'd gotten my wedding dress taken care of, and Seth and I had decided on our honeymoon, but Brigit had found a way around the childproof latch Seth had installed on the kitchen cabinet. She and Blast had eaten an entire box of my favorite crackers. I'd been tempted to eat her treats in return to teach her a lesson, but one sniff of the hard, liver-flavored squares and my stomach had turned.

Seth, the dogs, and I had spent a good part of the day Sunday making our way around Lake Worth, looking for any evidence of Greg's body. We'd even borrowed a canoe from one of Seth's firefighter buddies and rowed out to Goat Island in the middle of the lake. We'd searched all through the brush for a bloated corpse, but all we'd come across were some turtles, a gray heron, and several tangles of fishing line with rusty hooks left behind by irresponsible fishermen. We'd even hiked our way down a mile or so of the Trinity, checking the banks and water for any sign of Greg Olsen. We'd gotten nothing for our efforts other than exercise.

I'd placed a call to the phone number for Stormchaser's crew chief, but got only the standard automated voice-mail greeting, inviting me to leave a message. I had, telling the man my call was urgent and asking him to call me back right away. Nevertheless, the crew chief had yet to return my call.

It was Monday now, and thankfully I was back on the day shift. Before I could even leave the station that morning, Captain Leone cornered me. "Remember that roofing outfit you mentioned?"

"Stormchaser?"

"Yeah, yeah." He waved his hand impatiently. "We got another complaint about them on the non emergency line this morning. I told them I'd send an officer by. Get the caller's contact information from Melinda and go see what you can find out. Report back to me."

"Yes, sir."

I stopped by the reception desk, which was staffed by a fortyish woman with blonde hair, blue eyes, and supreme power, as she controlled the key to the supply closet. Melinda was speaking on the phone, but she looked my way, seemingly read my mind, and held up a pink phone-message slip. I took it from her. The slip indicated that a man named Barney Hashim had called and provided an address and phone number. I thanked her and she gave me a nod in acknowledgment.

Once Brigit and I were in our cruiser, I aimed it for Mr. Hashim's house. Just after I pulled to the curb and parked, a teenaged girl in a Prius pulled into the driveway and honked her horn. *Beep-beep!* She glanced over as Brigit and I made our way to the porch. As her brows knit in concern at the presence of police, her mouth simultaneously spread in a smile on seeing my fluffy partner.

Mr. Hashim and his wife answered the door right

away. They appeared to be in their late thirties or early forties. Mr. Hashim was in a business suit, ready to leave for work. His wife wore workout clothing and a head-scarf, ready for Zumba or maybe a spin class.

"Thanks for coming so quickly," Mr. Hashim said.

Maybe this job isn't entirely thankless, after all. "I understand you've had a problem with your roofing company?"

"We signed a contract with them nearly two weeks ago but no one has come to replace the roof. The represen-tative told us that our house would be the first one they would work on."

This story sounds familiar. It was the same spiel Tommy Perkins had given to Mrs. Nomikos. Probably all of Storm-chaser's sales team performed the same song and dance.

Mr. Hashim continued. "He gave me some excuses at first, but now he is not answering my calls."

A snarky, disembodied female voice came from behind the couple. "It's called *ghosting*, Dad." A dark-haired teenaged girl in a pink head scarf, jeans, a puffer jacket, and a cute pair of faux-fur-lined boots squeezed between Mr. and Mrs. Hashim, not once looking up from her phone as she slipped past Brigit and me and continued out to her friend's car.

Her mother scoffed and muttered "Teenagers." She cupped her hands around her mouth and called after her daughter. "We love you, too, sweetie pie!"

Her daughter looked up from her phone just long enough to cast a look of disgust back at her parents. The Hashims chuckled before returning their attention to me.

I asked, "Have you left messages for the roofing com-pany's salesman?"

"I have not been able to," Mr. Hashim said. "The recording tells me that his voicemail box is full."

Not surprising. Their inboxes were likely full of messages from upset people wondering why their new roofs hadn't been installed yet. "Have any shingles been delivered?" I asked.

"Only one package," the man said. "I put it in the garage. Several of our neighbors also signed contracts with Stormchaser Roofing. Their calls have also been ignored."

"Do you have your contract handy?"

Mr. Hashim strode to an antique roll top desk in the living room, retrieved the document, and handed it to me. Sure enough, a business card with the name Tommy Perkins on it was stapled to the agreement. I quickly looked it over. It appeared to be the same contract as the one Althea Nomikos has signed. In fact, the purported project start date listed was the same as hers, 2/17 or February 17th. A roofing company often had multiple crews, so the fact that the dates were the same didn't necessarily mean Perkins had intentionally misled the customers. On the other hand, it was concerning that yet another customer couldn't seem to get much in the way of results from Stormchaser.

After snapping pictures of each page of the contract, I said, "You aren't the first to complain about Stormchaser Roofing. Let me see if I can get you some answers." I dialed Tommy Perkins, but after five rings the number switched to an automated recording telling me the voicemail box was full. *Ugh.* I settled for sending Tommy Perkins a text. *This is Officer Luz. Call me right away.* I tried the crew chief's phone, too, with the same results. I sent him a text, as well.

Mr. Hashim shook his head. "Is Mr. Perkins a crook?"

"Honestly, sir? I'm not sure." At best, Perkins appeared to be an unscrupulous salesman, bending the truth and telling customers what they wanted to hear so that they'd sign contracts with the company he represented. "I'll go see what I can find out and be back in touch." When I made a promise, I intended to keep it.

I loaded Brigit back into the car and drove over to the rental unit to see if Tommy Perkins might still be there. No such luck. His truck wasn't in the drive, and nobody answered the door. Looked like he'd already headed out to work for the day.

When I returned to my cruiser, I drove over to speak to Althea Nomikos. Once again, there was no roofing crew at her house, no additional shingles delivered. "Any word on your crew?"

"Of course not," she said. "I've tried Tommy Perkins a dozen times and can't reach him. Seems he's turned his phone off."

I informed her that the department had received other complaints about Stormchaser. "I'll talk to my captain again, see how he wants to handle it."

"I can't keep waiting," she said. "There's rain in the forecast for later in the week. I've got another roofing company coming out here this afternoon. They say they can start work on Thursday and cover my roof with a tarp in the meantime. I talked to my bank about getting my money back, but they said they can't do anything now that the check has been cashed. I'll have to chalk up that five hundred dollars I gave to Stormchaser as a loss. That was an expensive lesson."

She glared at me as if the situation were my fault. Not fair, but not unusual, either. When people couldn't directly confront the person who'd caused them trouble, they often directed their rage at the person who couldn't make things right. In many cases, that person was me. I'd learned not to take things too personally. Still, it rankled a bit.

I drove back to the station, led Brigit inside, and sat down at one of the desktop computers where I could perform research more comfortably than in my squad car.

Through the open doorway, I saw Derek walk into the station and hit up Melinda for the key to the supply cabinet. He came into the room and went to the cabinet to round up a fresh citation pad for writing traffic tickets. When he saw me at the computer, he scoffed. "Desk jockey."

I didn't bother looking up at him. It was a lame insult, and I had better things to do with my energy than return the slight. Instead, I ran the name "James Thomas Perkins" through the criminal database. Although I received several hits, none of the men with the name were the same guy I was looking for. A couple were African American, not Caucasian like the James Thomas Perkins I was after, and all were too young, anyway. So, for what it was worth, Tommy Perkins didn't appear to have a criminal record.

I moved on to type "James Thomas Perkins" and the word "roofing" into my browser. Nothing came back. I tried the man's name again, along with the word "fraud." Still nothing. Finally, I tried his name alone. The Internet spit out a long list of obituaries for men with the same name who'd already passed on, as well as other useless information about various men with the name James Thomas Perkins. A disparaging hotel review one of them had posted. An employee-of-the-month award earned for selling the most used cars at a dealership in Nashua, New Hampshire. A James Thomas Perkins served as treasurer for his local Rotary Club. A man with the name had placed third in a popsicle-eating competition in the Florida Keys, winning a T-shirt and a coupon for twenty-five percent off at the souvenir shop that had held the event.

Discouraged, I sat back in my chair and ran my hand over Brigit's back. The motion not only soothed her, it helped calm my mind so I could think. Brigit turned her head so she could lick my hand in gratitude. She too, let me know this job wasn't entirely thankless. "You're welcome, Briggie Boo," I said.

A moment later, it dawned on me. Just as I used Briggie Boo as one of many endearing nicknames for Brigit, James Thomas Perkins was going by the nickname Tommy. *What if he's used different nicknames before?*

I ran a search for fraud committed by Thomas Perkins, and Jim Perkins, but got nothing. But when I tried the name Jimmy Perkins, I hit possible pay dirt. An article dated eighteen months ago from the *Dodge City Daily Globe* newspaper noted that a man named Jimmy Perkins had been associated with a company called MixMaster Cement & Asphalt, Ltd. Jimmy Perkins had solicited contracts in rural areas to replace gravel drives with concrete or asphalt. After canvassing the area for a week or two, he'd disappeared into thin air and the work had never been started.

Neither law enforcement nor any of the victims or their attorneys could reach anyone associated with the company. The incorporator of MixMaster, whose name was listed as Richard Jones, could not be positively identified. No personal identification was required when submitting articles of incorporation to establish a business, and many people filed the documentation by mail or online. It would have been easy for an unscrupulous person to submit paperwork under a fictitious name. The article went on to say that, when law enforcement contacted MixMaster's bank, they discovered that only $2.83 remained in the company's business account. The name and Social Security number used to open the business account at the online bank belonged to a Nebraska man who'd been deceased for over a decade. The dismayed customers lost their money and never got justice.

Could this concrete con man be the guy who's now going by the name Tommy Perkins? Unfortunately, I couldn't be certain. Because Jimmy Perkins could not be located, no arrest had been made and no photograph was included with the news article.

I continued to scuttle around on the World Wide Web, looking for any other evidence that Tommy Perkins had previously engaged in fraudulent conduct. Again, I hit potential pay dirt. A few inches of newsprint in the Pueblo, Colorado *Chieftain* detailed a scam involving a Jimmie Perkins. The man had enticed small business owners to hire Surefire Snow Plow Service Corp. to remove snow and ice from their parking lots. Back in November and December, dozens of customers had paid several hundred dollars each in up-front fees only to suffer distress and sore backs when no snow plow arrived to clear their properties and they had to do the work on their own with a handheld shovel. The article noted that calls to Jimmie Perkins were not returned, and that no other valid contact information for the company could be found. While the pool of victims had been scammed out of over eighty grand, no single victim had lost more than $750, the amount of their down payments. When the police department had been unable to bring about justice, the victims had likely done what Althea Nomikos had done—chalk the incident up to experience and moved on with their lives.

Once again, the article contained no photo or other means by which I could verify if the man who'd scammed the small business owners was one and the same with the Tommy Perkins now securing contracts for Stormchaser

Roofing. But even though paving and plowing services were different from roofing, the similarities in the over-all schemes could not be ignored. While Brigit dozed on my toes, I phoned the Dodge City, Kansas, and Pueblo, Colorado, police departments to see if I could get more information.

The detective in Dodge City admitted the case hadn't gotten far. "The company used an online bank, and the identity of the person who opened the account belonged to a man who'd passed away years ago. Someone obviously stole his information. We never could find Jimmy Perkins and positively identify him. We also weren't sure whether he was the one running the scam, or whether he was an unwitting dupe for the owner of the business. Everything was smoke and mirrors."

"Did any of the victims mention whether Mr. Perkins drove a vehicle with New Mexico license plates?"

"I can't recall. I'd be happy to forward the reports to you so you can take a look."

In other words, he didn't have the time to review the reports himself, and if I wanted the information I'd have to dig through the pages for it. But who could blame the guy for passing the task on to me? After all, he'd already closed the case and probably had dozens of others demanding his attention now.

"Yes. Please send the reports." I thanked him, ended the call, and immediately placed another, this time to the Pueblo PD.

The detective in Pueblo said the Jimmie Perkins who'd signed small business owners up for snow plow services had driven a truck with Colorado license plates, not New Mexico plates. "Problem was," she said, "nobody made a note of the number. The most anyone lost was around three hundred dollars, nothing that would set them back too much. Besides, we weren't sure we'd be able to pin anything on Perkins. I spoke to the guy on the phone once, and he told me that the owners of the plowing business had up and disappeared, and that they still owed him a commission check. Sounded to me like he was a victim himself."

Her conclusion had been reasonable, but taking into consideration that the man had been associated with another similar scheme, it was highly unlikely that he'd been a victim rather than a willing participant, even the mastermind, in a complicated con game.

She agreed to forward her documentation to me, also. "It might be a day or two," she said. "We're working a triple homicide."

Three murders? She'd one-upped me. Or, rather, *two-*upped me. Suddenly, my single homicide, without even a corpse to show for my efforts, seemed like small beans. A disturbing and ironic thought, huh?

We ended the call and I ran a search through both the New Mexico and the Colorado DMV records for a pickup truck registered in the name of James Thomas Perkins. I got squat. Were the trucks rentals? Could be. Perkins could have rented the truck he was now driving in New Mexico before heading to Texas. Or he could have flown or taken a train or bus to Texas, then rented the truck here. After all, it wasn't unusual for rental vehicles that were registered in one state to end up in another. Customers sometimes rented cars for one-way trips and returned them to different locations.

Deciding to try another tack, I used the number I'd pulled from Perkin's driver's license to find his record in the system. I made note of the address listed and searched for vehicles registered at the address. Two vehicles came up. A Toyota SUV and a Subaru Crosstrek. Neither was the truck Perkins had been driving. What's more, the names associated with the registrations were Brody and Abbie Bingham. A search of earlier records showed that the Binghams had updated the addresses on their vehicle registrations and driver's licenses approximately three years prior. Could the Binghams be related to Tommy Perkins? Maybe a daughter and her husband?

I ran a search of the New Mexico vital records, but found no birth certificate linking James Thomas Perkins to any child, let alone a daughter named Abigail. Of course, she could have been born elsewhere. I found no marriage license for him, either. Was the wedding ring also a farce, or had he been married in another state? Although I was curious, I didn't spend more time on the matter. Whether he was a father or a husband was far less important than whether he was a darn thief.

According to the images on Google Earth and the property records, the address on Perkins's driver's license was for a single-family home that he had sold to the Binghams a little over three years ago. A quick look at Mrs. Bingham's Facebook page told me she was a sixtyish woman who was into knitting, cats, and cooking. She looked too old to be his daughter. What's more, her page gave no indication of any relation to Perkins. *Hmm.*

A call to the home got me no further. Mrs. Bingham had no idea where the previous owner of their house now lived. "We never met Mr. Perkins," she said. "We only met his realtor when we were shown the house."

"What about Mrs. Perkins?"

"Far as I know," the woman said, "he wasn't married. His name was the only one on the deed and nobody else was listed in the documentation when we bought the place."

This fact supported my belief that the wedding band

Tommy Perkins wore was a ruse, a subtle symbol he'd adopted to make himself seem more stable or honest. People might assume, rightfully or not, that a married man would be more reliable than one who was single. Perkins hadn't updated his driver's license as the law required, and during our conversation he had commented about returning to Las Cruces, leading me to believe the address on the card was valid. That behavior alone was dubious. But when you added in all of the other factors, I felt fairly certain now that Tommy Perkins was a shyster. Even so, without a photo or eyewitness to identify him as one and the same with Jimmy and Jimmie Perkins, a small sliver of doubt remained.

I checked my email. The reports from Dodge City had arrived. Unfortunately, they were vague on details. Nobody had a license plate for the vehicle the so-called "Jimmy Perkins" had been driving, nor did anyone know where he lived or was staying. The phone number he'd been using to conduct business had been deactivated, and the mailing address the business had provided to its online bank was phony, belonging instead to a beauty salon that had been in business at the same location for years.

I checked back in with Captain Leone, updating him on the information I found and handing him the reports from the Dodge City PD.

His eyes narrowed as he read the reports. Frowning, he tilted his head from one side to the other, as if mentally weighing the evidence, before holding his head upright again. "This evidence isn't quite enough to arrest him, but it's enough to raise serious suspicions. Beside the fact that the other men were using the last name Perkins, there's no proof they are the same guy who's working for the roofing company here. There's not even any proof that Perkins was their real name. Let's see what the reports from Colorado say when they come in. In the meantime, go talk to Tommy Perkins again. If he confesses or admits to having any connection to those companies in Kansas and Colorado, you can bring him in for further questioning."

Having obtained my marching orders, I ran by the Airbnb Perkins had leased. Once again, I found no truck in the driveway and nobody at home. Not a surprise, really. He was likely still out and about, drumming up more business for Stormchaser. The thought that he could be racking up more victims made my gut twist. While people generally thought of the police as their defenders against violent crime, the vast majority of our work involved protecting the public from non-violent offenders.

I set back out on patrol, cruising slowly up and down the streets, keeping a close eye out for a pickup truck with New Mexico plates. No such luck. Looked like Tommy Perkins was working another part of Fort Worth today. Or maybe he'd left town entirely. Had I missed my chance to nab him?

Late that afternoon, Detective Jackson called my cell phone. I turned into the parking lot of a fast-food joint so I could speak with her safely.

"I just got off the phone with Trish LeGrande," she said.

The television reporter had called? Why? "Did she want information about Greg Olsen's murder investigation?"

"No," Jackson said. "She didn't ask me for information. She gave me some instead. She told me Shelby Olsen has filed a petition with the court to have her husband declared dead."

"She did?" Greg couldn't have survived losing as much

blood as he had, yet there was no body to prove his demise. What, exactly, was required for a judge to rule someone deceased? I'd never run into the issue before, and I was curious. "I thought a person had to be missing seven years before they'd be considered dead."

"There are exceptions," Jackson said. "Under Texas law, a person who is missing and unheard from for seven years is presumed dead. But a judge can declare a person dead sooner if the circumstances show that the person is likely dead, even if there is no direct evidence. The court decides what evidence is sufficient."

I supposed it made sense. After all, in some cases, bodies could not be recovered. Boats sunk at sea, for example, or explosions and fires destroyed human remains and made identification difficult if not impossible. Sometimes, only parts of a person could be found, such as when animals scattered their bones in the woods. Why force a family to wait seven years to probate a will or collect insurance proceeds when it was clear their loved one was no longer alive? "How did Trish LeGrande learn about Shelby's petition?"

"The TV station's intern came across it when he was looking over the recent filings. Trish called to find out what I thought about the development."

Reporters regularly reviewed recent court filings, which were public record, to determine if any of the legal matters were newsworthy. With Greg Olsen's body yet to be found, Shelby's case certainly could be.

"What did you tell her?"

"I told her I had 'no comment on the matter at this time.' I'm not sure what to make of the situation."

I wasn't sure, either. While I'd been wondering before if Greg had scripted his death, I now wondered if Shelby had brought about her husband's demise. She'd be able to access any assets she and Greg had held jointly, but she'd need to have Greg declared dead if he held assets in his name alone, or to obtain a life insurance payout. Could she have had him killed for insurance? If so, why not leave the body in the house, where his death could easily be proven? Had she been afraid that something about his death would point fingers at her, and decided to have the body taken elsewhere? Going to court took time and money, yet even if Shelby was innocent she couldn't be expected to wait around forever for Greg's body to be found, could she? Did she know somehow that his body would not be found? Had she ensured it was hidden somewhere it would never be discovered?

I shared my thoughts with the detective. "You think she had him killed for the life insurance money?"

"Greg Olsen died for one reason or another," Jackson said. "Insurance seems as good a reason as any. Go to the courthouse, get me a copy of the petition. Then swing by the station and pick me up. Let's go have another chat with Mrs. Olsen."

I did as instructed, and an hour later, Jackson and I stood on the front porch of the Olsens' home, speaking with Shelby. Though she wore no makeup and was dressed in yoga pants and a long-sleeved T-shirt, the woman had at least brushed her hair and washed her face today. Baby steps.

Jackson held up the petition, which had been prepared on Shelby's behalf by a partner at the law firm where she worked. "I understand you've filed a petition to have your husband declared deceased."

Shelby hugged Marseille tighter against her chest and nodded. "I hated to do it. I feel like it's giving up all hope that Greg could still be alive. But I can't live like this anymore. It could be weeks or months before his body is found, if at all. I need closure." She lifted her chin to indicate me. "Officer Luz told me I should move on. She was right."

While I took no offense to being told I was right, I felt a little put off that Shelby seemed to be saying it was my idea she file to have her husband legally declared dead. I'd said no such thing when we'd spoken before. In fact, Shelby had been the one to ask if she should move on. I'd only agreed that it might be for the best. She seemed to be putting words in my mouth.

Jackson cut a look my way before turning back to study Shelby. "Why do you need a formal declaration that your husband is deceased? Did he own some assets in his name only?"

"Only his retirement account," Shelby said. "We owned everything else jointly."

"What about life insurance?" Jackson asked. "Did Greg have any?"

"Yes, but the company won't pay out without a death certificate or a court order finding that Greg has died."

"Understandable," Jackson said. "They've got to cover themselves, dot their I's and cross their T's, so to speak."

Shelby's head bobbed in agreement.

"Glad you've got coverage," Jackson said. "Some folks don't bother with it, think that nothing will happen to them, and then their family ends up in a bind after an unexpected death. How much is Greg's policy for?"

"One million dollars," Shelby said without hesitation. "We both have policies in the same amount. Greg got them a couple of years ago. Honestly, I was kind of upset at the time. We'd agreed to get policies for fifty-thousand each, just enough to cover funeral expenses plus some time off from work to grieve. But the agent pressured Greg into the higher coverage. He said it was a good idea,

especially since we were planning to have children someday and there'd be their support and education to think
about. He told Greg it cost nearly a quarter-million dollars to raise a child from birth to age eighteen, and it's another sixty thousand on average for college. The policies
were relatively cheap—luckily, since we're both healthy
and young. Once I realized the insurance wasn't going to
cost an arm and a leg, and that we could be denied coverage later if either of us was diagnosed with a health issue,
it made sense to go with the higher amount."

Shelby seemed forthcoming, and her story made sense.
Living in limbo would be hell. Still, a million dollars was
a lot of money. Would she have been tempted to kill her
husband for it? Some women might, but I had a hard time
seeing Shelby Olsen as a black widow. She didn't strike
me as a particularly materialistic person who would want
the funds to buy a fancy car or an ostentatious house. She
seemed like the type of person who would rather have a
loving husband than possessions. I wondered about the
children she'd mentioned, the ones they'd purportedly
planned to have. Had they had trouble conceiving, or had
they decided to put off children for a while longer? Judging from Shelby's age, they didn't have much more time
to wait.

"I'm glad you came by," Shelby said. "I was planning
to get in touch with you. My boss is handling the petition
for me. She asked me to get the name of the person in the
crime scene department who computed how much blood
Greg had lost. She'll need to call that person as a witness,
or at least get an affidavit from them."

"Of course," Jackson said. "I'll have him get in touch
with your boss."

Shelby thanked us and we returned to the cruiser.

Once we were seated, I asked, "What do you think?"

The detective let out a long, exasperated breath. "This case would be easier if we had a body, something more to go on than suppositions and hunches." She turned my way. "What do *you* think, Megan?"

"Part of me is surprised that Shelby is moving ahead so quickly, but another part of me can understand why she'd want to wrap things up. If Greg's body hasn't been found yet, it's not likely to be found for some time, if at all. The uncertainty would be agonizing. Maybe this is the only way she can get some relief."

"And a million bucks."

"That, too. Which brings us back to the possibility she hired a hit man. Maybe she even used the cash that Greg withdrew to pay the hit man. Maybe she asked Greg to make the withdrawals so it would take suspicion off her. She could have made up some excuse for needing the cash, maybe visits to a salon or to pay a maid or gardener or something. Who knows?"

"Who knows?" Jackson repeated with a scowl. "Not us, that's for sure."

THIRTY-THREE
NO ANSWER, NO ANSWERS

Brigit

Right before their shift ended, Megan took her back to the house where they'd spoken to the man before. It was fully dark and dinnertime. Brigit lifted her snout as Megan let her out of the cruiser. Her nose told her that the next-door neighbors were cooking beans and cornbread for dinner. She wished she could have some. It smelled darn good.

No dinner smells came from the man's house. No sounds, either. The man didn't come to the door when Megan knocked.

As they crossed the yard to return to the cruiser, Brigit felt a necessary urge and popped a squat in the dry grass. After depositing her droppings on the lawn, she took a step forward and kicked her feet back, wiping her paws on the lawn. Instinct told her to cover the mess. It also told her to wipe some of the pheromones from the glands on her feet on the property, to mark it as her own, a dog's way of claiming dibs or stating "Brigit was here."

Megan normally scooped Brigit's poop up in a bag, but she didn't tonight. Brigit could sense that Megan was annoyed and angry, though she knew the feelings weren't directed at her. After all, she'd done nothing wrong today and Megan had even given her a liver treat earlier for no reason. She hoped whatever was bothering Megan would be over soon. She didn't like seeing her best friend upset.

THIRTY-FOUR
INVADED

The Slasher

With his appearance so transformed now, he no longer felt the need to rush down to breakfast early. He returned from the buffet Tuesday morning at 8:30 with a heaping plate of food. He nearly dropped it when he saw the door to his room standing wide open. He rushed forward, hot coffee sloshing over the top of his cardboard cup, burning his fingers and leaving spots on the hallway carpet.

He stepped through the door to find the housekeeper on the far side of the room, facing away from him, vacuuming. She'd opened the closet door to vacuum the floor. She wasn't even aware that he had entered the room. Anyone could have darted in here, reached into the open closet, and grabbed his backpack with the stash of cash zipped in the inside pocket. Or they could have quickly gone through the bag and removed the cash from it. Where would he have been then? Totally screwed. That's where.

He set his plate and coffee on the table and rounded up his backpack from the closet, carrying it to the table. The woman finished vacuuming on the other side of the bed and turned around, giving him a smile when she noticed him at the table. She had no way of knowing if he was a legitimate guest in this room, yet she did nothing to stop him from riffling through the bag. She probably didn't want to risk offending a guest. He surreptitiously peeked into the inside pocket, relief calming him when he saw the wad of cash still there. He'd need it today. He had to load more funds onto the prepaid credit card he'd used to pay for the room. His charge for the upcoming week was due today.

He wondered how much longer he'd have to hole up here. He was lying low to avoid prison, yet staying in this room felt like he'd been sentenced to solitary confinement. He'd had no companionship, nobody to talk to. Tomorrow night's meet-up couldn't come soon enough.

THIRTY-FIVE
DEAD AND GONE

Megan

I'd woken extra early Tuesday morning and made a stop at the Airbnb at 6:30, hoping to catch Tommy Perkins before he headed out on sales calls for the day. No such luck for this early bird. The worm was already gone when I went by. Was Perkins delivering shingles? Had he gone out for breakfast? Gotten the heck out of Dodge? I'd cruised through the parking lots of breakfast joints and fast-food places near the Airbnb, looking for him or his truck. No luck there, either. *Argh!*

It was nearly time for my lunch break now and I had some paperwork to deal with, so I decided to eat my lunch at the station. After wrapping up the administrative tasks, I took my thermos of hearty vegetable stew to a desk and took a seat. Something had been niggling at my mind all morning.

I filled my mouth with a spoonful of soup, and then I logged into the system and ran an Internet search to educate myself about Oklahoma law regarding declaration of death. After reading over the statutes and legal summaries, I learned that Oklahoma had a statute similar to the one in Texas. Oklahoma law provided that any person missing from their usual residence and whose address is unknown by their family or others who would be expected to know the person's whereabouts, and who was continuously absent and unheard of for a period of seven years, shall be presumed to be dead. The court had the authority to declare such person legally dead and to issue orders necessary for the administration of the person's estate. Unlike Texas law, however, Oklahoma law appeared to have no provision for having a missing person declared legally dead before the seven-year period had expired.

Hadn't Shelby's boss at the law firm said that Shelby's prior experience had been primarily in estate and probate? Was Shelby aware of the law pertaining to declarations of death? Could Shelby have convinced Greg to relocate from Oklahoma to Texas because it would be easier and quicker to have him declared dead here? While scarfing down the rest of my soup, I printed out the information I'd found online, planning to share it with Detective Jackson.

Now that my suspicions had turned squarely to Shelby, I decided it couldn't hurt to take another look at her e-mail account before speaking with the detective. Maybe I'd spot something we'd overlooked before, or maybe something incriminating had landed in her inbox since the last time we'd looked it over.

Using the login information we'd snagged from their computers, I logged into Shelby's personal e-mail account. From the bold font and highlighting, I could tell which e-mails she'd read already, and which she'd chosen to ignore or were still waiting for her to take a look. She'd received multiple e-mails from Regina asking how she was doing and telling her that everyone at the law firm was thinking of her, praying for her, and missed her at the office. Regina's most recent e-mail asked if Shelby had decided when she'd be returning to work.

I checked the sent message box to see if Shelby had replied. She had. She told Regina she hadn't yet decided when, or if, she'd return to work. *I can't keep my mind straight. I'm not sure I'd be of any use at the office.* She noted that her boss had given her until the end of March to decide before they'd have to seek a replacement. I wondered if I'd continue to work if I had $1 million coming to me. Even if I knew I'd be financially secure, I couldn't imagine not doing something productive each day. I didn't have many hobbies to take up my time. I supposed I could volunteer at a shelter for animals or the homeless, but I wouldn't want to give up working with Brigit, have to turn her over to another handler. Besides, I liked the mental challenge of solving crimes. But I couldn't blame Shelby for feeling otherwise. Not everyone's work meant as much to them as mine did to me.

Many of the other recent e-mails in Shelby's inbox were from hotels, airlines, and resorts, informing her of special pricing or attempting to entice her into planning a vacation. Others were bills or solicitations from stores she'd made online purchases from before, the same types of e-mails I'd seen in her account earlier. When I finished looking over her inbox and sent box, I figured it couldn't hurt to take a quick look at her spam box since I was already in her account.

I ran my gaze down the list. There was the usual assortment of junk. Messages claiming she'd won a lottery. Another telling her where to meet hot singles in her area. *Huh.* One of the spam e-mails was highlighted, indicating it had been read. *That's odd, isn't it?* I mean, who reads the junk that comes into their spam folder? The e-mail was sent from an account identified as LastingLovePleasurePills. *Ew.*

I logged into the message to find an ad for a nutritional supplement that allegedly allowed men to maintain "a ready manhood" all night long. *Sheesh.* Sounded exhausting to me. Some romance was nice, but so was sleep. The ad was basic, with exaggerated language in bold, blue type and all caps, promising the capsules would KEEP THE PARTY GOING FOR HOURS! The e-mail included a stock photo of a man and woman entwined in an embrace. Interested parties were directed to click on the designated link, which would take them to a website for more information.

Though I might have been hesitant to click on the link had I been running this search on my personal computer, I knew the department's IT team regularly updated the network's virus protection so I went ahead and clicked. I was taken to a professionally designed nutritional supplement site that looked nothing like the cheesy e-mail. *Weird.* Why would a legitimate company send such a poorly designed e-mail solicitation that didn't tie in with its branding? And why would Shelby click on an e-mail for a performance enhancement drug for men, especially now that her husband was gone? Could this be evidence that she had been cheating on Greg, had something going on the side?

I backed out of the website and ran a search of Shelby's spam folder. She'd received five messages from the LastingLove account in the past but, unlike the recent e-mail, all of the earlier messages remained unread. I returned to the recent e-mail. As I scrolled down through the short solicitation, I noticed that there was what appeared to be a single blank line after the text ended and the reply and forward prompts appeared. Not a large space, but enough to catch my eye. Why did there seem to be an extra margin?

I stared at the e-mail for a long moment, thinking there had to be a reason why Shelby opened this particular one. Even if she were having an affair, why click on an e-mail that was so obviously junk? *Something isn't right here . . .*

As I stared at the screen, my mind went back to my childhood and the invisible ink pens Santa had slipped into my stocking at Christmas. Even as a young girl, I'd been intrigued by all things detective and spy-related, and Kris Kringle knew me well. Using the pens, I would write a message on a piece of paper, and the page would appear blank until the secret decoder pen was run over the page, revealing the words. As I grew older, Santa brought me more sophisticated, high-tech invisible ink sets with pens that wrote messages that would be revealed only under a black light. Could there be some type of secret message here in this extra space? Or was I nuts?

I moved my cursor to the beginning of the blank line and copied from that point down to the end of the line. I opened the word processing program and pasted the section I'd copied into a blank document. Nothing showed up on the screen, but when I looked down at the word count readout in the bottom left corner of the screen, it told me that there were twelve words on the page. *Holy guacamole, I'm not nuts! I'm actually on to something!*

I highlighted the invisible text and changed the text color to black. In an instant, a cryptic message appeared on my screen as if by magic. *Be at the Starbuck's on Camp Bowie Blvd Wednesday at 8:00 p.m.*

My mouth fell open. Who had sent this e-mail to Shelby? Could it be from someone she'd been having an affair with before Greg's death? Could that person have killed Greg and gone into hiding to avoid suspicion and arrest? Or had whoever killed Greg only meant to kidnap him? Had they taken his body so that Shelby would think he was still alive and pay a ransom? Had they told her to look for these hidden messages? Didn't that type of thing only happen in the movies?

I printed out the message, rousted my sleeping partner, and sprinted down the hall to Detective Jackson's office, virtually dragging a drowsy Brigit behind me. I skidded to a stop in the doorway, grabbing the jamb with my free hand to keep from banging into the door. Panting, I held up the printout. "I found something!"

Jackson looked up from her desk, brows raised. "Oh, yeah?" She reached out for the paper and I handed it to her. After reading it, she said, "Where'd you get this?"

"It was in an e-mail in Shelby's spam folder. One she'd read." I told her how I'd taken a fresh look at Shelby's e-mail account and noted the extra blank line at the end of the solicitation. "I copied and pasted the text into a document, and changed the color from white to black." I gestured to the printout. "That's what showed up."

"Tricky." She motioned for me to come around the back of her desk. "Walk me through what you did."

I took her through the steps, showing her the highlighted e-mail in Shelby's spam folder, and directing her how to make the invisible message appear.

She sat back in her chair, mouth gaping as she stared at the screen. "I never would have noticed that single extra line." Her gaze shifted to me. "You're a genius, Megan."

"Just observant." Maybe even obsessive.

"Don't argue with your superiors."

"Okay," I said. "Genius, then." I took a seat in one of her wing chairs. "Who do you think sent the message?"

She read the page over again, her brows inverting. "Sounds like a lover."

"That's what I thought, too. Think he could be responsible for Greg's death?"

"Maybe. That might be why this person and Shelby have kept their relationship under wraps. At the very least, it gives us a motive for Greg's death. Shelby might have had her husband killed so she could pursue a relationship with the guy who sent the e-mail. If so, the guy may or may not know Shelby was responsible for killing her husband. Or her lover might have killed her husband so that he could have Shelby to himself. If that's the case, Shelby may or may not be aware that her lover was responsible."

"In other words," I said, "we still can't definitively pin anything on Shelby."

"Not yet," Jackson said. "But we'll stake out the coffee house. We just might get some answers Wednesday night."

I'd keep my fingers crossed. I wanted this case solved.

After speaking with Detective Jackson, I'd examined the other e-mails in Shelby's spam folder but found no others containing hidden messages. I'd also swung by the Airbnb at the end of my shift. No Tommy Perkins. I jotted a note on one of my business cards—*Call me right away!*—and left it stuck in the door. I'd also left another voicemail for the crew chief.

People tended to give law-enforcement K-9s a lot of leeway, so I remained in uniform and dressed Brigit in her police-dog vest as I met up with Seth for dinner. He sported a Fort Worth Fire Department sweatshirt. We brought Brigit and Blast into the Italian restaurant with us. As usual, our canines were given carte blanche. They were also given an antipasto platter full of delicious meats and cheeses on the house. I knew the feast would make Brigit gassy later, but how could I deny her such a yummy treat? I'd just have to rub some Mentholatum under my nose to block the smell.

Seth and I discussed some of the pending wedding matters.

"We need to find a florist," I said. "I'll need a bouquet, and you'll need a boutonniere. Corsages for our mothers and boutonnieres for my dad and your grandfather." Floral centerpieces for the tables would be expensive, so I suggested a more affordable alternative. "Gabby and Frankie want to be involved. We can take a look on Pinterest and come up with some fun ideas for centerpieces that we can make ourselves."

"My mother would be happy to help with that, too."

"Good. We could use a lot of hands. Got any opinion on flowers?"

"None," Seth said. "I don't know a daisy from a daffodil."

"I'll see what the floral designer comes up with."

We decided we'd leave our wedding amidst the glow of sparklers. Seemed appropriate for a firefighter's ceremony. Fortunately, there'd be plenty of trained first responders on hand in the unlikely event something went up in flames. When it came to party favors, I suggested something useful, like a personal security device.

Seth arched a brow. "Are you suggesting we give everyone a canister of pepper spray?"

"Why not?" I asked. "It's practical. We could get the cylinders embossed with our names and the wedding date."

"It's not exactly romantic."

He had me there. "What about those reflective slap bracelets? It would make people more visible if they're out at night walking their dog or jogging."

"That's a little more like it."

"Flowers are romantic. Let's include a packet of seeds, too. Bluebonnets, maybe?" The official Texas state flower blanketed roadsides in spring, providing a beautiful splash of color and the perfect backdrop for photos. It wasn't unusual to see cars pulled over on the highways or county roads, parents snapping pics of their children sitting among the blooms.

"Works for me."

"Let's do bookmarks, too," I added. "We can order some with photos of us with Blast and Brigit on them. We can put the gifts in little bags and fill the rest with pastel mints."

Seth smiled. "Whatever you say, dear."

I raised my water glass in salute. "You're already sounding like a husband."

When we finished dinner, we parted with a warm kiss in the parking lot. I drove back to the Airbnb once more. It was fully dark now, and after 7:00. Tommy Perkins wouldn't be out this late after getting such an early start to his day, would he?

I pulled up to the house to find the driveway empty, once again. *Argh!* Had Perkins come back here yet? With the porch light off, it was impossible for me to tell if my card was still in the door. Maybe he'd stopped somewhere for dinner.

I released Brigit from her enclosure, let her take a tinkle on the lawn, and led her to the door. My card was gone. Someone had been here, had seen my card. Just in case Perkins was here but had left his truck elsewhere for some reason, I knocked several times and rang the bell.

There was no answer. It appeared Perkins had come to the rental, found my card, and taken off.

I stepped over to the living-room window, cupped my hands around my face, and peered inside through a narrow gap in the curtains. It was too dark for me to see anything other than the tiny glow of the light on the smoke alarm and the readout on the DVR. I whipped my flashlight from my belt and shined it through the window. The only signs of life were a cereal bowl, a drinking glass, and a crumpled napkin that had been left on the coffee table.

I returned to my car, logged into my computer, and ran a search on the Airbnb website to see if I could track down the owner of the house. The listing came up on the first page, one of the more affordable ones in the area. Luckily, the owner had noted her cell number so that prospective tenants could call or text her with questions.

I dialed her number and explained my situation. "I'm afraid Mr. Perkins has taken off."

"Really?" the woman said. "He's booked the place for three more days. Already paid and everything."

A few days' rent would be nothing to lose compared to his freedom. "Any chance you could let me take a look inside, see if Mr. Perkins left anything behind that might tell me where he's gone?"

"Of course, officer. I'll be right there."

The woman arrived less than ten minutes later. She typed a four-digit code into the electronic keypad and stepped inside, flipping on the light switch. Brigit and I followed her in.

"It's the landlord!" she called out. "Anybody here?"

There was no answer.

"Fort Worth police!" I called. "If anyone is in here, respond now!"

Sill nothing.

I turned to the woman. "Wait here. Let my K-9 and I check things out, make sure it's safe." The last thing I'd want is for her to be hurt by Perkins if he was inside and decided not to go down without a fight. This was Texas, after all. For all I knew, he'd blast his way out of a closet, a gun in each hand.

Walking side by side, Brigit and I made a quick but careful sweep of the place, checking behind curtains, in closets, in the shower, and under the beds. *Nope. Nobody here.* There was no luggage in the bedroom, either, no clothing hanging in the closet, no toiletries in the bathroom. Perkins had left in a hurry, leaving behind an unmade bed and dirty towels but no evidence of where he might be headed.

I returned to the living room. "It's clear."

As the woman came inside and closed the door behind her to keep out the cold, I donned a pair of latex gloves and rummaged through the trash bins, searching for anything that might tell me where Tommy Perkins might be headed. Unfortunately, I found only discarded takeout wrappers, food scraps, and an empty bottle of dandruff shampoo. The jackass hadn't even bothered to recycle. *Jerk.*

I looked around for a pad of paper he might have jotted a note on. In the movies, there always seemed to be such a pad, and a ready pencil to scratch back and forth across the top page to reveal the hidden message. But no, no pad. The only secret messages were the ones I'd found in my other investigation, hidden in Shelby's spam folder.

I pulled off the gloves and added them to the trash bin before addressing the landlord. "If you see Mr. Perkins or hear from him again, don't tell him you've spoken with me, okay? Try to find out where he's gone, and get me whatever phone number he's using now."

"I will."

I thanked the woman and led Brigit back to the cruiser. While I was frustrated as heck that Perkins had slipped through my fingers and Brigit's claws, at least I had tomorrow evening to look forward to. With any luck, Detective Jackson and I might finally get an answer to the question that had been dogging us for more than two weeks. *Who killed Greg Olsen?*

THIRTY-SIX
THE SCENT OF GOODBYE

Brigit

The house had smelled strongly of the man that Megan had spoken to several days ago at that other place. It also smelled strongly of his adrenaline. He'd been at the house very recently, and he'd been frantic. But he was gone now. All he'd left behind was a bran flake stuck to a bowl. Brigit licked it, but the darn thing was firmly glued to the dish. As far as the dog was concerned, the entire visit to the house had been a colossal waste of time.

THIRTY-SEVEN
MISSION IMPOSSIBLE

The Slasher

As the bus rolled down Camp Bowie toward the coffee shop, the Slasher grew increasingly excited and anxious at the same time. His skin felt warm and tingly. He couldn't wait to see Shelby again. The two weeks since he'd last seen her had been pure torture.

The brakes squeaked and a rotating mass of people got on and off the bus, mere movements and colors in his periphery as he stared out the window, every cell in his body prickly with anticipation. A voice came over the loudspeaker, announcing that the next stop would be the one at Camp Bowie and Bryant Irvin Road. He looked over at the coffee shop as they rolled slowly past. *There she is!* Shelby stood in line at the counter, her strawberry blonde hair like a beacon in the night.

As the bus rolled to a stop, he began to stand, turning to the woman next to him and saying "Excuse me" so that he could ease past the grocery bags littering the floor at her feet. As he stood, he cast a glance across the street and instantly went cold.

Holy shit!

Parked at the edge of the lot across the wide boulevard

sat a plain four-door sedan, the type driven by little old ladies and cops working undercover. It sat under a tree, the bare limbs obscuring his view inside the vehicle. He'd barely gotten a glance at it when the lights came on inside the bus, reflecting off the windows and obliterating any view he might have outside. He dropped back into his seat, panic rendering him paralyzed.

The woman next to him cast him a confused glance, the handles of her grocery bags gathered in her hands. "Ain't this your stop?"

"No," he said. "I was mistaken."

She shrugged and released the handles of her bags, returning her attention to the paperback she'd been reading.

He looked down at his feet until the lights went off in the bus and it began moving again. He scrubbed a hand over the short stubble on his head and cast a glance back at the car. *Is anyone inside?* Between the dark of the night and the large SUV parked beside it, casting it in further shadow, it was impossible to tell. There was some clutter on the dash, which could mean it was a personal car, not a government vehicle. But he couldn't take a chance, not for himself or for Shelby. He rode the bus farther into the city, leaving Shelby to wonder why she'd been stood up.

THIRTY-EIGHT
TABLE FOR ONE

Megan

Detective Jackson and I sat in her car, our eyes glued on the Starbucks across the street, while Brigit lay in the backseat, happily gnawing a new squeaky chew toy I'd bought her. It was shaped like a leprechaun in recognition of the upcoming St. Patrick's Day holiday. For many people, Valentine's Day was now only a fond memory, the chocolate long since devoured, the flowers dried, dead, and disposed of. But for Detective Jackson and me, Valentine's Day was still heavy on our minds, marking the night we launched an investigation into a murder we had yet to solve.

Squeak-squeak. Squeak-squeak-squeak.

Jackson groaned and slid me some side-eye. "You couldn't have bought her a quiet toy?"

I raised my hands in innocence. "She picked it, not me."

The smell of fresh-roasted coffee wafted across the boulevard, making me wish I had a cup of my own to fight the chill. A bus had just stopped nearby. We eyed those who'd disembarked, assessing them, but the only people who'd climbed off were two fortyish women and a young boy one of the women held by his mitten-clad hand. The boy hopped along the sidewalk as if playing hopscotch, jerking the woman's arm. She tolerated being yanked on, leading him down the sidewalk past the small shopping center, heading for the apartments that sat behind the retail shops.

Knowing Jackson's plain, four-door sedan was the type favored by undercover law enforcement and grandmothers seeking comfortable cars big enough to safely transport precious grandchildren, we'd done our best to make it look like the latter. We'd put a plastic baby bottle and one of Brigit's plush toys on the dashboard, as if children regularly rode in the vehicle. We'd disguised ourselves, too. I'd worn a knit cap and draped a plaid blanket over my shoulders to hide my uniform. The detective had donned a colorful crocheted shawl.

Jackson raised a small pair of high-powered binoculars to her face. "Shelby's paying for her order."

I raised my glasses, too, waiting eagerly to see what Shelby would do once her coffee was ready. Would she take a seat with someone already in the shop? There were two men in their thirties or forties sitting alone at tables. Two women, one of whom was built like a WNBA player, lounged in arm chairs situated around a coffee table. Surely the tall one had large feet, maybe even a women's size eleven. Would Shelby sit with them? Three young men who appeared to be working on a group project for either work or college huddled around an open laptop at another table, while a single thirtyish woman in fashionable clothing and high-heeled boots rested her feet on the chair across from her as she sipped a coffee and chatted on her cell phone. Was one of them the person Shelby had come here to meet, or was the person who'd sent her the e-mail yet to arrive? Shelby had glanced around when she'd entered the shop a moment ago, but hadn't acknowledged anyone. My guess was that whomever she planned to rendezvous with here tonight was still on their way.

Squeak-squeak.

A barista stepped to the far end counter, his lips moving as he called out a name. Shelby walked over and claimed the cup.

Jackson leaned forward in her seat, still watching through her binoculars. "Where are you going, Shelby?"

Squeak.

Shelby glanced around the space and took a few steps toward an empty table at the front before doing an about-face and walking to another empty table at the back where she could have more privacy. She sat facing the door. Unlike all of the others who were sitting alone, she didn't take out her phone, a computer, a tablet, or a book. She just perched stiffly on the edge of her chair, occasionally taking a sip of her coffee, watching the door with the same intensity Brigit watched her treats when other dogs were around. Even if we hadn't known Shelby was waiting for someone, her body language would have made it clear.

Unfortunately, she was still sitting an hour later, and so were we. After two hours in my seat, my bum had fallen asleep. Going so long without turning on the heater had turned my toes to ice, too. Everyone else in the coffee shop had gone, and a green-smocked staff member wandered over to Shelby's table to speak with her, probably to tell her they needed to close up for the night. Shelby nodded and stood, her shoulders slumped as she dropped her now-empty cup into the trash can and exited the store. She stopped on the sidewalk and glanced around the area, as if searching for the person who was supposed to meet her or some explanation as to why the person hadn't come. When she found neither, she pointed her key fob at her car and pushed the button, lighting it up inside. She slid into the driver's seat, swiping at her eye with her right hand as she shut the door with her left.

"She's crying," I said, instinctively narrowing my eyes to focus, though the motion did nothing to help me see better through the field glasses.

Jackson started her engine. "Let's see where she goes."

Maybe she'd do something stupid, like drive by the person's place to find out why they never showed, lead us directly to Greg's killers. It was unlikely, but there was nothing wrong with hoping for the best, was there?

Ten seconds after Shelby had pulled out of the lot, we surreptitiously pulled out of our lot across the street. Shelby was headed east on Camp Bowie. Was she going home?

I slid my binoculars back into their case. "What do you think happened back there?"

Jackson stared through the windshield and issued a frustrated growl. "Maybe whoever she was supposed to meet changed their mind. Or maybe they somehow realized we'd seen the e-mail. Or maybe the person spotted us."

I reached out to turn on the heater. "Or maybe the person is dead."

"Wow." Jackson slid a glance my way. "This took a dark turn."

"I'm just saying, if the person who sent the e-mail is someone Shelby was having an affair with, and if he's one of the people who killed Greg, maybe the person who helped Shelby's lover kill Greg has since killed the lover, too. Maybe that person was afraid Shelby's lover would get caught meeting her here and would lead police to the accomplice."

"Could be. Sometimes people who might otherwise get away with their crimes get caught when they try to cover it up."

That's irony for you.

We followed at a distance until Shelby turned down her street to go home.

Jackson snorted. "Well, this was one way to waste an evening."

As we drove back to the station in silence, I mulled things over some more. Who had sent that e-mail? Could that person actually be dead now, too? If not, what would happen now if that person realized we'd seen the message about their plan to meet Shelby at the coffee shop? We might have just frightened the person back into hiding, much like Brigit scared squirrels out of the yard and back up into the trees. I could only hope that wasn't the case, that our attempts to gain intel hadn't backfired.

Thursday morning, as Brigit and I were wrapping up a false alarm call at a home in the Frisco Heights neighborhood, Detective Jackson called on my cell.

"I just spoke with Shelby's boss," she said. "She was returning my call about the blood evidence she needed to have Greg declared dead. She mentioned that Shelby returned to work today. Sounds like she decided all of a sudden, said she couldn't bear to be at home alone anymore."

Once again, I wasn't sure what to make of the behavior. A two-week bereavement period was the norm, and that time had expired. Getting back on a routine would provide a distraction, maybe even some comfort, to a person who was grieving the loss of a loved one. But could this also mean she was putting Greg behind her now? Letting go? Did it show that the insurance money didn't mean that much to her, wouldn't change the way she lived? Or was she simply trying to avoid both suspicion and depleting her savings while she waited for her husband to be declared dead and the insurance proceeds to be paid out? The timing, immediately after the failed meeting at Starbucks, seemed suspicious. Still, it could be mere coincidence.

"When's the hearing on Shelby's petition?" I asked.

"First week of April," Jackson said.

"Really? That soon?" Criminal matters often took months, if not years, to make their way through the court system. I knew civil matters were different given that only money was at stake—not freedom or lives—but the civil courts, too, were known for their sluggish pace.

"Shelby's boss was able to get an expedited hearing because there's no opposing party to contend with and it won't take long to present the evidence. Ten, maybe twenty minutes, tops. Probably didn't hurt that she donated two grand to the judge's campaign fund during the last election, either."

In only five more weeks, Shelby Olsen would be a millionaire. It must be odd to know a windfall was coming your way, especially when it was born of tragedy. Of course it was likely much less odd for Shelby, who seemed to have had a hand in the tragedy.

During my lunch break, I decided to stop by the station, where I could nuke the leftover pasta I'd brought for lunch in the microwave and check my e-mails. After warming up my meal in the station's break room, I carried it to a desk in the administrative area and logged into a desktop computer.

First, I checked Shelby's e-mail account to see if there was evidence of any new suspicious activity. I discovered that the e-mail from LastingLovePleasurePills was now marked as unread. *Hmm.* Shelby must have checked her spam folder and realized she'd forgotten to cover her digital tracks. She must not know we were already on to the secret communications or she would have left it alone.

I looked over the more recent e-mails that had come into her spam folder. There were no others from Lasting-Love, but one from SnoreSolutionzzz caught my eye. I opened it to find a message that read *Snore no more! Our patented mouth guard is guaranteed to stop snoring or your money back!* Again, the e-mail contained a simple photo of the device, which resembled a dental mold, as well as a link that took me to a legitimate site for the device. But also again, there were earlier unread e-mails from the same sender, as well as extra space at the bottom of the most recent message.

I performed my copy-and-paste process once more and was thrilled to find a new message. *Cops might have followed you last night. They're less likely to watch your office. Burnett Park at noon Friday. Keep an eye out.*

The phrasing gave no clue as to who had sent the message. It could as easily be from a kidnapper as from a boyfriend. Whoever had sent the e-mail had spotted Jackson's unmarked cruiser, after all. *Damn.* But at least they didn't realize we'd intercepted the e-mails. Instead, they'd assumed we'd tailed Shelby from her house to the coffee shop. They'd be on the lookout for a tail tomorrow, too. Little did they know we wouldn't have to follow Shelby. We would already be in place at the park, ready to ambush them and finally get some answers.

Burnett Park was a three-acre urban park downtown. The park also served as an event venue and public art space, and included stone sculptures by famed artist Isamu Noguchi. While the park's design incorporated trees and grassy spaces, its most distinguishing feature were its walkways. The walks were laid out in a geometric pattern of twenty-four squares in a grid. From above, they looked like starbursts. The park sat in front of a tall bank tower, one of the many skyscrapers making up the Fort Worth skyline. On fair-weather days, workers in nearby buildings often took their brown bag lunches or takeout orders to the park to enjoy some outdoor time before returning to their offices. Fortunately, while the evenings and nights remained cold, daytime temperatures had been in the upper sixties the past few days. The pleasant weather meant more people would be outside, providing more cover for us.

The person who had sent the e-mail didn't seem to know that Shelby hadn't returned to work yet. Their communications must be one-way only. A smart system, because any response or communication initiated by Shelby by phone or e-mail would have been easier for law enforcement to catch and could directly implicate her in her husband's disappearance, assuming, of course, that she was involved. This way, she could deny ever seeing these messages, or even knowing they existed. Heck, she could claim to have no idea who'd sent them, or that they must have been sent to her by mistake. They were smart to communicate via her already established e-mail account, too. Any new or unusual accounts would have been more likely to raise suspicion and undergo more scrutiny. Shelby must have thought we'd stopped looking at her e-mails after I returned her and Greg's computers. Of course, she'd be wrong about that.

Had I not had my epiphany about the invisible ink, the hidden, cryptic messages sent to her spam folder could have very easily flown under our radar. Could there be other clues we'd missed, ones hiding right under our noses?

The message could also explain Shelby's sudden decision

to return to work. She'd be less conspicuous walking to the downtown park from her office a few blocks away than she would driving there from her home. They feared law enforcement was keeping an eye on her, and they assumed she'd be less likely to be watched while she was at work. They would have been right, too, had I not found their secret communications.

I printed out the message and took it down the hall to Detective Jackson.

She read it over and looked up at me. "Heck, Megan. You've found more clues than I have. Maybe you should be in charge of this investigation."

Though I was flattered and glad to have helped, I was smart enough to realize that there was a lot more to know about running an investigation. That said, this experience reinforced the idea that two heads are better than one. When I made detective one day, I'd find a sharp aspiring investigator among the police recruits and take him or her under my wing, too, get their thoughts and ideas on the investigation and evidence.

Jackson set the printout down on her desk and drummed her fingers on the desktop. "We'll need backup to keep an eye on the area with us, make sure we don't miss our chance to nab them together. I'll round up a couple of the other officers to help us out tomorrow. We'll have to be inconspicuous. I'll work on some disguises."

"Brigit has a hula girl outfit she could wear," I joked.

"As much as I would love to see that, a flower lei and a grass skirt wasn't exactly what I had in mind. You two will be stationed inside the bank building. Bring your binoculars."

I gave her a salute. "Yes, ma'am."

I returned to the computer to finish both my lunch and checking my e-mails. To my delight, my inbox included the reports taken by the Pueblo Police Department from the victims of the snow-plow scam.

I took a bite of my now lukewarm pasta and pulled the first report up on my screen. Nothing in it definitively linked the Jimmie Perkins who'd been involved in the snow-plow scam to the Tommy Perkins who purportedly represented Stormchaser Roofing, Inc. *Darn.* I pulled up the second report. Nothing helpful there, either. A description of Perkins in the third report proved promising. The woman who'd filed the report said that Jimmie Perkins resembled Paul Newman. *My thought, exactly.* But while a resemblance to the Hollywood icon might not be enough alone, the fact that she said he wore a watch with a silver-and-turquoise band, the same type I'd seen Tommy wearing, pegged Jimmie and Tommy as very likely the same man.

I shoveled the rest of my lunch into my mouth and let Brigit lick the bowl clean. After printing out the Pueblo police report, I carried it down the hall to show Captain Leone. Once he'd read it over, I'd told him that I'd also seen the turquoise watch band on Tommy Perkins. "May I have permission to arrest the guy now?"

"You got it," he said.

"I'll have to look for him. He's vacated the Airbnb. I don't know where he is at the moment."

"I'll get a warrant to ping his cell phone. What number do you have for him?"

I gave Captain Leone both the number for Tommy Perkins and the one he'd given me for the crew chief.

"I'll have Melinda put a note in the system, too," the captain said. "If anyone comes across him in the meantime, they'll haul his ass in. We'll need some luck, though. I'd bet dollars to donuts he's already back in New Mexico someplace."

The captain was probably right. I was a day late and

a dollar short. I'd let a criminal slip through my fingers, two if you counted whoever had planned to meet up with Shelby last night. While I tried to tell myself that I'd done what I could, done even more than required of me, it didn't relieve my sense of guilt. I'd let down the people on my beat, and that didn't sit well with me. But, if nothing else, I was more motivated than ever to get these two cases resolved and the guilty parties behind bars.

Sure enough, the captain called my cell later that afternoon to tell me that the tech team had gotten no pings on either number. Either the phones had been turned off and their batteries removed, or they'd been destroyed entirely. With no way to track Perkins digitally, he'd have to be nailed the old-fashioned way—by being otherwise located, perhaps when pulled over for a traffic violation. If he obeyed the traffic laws, he might never interact with law enforcement. He might once again get away with his fraud scheme, head off to a new locale to dupe another set of unsuspecting victims. The thought enraged me to no end. I wanted that man stopped, and I wanted him stopped *now*.

Frankie was off duty that evening, and we decided to go out for Mexican food and margaritas. I could use a lime-flavored libation to ease my frustrations.

Over a basket of chips and salsa, I told Frankie about the cryptic e-mail and the aborted meeting at Starbucks. Frankie was discreet, and I knew I could trust her. The information would go no further than our table.

She sipped her frozen drink. "So Shelby Olsen might have been having an affair and duped her husband into withdrawing the cash to pay for his own hit?"

"It's one theory I'm working," I said. "But there's a small problem."

"What's that?"

"By all accounts, she and Greg were happily married. Nobody suspected they were having any problems."

"That's not unusual, though, is it?" Frankie asked. "People often don't know what's happening in other peoples' relationships, about abuse or money problems or things like that."

It was true. A number of murders had made the headlines in recent years, women and sometimes even children killed by men they thought loved them and who'd seemed to everyone else to be loving husbands and fathers. While much rarer, the roles were sometimes reversed, with the wife being the one to do away with her husband. Still, I couldn't see it. "She really seems to love him and miss him."

"It could be nothing more than a good act." Frankie pointed a tortilla chip at me. "But I think you're having trouble believing Shelby could have killed her husband because you can't imagine ever killing Seth. It's so inconceivable for you, that you can't imagine anyone else doing it."

Was she right? Were my thoughts about this case clouded by my own personal feelings? It was hard to say. The lines often blurred between Megan Luz, the engaged young woman in love with her broad-shouldered firefighter fiancé, and Megan Luz, the dedicated and logical cop.

We turned our conversation toward more upbeat topics. The wedding dress Beverly Rubinstein had designed for me. My fall honeymoon in Utah and the state's gorgeous scenery. The fact that the Fort Worth Whoop Ass was currently ranked first in its league.

"Congratulations," I said. "That's quite a feat."

"We're a top-notch team," Frankie said. "That goes

without saying. But I have to give some credit to my lucky socks. We haven't lost a game since I stopped washing them."

"Ew."

"Maybe you'd solve your two cases if you stopped washing your socks."

"That's ridiculous."

"Maybe," she said. "But it's all about the confidence, about believing in yourself."

"It's hard for me to believe in myself when I let a crook slip through my fingers."

She sipped her margarita. "You need to stop beating yourself up about that."

"If I don't beat myself up, who will?"

She snorted. "Now you're the one being ridiculous."

When we returned home that evening, I decided to take a bubble bath. I did some of my best thinking in the tub, where there were no distractions and both my body and mind could relax.

Brigit trod after me as I went to the bathroom, but took off at warp speed when she saw me turn on the tub's tap. "Don't worry, girl!" I called after her. "This bath is for me, not you."

Once I was in the tub, she peeked around the edge of the door. Realizing she was in no danger of being bathed, she wandered over and sniffed at the bubbles, sneezing when they popped in her nose. *Snit-snit!* She pawed at the bubbles, popping them with her claws. When she'd cleared a spot, she lowered her snout and lapped at the water.

I gently pushed her away. "No, girl." The bubble bath was too diluted to hurt her, but surely the water wouldn't taste good.

She ignored me and returned for another drink. I gave

up. If she thought lavender water tasted yummy, who was I to tell her different? Lying back with only my face above water and closing my eyes, I let my mind and body drift.

Earlier, I'd thought how I would take an aspiring investigator under my wing once I made detective, how doing so would not only allow me to serve as a mentor like detectives Jackson and Bustamente had done for me, but would also provide a second opinion on evidence, a fresh perspective on the cases and clues. When Brigit licked bubbles from my knee, I realized I already had someone who could give another perspective on the clues. A furry, four-footed someone.

My mind went back to Valentine's Day, to the horrific crime scene in the Olsen's kitchen, to the numerous puddles of blood individually designated with evidence markers, to Brigit paying special attention to the puddle marked with the number 23. Was there something to that? Was it different somehow? The lab had confirmed that all of the blood was Greg's. What could be different about that sample?

My mind was still swirling when the bath water cooled and I climbed out to dry off. I might not have answers now but, with any luck, we'd get some tomorrow when we detained and questioned Shelby and whoever had sent her the mysterious e-mail.

THIRTY-NINE
DOWN DOG

Brigit

Megan led Brigit into a tall building and across a hard, cool floor. Brigit's nails clicked as she strode along beside her partner. Brigit preferred soft ground, where her claws could dig in for traction and she could sneak up on prey without her toenails making such a racket. But when they were on duty, Megan called the shots.

Her partner stopped to speak to a man sitting at a counter in the building's foyer near the doors. She had no idea what the humans were saying. She didn't speak human. But the next thing she knew, the man had offered a spare stool to Megan and placed it next to a potted tree by the front windows. Megan told Brigit to lie down on the floor while she took a seat on the stool, lifting her binoculars to her eyes. Megan smelled of adrenaline and her body language told Brigit that whatever they were doing, it was important. Brigit didn't know who Megan was looking for, but she hoped it was someone she'd get to chase.

FORTY
LUNCH DATE

The Slasher

He wasn't taking any chances. He'd dressed in a business suit he'd bought at a thrift store so he'd blend in with the professional downtown crowd. He'd also arrived an hour early and circled the park, walking in increasingly larger circles around the block, then around a four-block area, scoping things out. It was a sunny day, and he kept his eyes peeled behind his dark sunglasses, searching for uniformed law enforcement. In case any of them were working undercover, he also kept an eye out for anyone who might be a cop in a disguise.

He saw a white woman with blonde curls and a sketch-pad sitting on a blanket in a grassy area of the park. She was dressed in Lycra and sneakers, and had a lean, athletic build. Like him, she wore sunglasses, but she seemed far more interested in the city skyline she was roughing out on her pad than she was in any of the people milling about the park. He supposed she might have dressed in exercise gear to be ready for a chase, and she could have a gun and handcuffs in her bright pink tote bag, but it seemed unlikely. Lots of women wore yoga pants these days. Besides, if the police were on to him, they'd send men, wouldn't they? And big ones at that?

He scanned the area. A beefy guy ambled along the perimeter of the park. A white hardhat sat atop his rust-colored hair. He also wore safety goggles, work gloves, and a bright orange safety jacket that hung down to mid-thigh. He carried some type of long-handled landscaping tool. He knelt down and appeared to be inspecting one of the automatic sprinkler heads under a row of bushes. Another muscular man stood behind a nearby hot dog cart. He wore a white paper cap and a white apron that bore ketchup splotches, taking the Slasher back to that bloody night in the kitchen and the spots he'd left on the walls and floor. A short line had formed in front of the cart, hungry workers looking for a quick, inexpensive lunch.

After watching them for a moment or two, the Slasher dismissed the two men. They looked legit. He stopped at the corner of the bank building and pulled out his phone, pretending to be dialing a number. He held the phone to his ear and mumbled nonsense as he continued to scan the area.

Shelby emerged from between buildings across the park, a takeout bag from a sandwich shop clutched in her hand, her strawberry blonde hair shining in the sunlight. He inhaled sharply, a gasp of joy. *She's here!* Reflexively, he took a step toward her and began to lower his phone, when his senses caught up to him. *Give it a minute or two. Make sure she wasn't followed.*

He raised the phone back to his ear, occasionally saying, "Sure," or "Yes," or "That's right" enough to make it look like he was having a conversation. Meanwhile, Shelby took a seat on a bench under a tree, not far from the artist, and proceeded to pull a sandwich and napkin out of the paper bag. It took every bit of restraint he had not to run to her and take her in his arms.

He scanned the area again. Nobody seemed to be paying Shelby any mind. A black woman in a gray pantsuit stepped out of a building on the other side of the park, behind Shelby. She stopped next to the revolving doors to dig through her purse. A felt hat with a narrow brim hid her hair and shaded her eyes, and a lightweight blue fashion scarf was looped loosely around her neck, obscuring her jawline. Between the hat and the scarf, it was nearly impossible to make out her facial features. *Could she be a cop?* He tossed the possibility around in his mind before dismissing the thought. The woman hadn't followed Shelby here. She'd already been inside the building. *All those days holed up in the hotel have made me paranoid.*

Deciding the coast was clear, he said "goodbye" into his phone, and slid it into the breast pocket of his suit jacket. He wondered how long it would take for Shelby to recognize him with the short, dark hair and thick beard. He'd seen her glance his way with no reaction. Of course he was still sixty yards away, too far for her to get a good look. Surely she'd spot him as he drew closer, maybe even get a laugh out of it.

He'd taken three steps in her direction when the sprinkler-repair guy strode over to the hot dog vendor. He placed his order and reached into his back pocket to remove his wallet. As he did, the bottom of his jacket lifted, revealing a gun holster. *Shit-shit-shit!*

His body temperature spiked as his pulse sent his blood through his veins at the speed of light. Thoughts zipped through his mind, too, at the same speed. Had he dismissed the woman in the hat too soon? Was she a cop, too? The artist was glancing around the park now, nonchalantly chewing on her pencil eraser, but was it an act? Was she actually a police officer?

Realizing he'd faltered in his step, he reached into his breast pocket and removed his phone again, pretending he'd received a call. He put a finger to his opposite ear, as if to block out sound so he could hear the nonexistent caller better, but in reality hoping the hand would block his face. The last thing he needed now was for Shelby to spot him from across the way, to clue in any cops with a flicker of recognition. Looking down, he strode across the pavement in front of the bank and turned down the side of the building, moving as fast as he dared so as not to draw attention to himself.

Their plan had seemed cunning and clever, their communications virtually undetectable, sure to pass right under the nose of law enforcement. *How the hell had the cops discovered the secret messages?*

FORTY-ONE
ONE DOWN, ONE TO GO

Megan

From my vantage point inside the bank, I repeatedly scanned the park and streets, watching and waiting for someone to approach Shelby. She sat on the bench, eating her sandwich slowly, tiny bite by tiny bite, as if trying to make it last as long as possible, to give her a reason to remain on the bench. A dark-haired businessman strode past in front of the building, his head ducked as he spoke on his cell phone, the device to one ear and a finger to the other. He blocked my view for a brief instant, but then there Shelby was again, still nibbling at her lunch. Meanwhile, across the park, Derek, disguised as a maintenance worker, wolfed down a series of three sloppy chili dogs he'd bought from a vendor. Sauce dripped from the hot dog in his hand onto his orange safety jacket. *Sheesh. At least he looks legitimate.*

Summer, one of my fellow female officers, sat cross-legged on the grass, pretending to be an artist sketching the nearby trees. She'd dressed in yoga pants, an athletic top, and tennis shoes, ready to drop her sketchpad and pencil to run and wrangle a suspect if needed. Detective Jackson was in place near the doors of a building behind

Shelby, hiding in plain sight so to speak. She looked about purposefully, as if waiting for a lunch date herself. In actuality, she was scanning the surroundings for someone who might be aiming for the bench, preparing herself to close in when he appeared.

As the lunch hour wore on, more and more people milled about the park. To some, it was a destination, a place to eat their lunch outdoors and enjoy some direct sunshine before returning to their offices or cubicles. For others, the park was simply a shortcut, a way to get from their office buildings to the nearby lunch spots faster than taking the sidewalks along the streets.

A tall, middle-aged woman approached Shelby and addressed her. Could this woman be the person who'd e-mailed Shelby? We'd been expecting a man. Had we made an incorrect assumption? The woman seemed unconcerned whether anyone might be watching her. Shelby, on the other hand, glanced around before responding to the woman with some quick words and a hand gesture, inviting her to share the bench.

I raised my binoculars to my eyes for a closer look. The older woman took a seat at the other end of the bench. The two said nothing more to each other. While the older woman pulled what appeared to be a day planner from her purse and jotted notes in it, Shelby finished her sandwich and crumpled up the wrapper. Looked like the woman had merely been asking if the other half of the bench was taken so she could sit and get organized.

A quarter hour passed. Shelby's gaze surveyed the area as she sipped her drink. When she lowered the bottle, her eyes welled with tears and her lip quivered. Whomever she had been expecting had not arrived . . . again. I'd never seen someone look so lost and lonely.

Was the person who was supposed to meet Shelby here

running late? Had they hit some type of snag? I waited and waited, watching and wondering. Brigit went stiff when she spotted a squirrel sneaking across the closest corner of the park to grab a French fry someone had tossed its way. I knew Brigit wanted to bark and run outside to chase the rodent, but I'd given her the commands to be quiet and still, and she knew better than to make any moves or noise while under those orders. Liver treats were at stake and, while they were a sure thing, she had yet to catch a squirrel despite approximately ten thousand attempts.

Shelby pulled her phone from her purse several times to check the time. Finally, she logged into her phone and appeared to be reviewing her e-mails, probably looking to see if another had come in, explaining why the person she was supposed to meet had not arrived for their rendezvous. She returned her phone to her purse, leaned forward with her elbows on her knees, and dropped her head into her hands, her shoulders visibly shaking as she sobbed. The woman sitting on the bench next to her looked over and said something, probably asking if Shelby was okay or needed help. Shelby kept her head in her hands, but shook it in a "no" gesture. The woman's face contorted in concern.

A long moment later, Shelby lifted her head and reached into her takeout bag, removing a napkin that she used to wipe her face. She pulled a compact from her purse and opened it to check her appearance. After dabbing under her eyes to remove traces of runny mascara, she dropped the compact back into her purse, gathered her things, and stood. She tossed her trash into the can nearby and walked slowly and somberly away in the direction of her office.

A few seconds later, my cell phone jiggled with a group

text sent by Detective Jackson to the rest of us. *Summer—follow Shelby. I'll trail you. Derek and Megan—stay here another half hour, see if anyone shows up.*

We all did as we were told. Unfortunately, our efforts here at the park were for naught. When nobody suspicious showed up within thirty minutes, Derek carried his tools and headed off down the sidewalk. Brigit and I exited the front of the building and aimed for my squad car, which I'd left in the parking lot of a church several blocks away, where it wouldn't be spotted. As we made our way, Brigit raised her snout in the air and sniffed, her nostrils flaring as she took in the scents. She stared off to the left for a few beats before looking up at me, as if awaiting instruction. More likely, she was awaiting a treat to reward her for behaving so well despite the squirrel. She had indeed been patient and silent, exactly as instructed. I fished a liver treat out of my pocket and tossed it to her along with a "Good girl, Brigit." I ruffled her ears, too, for good measure.

We were nearly back to the cruiser when my phone jiggled with another text from Detective Jackson. *Shelby's back in her building. Summer and Derek—you two are dismissed. Thanks for your help. Megan—meet me at the station.*

A half hour later, Jackson and I slouched in chairs on either side of her desk, feeling defeated. We'd checked Shelby's e-mail account, but found no new communications from the elusive individual who'd evaded our ambush. What had gone wrong? Could the person have spotted Brigit and me hiding behind the potted tree in the bank lobby? Had he noticed that Summer had a gun, pepper spray, and handcuffs in her bag? Or identified

Detective Jackson despite her face being obscured by her scarf and hat? Had he realized that the idiot dripping chili onto his clothing sported a utility belt and holster under his oversized orange safety jacket?

Jackson threw up her hands. "I'm out of ideas. I suppose all we can do now is go to Shelby and hope she'll break down and reveal who the e-mails were from. She's an intelligent woman, and she knows something about the law. She's probably put two and two together and realized law enforcement is on to the covert e-mail messages. But if she refuses to identify the person, or says she doesn't know who they came from, we're out of luck. With her rock-solid alibi and no proof of an affair or a hired hit, we'd never be able to get a conviction."

"This might sound crazy," I told her. "But what if the messages are from Greg?"

"*Might* sound crazy?" She cut me a scathing look. "That absolutely sounds crazy, Megan. Unless they have Wi-Fi in the great beyond, there's no way Greg could have sent those messages. Nobody can lose nearly a gallon of blood and live."

"True," I said. "If they lose that blood all at once. But what if the blood loss was spread out over a longer period of time?"

The scathing look morphed into another look entirely, this one curious and intrigued. She sat up straight in her chair. "What are you saying, exactly?"

"What if Greg and Shelby scripted the crime to collect the insurance? What if the blood was a prop? What if Greg withdrew his blood a little at a time over several weeks or months so he could cover the kitchen with it and make it look like he's dead when he really isn't?"

Jackson cocked her head. "Spectroscopy can be used

to date a bloodstain with reasonable accuracy, but I don't know whether there's a way to date blood samples. I'd have to find out."

"That might not be necessary," I said. "When Brigit and I were in Shelby and Greg's kitchen the night he disappeared, Brigit kept returning to blood sample twenty-three, as if she were comparing it to the other samples. There might be something different about that sample, something that would distinguish it from the others and prove that Greg's blood had been drawn at different times."

She picked up her phone and dialed the lab, putting the lab manager on speakerphone. "Tell her your theory, Officer Luz."

I provided the lab manager with my latest theory, that Greg Olsen's death had been faked. "My K-9 kept going back to sample number twenty-three after sniffing the other samples. What types of tests can you run to compare twenty-three to the other samples? To see if it's different somehow?"

"I can run a test for blood-alcohol content," the woman said. "I can also run a test for legal drugs, medicines. I could run a basic metabolic panel, too. The panel tests for blood sugar levels, as well as sodium, potassium, calcium, carbon dioxide, things like that. Those levels vary over time. If the results aren't uniform, it would prove the blood was not released from his body all at once."

"Can you put a rush on it?" Jackson asked. "I want to speak to Greg Olsen's wife this evening, and it would be helpful if we had the results first."

"I'm short a tech," she said. "Darn flu took him down. But nothing else we're processing is particularly pressing. We'll make this our top priority."

We thanked her and signed off.

I stood. "We're short several officers, too. I better get out on patrol until we hear back."

"I'll be in touch," Jackson said.

As Brigit and I headed down the hall, Captain Leone called out from his office. "Luz! Get back here!"

We retraced our steps until we stood in the captain's doorway. "Yes, sir?"

"Two of the officers scheduled for tonight's swing shift called in sick. Can you cover for one of them?"

"I'd be glad to, sir." With an expensive wedding on my horizon, I wasn't about to pass up a chance to earn some overtime pay.

He looked down at my partner. "You on board, too, Sergeant Brigit?"

She wagged her tail, raised her head, and woofed as if to say, *"Of course! You can always count on this K-9 team."*

The captain gave us an appreciative nod. "You ladies make my job easier."

I hoped he'd remember this when I requested two weeks off for my wedding and honeymoon come fall.

Brigit and I had been back on the beat for a little over an hour, cruising the streets and keeping a keen eye out for a pickup with New Mexico plates, when an odd call came in. Dispatch sounded both amused and confused. "Got a call about some folks making a citizen's arrest at Park Hill Drive and University. Who can respond?"

A citizen's arrest? This is a first. While it was true that the Texas Code of Criminal Procedure allowed any person to arrest an offender who committed a felony or an offense against the public peace in their presence or within their view, the practice was certainly not the preferred method for rounding up a criminal. When people took the law into their own hands, matters could escalate and violence could ensue. Someone who misinterpreted a situation and wrongfully restrained another could find themselves charged with an unlawful arrest. The person making the citizen's arrest could also be liable for any injuries incurred by the person they captured and restrained.

Brigit and I were only a quarter mile away and headed in that direction. I grabbed my mic from the dash and squeezed the button. "Officer Luz and Brigit responding."

In no time, Brigit and I pulled into the parking lot of a small café. There, I was surprised to find Althea Nomikos and two of her neighbors, one male and one female, standing in front of an SUV that sat crossways behind other vehicles parked in the designated spots, preventing them from backing up. She raised an arm when she saw my cruiser and flagged me down. As I pulled up and unrolled my window, she danced a little victory jig that involved arm rotations and pelvic thrusts, an odd combination of disco and dirty dancing. Brigit stood up in her enclosure behind me, eager to see what was happening outside.

"We got him! We got him!" Mrs. Nomikos sang.

"Got who?" I asked.

She pointed to a green pickup truck sandwiched tightly between two other vehicles. "Tommy Perkins!"

I squinted to see a man at the wheel of the truck. He glared at me and the others in his rearview mirror. *Yep, those are Tommy Perkins's eyes, all right.*

Mrs. Nomikos filled me in. "I was driving by when I thought I spotted Perkins getting out of this truck and going inside the restaurant. I stopped and looked through the window. Sure enough, it was him. I phoned my neighbors and got them over here to help. I parked my car right up next to the truck so he wouldn't be able to get in it. When I confronted him on the sidewalk, he went around and climbed in the passenger door. The others blocked him from behind and on the other side so he wouldn't be able to move."

Crafty. Nearly as clever a move as the invisible ink e-mail messages.

Tommy Perkins unrolled his window. He wore his usual dress shirt and tie today, along with the fleece-trimmed shearling coat. "I'm glad you're here, Officer Luz!" he hollered. "You need to arrest these people for false imprisonment!"

Althea Nomikos hollered right back at him. "It's a citizen's arrest! It's perfectly legal!"

Although vigilante justice could be problematic, in the present case, where Tommy Perkins could have easily vanished again and where nobody had been physically harmed, I was glad that Althea Nomikos and her neighbors had taken the initiative. I never would have known he'd traded his earlier truck for another, and would have driven right past him, none the wiser.

"These people are out of control!" Perkins cried, ignoring the woman. "They've accused me of ripping them off when I'm a victim, too! Nobody at Stormchaser will return my calls. They're late with my paycheck, too!"

"Is that so?" I circled around to the front of the pickup where I could have a better view of him and address him more directly. "Seems you've had a run of bad luck. That's the same thing that happened to you with Surefire Snow Plow Service and MixMaster Cement, isn't it?"

On hearing me mention the other sham shell companies from his previous schemes, his expression changed from angry to apprehensive. He drew his head back, and his voice was softer when he spoke again. "I . . . I . . ." he stammered. "I have no idea what you're talking about."

"Really?" I said. "Because I think you do, *Jimmy.*"

His gaze darted about, from me to Brigit to the neighbors he'd scammed and who'd stepped up onto the sidewalk beside me.

"He's pulled this kind of thing before." I gave his victims a quick summary of the evidence I'd dug up. Keeping my eyes on Perkins lest he pull some fresh shenanigans, I said, "Mrs. Nomikos, I'll need you to back up the car on his driver's side so I can get him out and cuff him. Go slow, okay?"

"Sure." Mrs. Nomikos pulled her keys from her pocket and climbed into her car. As she inched the vehicle backward, I stepped forward, bringing Brigit along with me. I walked up to the open window of Perkins's truck. "You're under arrest. Step out, face the hood, and put your hands on it. Understood?"

"Understood," he snapped, scowling.

I kept a close eye on him as he opened the door to the truck. But rather than close it and come forward, he left it open, turned, and took off running. *Moron.* This was the type of moment Brigit lived for. She watched Perkins go, quivering with anticipation beside me. I bent down, unleashed my partner, and ordered her to take the shyster down. *Get 'im, girl!*

It took Brigit only three bounds and one leap to take Perkins to the parking lot pavement. As if that hadn't been enough fun for her, she grabbed the fleece collar of his coat in her teeth and yanked back and forth, shaking him, his head flopping one way then another. Seemed the shepherd in her was trying to keep his coat in line.

As the group of neighbors cheered Brigit on, I knelt down, yanked Perkins's hands up behind him, and slapped on the cuffs. *Click-click.* After ordering Brigit off the con man, I reached into my pocket for a handful of liver treats. I held them out to Mrs. Nomikos and her neighbors. "Would you like the honors?"

"Of course!" Mrs. Nomikos broke into a smile and, while she didn't apologize for her negative attitude toward law enforcement during our earlier interactions, it was clear my dedication to tracking down clear evidence against Tommy Perkins had caused her to change her attitude. She and I were finally on the same team. She took the treats from me and divided them up. She and her neighbors took turns tossing them to my partner, who expertly snapped them out of the air.

After ordering Brigit back to my side, I reached down and grabbed Perkins's forearm to lift him. "Up you go."

"Like hell I do!" Perkins refused to get up, lying on the pavement like dead weight. He glared up at me.

I left him on the pavement. "Have it your way, then."

I pressed the button on my shoulder-mounted microphone and called for backup to transport the guy to the station for booking. For once, I was actually glad to see Derek when he showed up a couple of minutes later. The Big Dick was far from the smartest cop on the force, but his sheer strength definitely came in handy on occasion. Without a word, he yanked the man to his feet and tossed Perkins into the back of his cruiser as if he were a rag doll.

FORTY-TWO
THE SWEET SPOT

Brigit

Earlier, when they'd left that tall building, Brigit had smelled the strong scent of the man she'd smelled at the bloody house days ago. She had expected Megan might tell her to chase after him, but when she'd looked up at her partner, Megan had given her no such instruction. Instead, Megan gave her a liver treat even though Brigit hadn't done anything. Oh, well. Humans were sometimes hard to understand. Too bad Megan didn't speak dog.

Right now, though, Brigit was getting all kinds of love from the two women and the man who had tossed her the liver treats. They seemed happy that she had tackled that other guy. One of them was rubbing her ears, while another scratched under her chin. She lifted her head higher, so they could get at her neck, scratch under that pesky lead. When she'd had enough head pats, she flopped down and rolled over onto her back to give them easy access to her chest. The two women dug in, giving her a four-handed scratch with their long fingernails. *That's it*, Brigit thought. *That's the sweet spot.*

FORTY-THREE
KARMA'S A BITCH

The Slasher

He'd had to abort their meeting, again! Could it be co-incidence that an undercover cop was in the park at the same time he and Shelby were to meet? He could hardly believe the police had intercepted their communications. It had seemed like a foolproof system. He'd send Shelby what appeared to be a spam e-mail, it would go directly into her junk folder, and she'd mark it as unread after she copied and pasted the hidden message into a document and changed the font color so that the words were visible. They'd used her existing e-mail account because having her establish a new e-mail account had seemed riskier, more likely to raise suspicions if the police came sniffing around a second time after the initial review of Shelby's computer. Something sent through the existing system seemed less likely to draw attention. Maybe the cop had been at the park for another reason. Maybe someone had been seen selling drugs there, or maybe there'd been a mugger or pickpocket preying on people in the area. After all, the park sat in front of a bank building, where people would be expected to make cash withdrawals.

Still, he didn't dare send another e-mail message using

this method. He wanted to get in touch with her, but he'd have to find another way. Had the police confronted her directly? Were they checking her mailbox? Had they put a camera in the parking garage at her office? Were they watching her building? He had no way of knowing.

For now, though, he needed a drink. A stiff one. Luckily, a liquor store sat on the next block.

He tucked sixty bucks into his wallet and took the stairs down to the first floor, exiting at the side door at the end of the hall. It was after 8:00 and fully dark, the sun having set over an hour before. The streetlights provided meager illumination but he stuck to the shadows anyway, trying to be as invisible as possible. The day's events had left him feeling exposed and vulnerable.

He reached the store and slipped inside on the heels of five college boys who were yukking it up about some stupid thing one or another of them had done at a frat party. He went straight to the whiskey section, grabbed a large rectangular bottle of Jack Daniel's, and headed to the register, avoiding eye contact with anyone along the way. On a Friday night, the store was packed and he had to wait in line behind three other people stocking up on spirits for the weekend. Finally, it was his turn to pay. He set the bottle on the counter and forked over two twenty-dollar bills when the cashier gave him the total. He took his change and the tell-tale tall, narrow paper bag the clerk had slipped the bottle into. He was out the door having spoken not a single word to anyone. While he used to enjoy the peace and quiet of solitude, it was becoming far too much. He felt disconnected, deserted, desolate.

As he drew near the hotel, he heard the sound of wheels on asphalt and saw a trio of what appeared to be teenaged boys riding toward him on skateboards. All were white, and wore dark hoodies, jeans, and the expressions of hungry predators seeking prey. When they spotted him, the one in the lead popped a wheelie with his board, the back end dragging across the road as he sailed to a graceful stop in front of the Slasher. The other two followed suit, pulling up on either side of their leader to form a semicircle around the Slasher, forcing him to a stop.

"Whatcha got there?" The leader reached out and yanked the bag out of the Slasher's hands. He pulled the bottle out of the bag and held it up in victory. "Score! Looks like there's going to be a party tonight!"

The Slasher grabbed at the bottle, but the boy jerked it back out of his reach. He signaled his two friends. "What else you got, dude?"

Before he knew what was happening, the other two boys had shoved him to the ground. His knee hit the asphalt, bearing the brunt of all of his weight, and a sharp pain shot up his leg. One of the kids wrangled with him while the other pulled his wallet from his back pocket. *If they take the driver's license and cash, I'm fucked!*

The boy held the wallet up in victory, like his friend had done with the bottle. "Let's see what's in here." He opened the wallet and looked inside. "Got about thirty-seven in cash and a credit card." He pulled out the driver's license and read the name on it. "Samuel Leftwich." He barked a laugh. "Sounds like one of the bunnies from Peter Rabbit."

The boy danced a little jig around him, putting out his pinky and pretending to sip tea. "Another scone please, Mr. Leftwich," he chirped in a terrible British accent. His friends cackled and hooted.

The Slasher reached up to snatch the license, but the boy held it up, out of reach. He used his other arm to backhand the Slasher across the face. *Smack!* His skin stung, as if seared by a branding iron. The damn kid was awfully strong for as skinny and scrawny as he looked. The second boy backed off, and the Slasher pushed himself to a shaky stand.

"Look," he said. "Take the money, but give me my license. I need it."

The kid sneered at him. "Tough shit."

He launched himself at the boy. *WHACK!* If he'd thought being backhanded across the face smarted, it was nothing compared to the agony of being whacked upside the head by a skateboard. His brain seemed to wobble inside his skull, and he stumbled involuntarily to the side. He fell on the same knee again, and this time it felt as if his kneecap had splintered into sharp shards of bone. He raised his head and howled in pure agony. The boys laughed and took off, skating away into the darkness. The one who'd taken his wallet pocketed the cash, but dropped the wallet and license behind him as if they were trash.

Drawing deep breaths to fight the pain, the Slasher forced himself to a crooked stand. He reached a hand up to his temple, finding it wet. He pulled his hand back and looked at his fingers. They were covered in fresh blood. His head nearly exploded as he bent over to round up his now-empty wallet and the driver's license.

A voice came from across the lot. The hotel desk clerk stood in the front doorway, the glass doors pushed aside. "Are you all right?"

He was anything but. Thanks to the shattered knee, he couldn't stand up straight. His head throbbed and his brain felt thick and gooey, his thoughts stuck in the muck.

Before he could gather his wits, the clerk hollered, "I'll call for police and an ambulance!"

"No!" The cry was like another blow to the brain, a

fresh explosion of pain ricocheting through the confines of his skull. He fought the urge to vomit as he raised a palm to stop the man. "I'll be fine. They were just kids. Besides, they're gone now and I didn't get a good look at them anyway." He staggered to the door.

The clerk eyed the Slasher's head and grimaced. "That wound looks bad. You should probably get it looked at."

"I'm an easy bleeder," he lied. "I'll be okay. Don't call anybody."

He stumbled into the hotel and headed toward the stairwell before realizing he was in no condition to get himself up a flight of stairs. He punched UP for the elevator. It dinged a few seconds later and he climbed on. By then, the clerk was standing in front of the elevator doors. "You sure you don't want medical attention?"

"Yes, I'm sure!" he snapped. "How many times do I have to tell you?" *This guy needs to mind his own damn business!*

FORTY-FOUR
BLOOD TRAILS

Megan

Brigit and I were working overtime that Friday evening and cruising our beat when dispatch came over the radio. "Police needed at the Studio Suites Hotel. The clerk called to report an attack on a guest in the parking lot. The suspects ran off. An ambulance is also en route."

Fleeing suspects were right up our alley. If anyone could find them, my partner could.

I grabbed the mic for my radio. "Officers Luz and Brigit responding."

Two minutes later, we pulled into the lot. The ambulance had yet to arrive. The clerk met me at the door, but my visual scan of the lot turned up no victim.

"What happened?" I asked.

"I was working the desk when I heard skateboards outside. Kids sometimes ride through the parking lot and bother people, so I went to the door to tell them to get lost. That's when I saw them attack one of our guests. They stole a bottle of liquor from him and pushed him down, then hit him over the head with a skateboard. It was a solid whack. I heard it from here. One of them took the money from his wallet before they rode off. I asked the guest if he wanted me to call for help, but he said no. I'm concerned he wasn't thinking straight. His head was bleeding pretty bad when he came inside. He was limping, too."

"Where is he now?"

"He went to his room, I guess. He got on the elevator. That's the last I saw of him before I called for help."

"What room number is he in?"

"I don't know. I don't know his name to look it up."

I looked down to see a trail of blood drops leading through the lobby to the elevator, where several of them had flowed together in front of the doors to form a small pool. "I'll see if I can find him." I led Brigit over to elevator and pushed the button. When the car arrived, we climbed on. More blood drops decorated the floor of the car. I pushed the button for the second floor. When the doors opened, I put my hand on the frame to keep them from closing while I peered out. Sure enough, a trail of blood droplets led down the hallway.

"C'mon, girl." Brigit followed me out the doors and down the hall. The trail led to Room 213, where another collection of blood stained the carpet in front of the door, indicating the man had stopped there momentarily while using his key to open it. While Brigit sniffed at the blood spot, I raised a hand and knocked. *Rap-rap-rap.*

An angry voice came from inside. "I told you I'm okay!"

"It's Officer Luz with the Fort Worth Police Department," I said, leaning into the jamb so he could hear me. "I need you to open this door, sir."

The man spat an expletive, but a moment later opened the door. He held what had once been a white bath towel to his head, though the towel was mostly red now, soaked with his blood. *Whoa.* This guy was anything but okay. My gaze moved down to his clothing. Blood stained the front of his jacket and had dripped onto his pants, too. I hadn't seen this much blood since the Olsens' kitchen on Valentine's Day. My stomach squirmed at the sight.

I pressed the button on my radio. "Instruct the ambulance coming to Studio Suites Hotel that the victim is in Room 213."

"I'm fine!" the man said. "I don't . . . don't need . . ."

With that, his eyes rolled back in his head and he crumpled to the floor. I was able to slow his fall by grabbing his jacket and doing my best to hold him upright. It wasn't easy with the fabric so slippery with blood. Once he'd settled on the floor, I watched his chest, looking for a tell-tale rise and fall. There was slight movement. He was still breathing. *Thank goodness!*

While we waited for the medical team, I hurriedly washed my hands in the kitchen sink, the runoff pink with the man's blood. I dried my hands on a paper towel and returned to the man's side, kneeling next to him to make sure he was still with us. The ambulance arrived in minutes. Alex, a relatively new paramedic with caramel blonde hair and lots of curves, appeared in the open doorway. She was gorgeous, sweet, and capable. She'd joined Seth's station not long before, and had promptly developed a hopeless crush on him. Who could blame her? Ironically, Seth's lack of interest in Alex made him realize how whipped he was over me. If she couldn't tempt him, nobody could.

Alex came into the room, took one look at the deep gash on the man's head, and flinched. "Ouch. What happened?"

I stood. "The clerk said some kids hit him with a skateboard."

She bent down and felt for a pulse while the other

paramedic rolled a gurney inside. "Do you know his name? Age?"

I reached for the wallet sticking out of the man's back pocket and fished out his license. "Samuel Leftwich." Noting his birthdate, I performed some quick math. "He's forty-one."

I compared the picture on the license to the man on the floor in front of me. His appearance had changed quite a bit since he'd had his driver's license photo taken. While the guy in the photo was clean shaven with medium brown hair, the guy on the floor had cut his dark brown hair short and sported a full but nicely trimmed beard. I didn't give the matter much thought. After all, it wasn't unusual for people to look different in person than they did on their licenses. Hairstyles, hair colors, and facial hair changed with the times. A person's weight could fluctuate, and lighting could make hair, eyes, and skin tone appear darker or lighter. In this case, the blood in the man's hair might have given it a darker appearance.

The address on his license was a local one here in Fort Worth. Why was he was staying in a hotel here in town? A glance at his left hand told me he wore a wedding ring. My eyes scanned the room for any indication of a woman staying here with him, but found none. Maybe he and his wife had an argument or were splitting up? I supposed it was none of my business and, besides, his reasons for staying here seemed to have nothing to do with the crime committed against him. I snapped a quick pic of the license with my phone, and stepped out into the hallway with Brigit to give the medical professionals room to work.

Alex and the other EMT carefully cut off the man's clothing to check for hidden injuries, then strapped him to the gurney, and rolled him out to the waiting ambulance. "I'll get in touch with the next of kin," I told them. "Where will you be taking him?"

"John Peter Smith," Alex said, naming the city's primary public hospital.

As soon as the ambulance took off, lights flashing and siren screaming, I confirmed Mr. Leftwich's address with the clerk. He searched the guest records. "Yes. The address on the license is the one we have in our system, too. We always ask guests to verify whether the address on their license is current to make sure we've got accurate records."

"Thanks." The address confirmed, I followed the blood trail out of the hotel to the front of the parking lot. A puddle of blood and surrounding spatter marked the site where the skateboard made contact with the man's skull. Also on the asphalt was a crumpled brown paper bag, the tall and narrow kind they put bottles in at the liquor store. I called for backup.

Once Summer arrived to help me, I gave Brigit the order to trail the disturbance. Summer rolled her window down and trailed Brigit and me in her squad car while we trotted along, following the scent the boys had left behind. They'd veered off into an older residential area. It wasn't long before I saw them in a yard up ahead sitting on the hood of an oxidized Chevy sedan that had been parked on the front lawn. They were laughing and passing a bottle of Jack Daniel's between them, rock music playing from one of their cell phones. They didn't even have the sense to hide inside the house. *Idiots.* Summer and I exchanged a glance and a nod, ready to roll.

The boys didn't notice us until we were only a dozen feet away.

"Shit!" The one with the bottle at his lips hurled it

aside, the glass shattering as it impacted the concrete steps of the porch. The boy sprang from the hood and made it about twenty steps before Brigit brought him down on the sidewalk, his shriek filling the night air. While I rushed up and slapped cuffs on the kid, one of the others took off like a rocket. Summer leaped from her cruiser and ran after him. Luckily for us, he got tripped up in his own feet when he turned to look back at his pursuer. He fell down in the road, skidding on his hands until his face met the pavement, too. In an instant, Summer had him straddled and pulled his arms behind his back to be cuffed. The third kid was the only one of the group who appeared to have any sense. Or maybe he was just slow. He slid down the hood of the car with his hands in the air. In minutes, all three were shackled and seated in the back of Summer's cruiser, muttering curses and sending death glares in our direction.

After tossing Brigit three liver treats and giving her an ear rub and a "good girl!", I turned to Summer. Rather than liver treats and ear rubs, I gave my friend a grateful smile to acknowledge a job well done. "Thanks for your help, Summer."

"Any time."

Congratulations complete, Summer opened her trunk to retrieve evidence-collection gear. We donned latex gloves and looked around for items that would definitively link these boys to the attack on Mr. Leftwich. While Summer carefully picked up the pieces of the broken whiskey bottle and bagged them, I looked around for the wheeled weapon. Three skateboards were scattered about. The first two were relatively clean, bearing only the expected road dirt and traces of motor oil on the wheels, but the third had a smear of what looked like blood on the bottom. Though I had no idea whether the blood was type A, B, AB, or O, the skateboard would no doubt be Exhibit A in the boys' assault trial.

Once the evidence had been secured, I rushed to the address on Leftwich's license to notify his family that he'd been taken to the emergency room. Leaving Brigit in the car with the windows down, I hurried up to the porch of the single-story brick home and rang the bell. A moment later, a man pulled the door open. He looked remarkably like the photo on Mr. Leftwich's license. A brother perhaps? Maybe even a twin? In the living room behind him, three young children sat on the floor in their pajamas, playing video games on the television.

"Hello," I said. "I'm looking for the next of kin of Samuel Leftwich. Are you related to him?"

"I can do you one better," the guy said. "I *am* Samuel Leftwich." He lifted his palms and turned side to side as if modeling for me.

My mind whirled. I whipped out my phone and pulled up the pic I'd taken of his license. "I just handled an incident involving a man with this license in his wallet."

Leftwich leaned in and eyed my screen. "That's my license. My old one, at least. I lost it on Thanksgiving along with the rest of my wallet. The man you mentioned must have found it. Wish he'd returned it to me. I had to wait in line for three hours at the DMV to get a replacement."

The man who'd been attacked had been hiding out under Mr. Leftwich's alias. *Why?* My mind began to twitch as it realized the *who* might be the answer to the *why.* "Any idea where you might have lost your license?"

"I thought it might have fallen out of my pocket when I took my kids to see a movie, but when I called the theater, the manager said nobody had turned it in."

Movie theater. Thanksgiving. Manager. Could it be?

"By any chance did you see the movie at the Take Two Theaters?"

"That's the one. How did you know?"

"A hunch," I said, having no time or inclination to explain, at least not until I verified my hunch. "I've got to get going. I'll be back in touch about the license."

I turned and rushed back to my car, putting the pedal to the medal as I sped to the hospital. I brought Brigit into the ER with me. The place smelled of antiseptic and stale coffee. Several people sat waiting in the chairs that lined the walls, all with pensive expressions on their faces. One man held his side and groaned. A kidney stone, probably. The sheen of sweat on his grimacing face said that, on a scale of one to ten, his pain was a 33.

I explained to the woman tending the reception desk that I needed to see the patient who'd been brought in under the name Samuel Leftwich. She called a nurse over to assist me.

"How is he?" I asked the woman.

"He's still unconscious," she said. "The doctors ran a CT scan to check for a skull fracture or brain bleed. We're waiting on the results. In the meantime, they stitched up his wound and put him on monitors and pain meds. We're checking in on him every few minutes."

"Where is he now?"

She pointed down a row of gurneys, some of which were closed off with curtains. "Last bed on the left."

"Thanks." I passed by several curtained-off spaces in which people sat or lay on gurneys, some alone, others with a loved one beside them. I'd nearly reached a back door marked with a sign that read AUTHORIZED PERSONNEL ONLY when I came to the last bed. The man with the head injury lay on the gurney, still unconscious. A large white bandage was wrapped around his head, holding gauze padding in place over his wound. He'd been loosely dressed in a medical gown. The back of the gown was untied, the strings hanging about his shoulders. He was covered from the lower chest down by a blue blanket, his bare arms resting on either side of his torso. Clear tubing taped to the back of his left hand connected him to an IV bag hanging on a shiny metal stand next to him. Wires led from various parts of him to machines that monitored his vital signs. The soft *beep-beep-beep* of the heart monitor said he had a slow but steady pulse.

I stepped up close and stared at the man's face for a long moment. *Is he Greg Olsen?* It was impossible for me to be certain. I'd never met the man in person and could only go on the photographs I'd seen. This guy was Greg's approximate height and weight as best I could tell. His eyes were closed, so I couldn't verify their color without lifting a lid, but I wasn't about to touch his injured head and risk hurting him further. How could I know?

Then it hit me. On Valentine's, when Detective Jackson had asked Shelby whether Greg had any identifying physical characteristics, Shelby mentioned two—Greg's appendix scar and his outie belly button. Fortunately, I could verify those traits without having to touch his body.

While I couldn't pull the blanket down from his chest without lifting his arms, I could lift it from the bottom without disturbing him. I reached out and eased the blue blanket upward. One of his knees was turning purple with a whopper of a bruise. He must have landed on it when the delinquents attacked him. The dressing gown still covered his thighs and abdomen, so I reached out a second time to lift the gown up, too. Standing on her hind legs, Brigit put her front paws on the bed to see what I was doing. *Yikes!* They'd removed the man's underwear. I got a full frontal view of his genitals in all their glory.

Not satisfied with just a look, Brigit extended her snout to take a sniff. "No, girl!" I pushed her back before raising the gown farther. Sure enough, an appendix scar ran across the right side of his abdomen. As I continued to lift the fabric, his belly button came into view. *An outie.* "Whoa."

"Whoa, indeed," snapped the stealthy nurse, who'd stepped up unheard behind me. "What are you doing?"

I had no choice but to lay the gown to the side, leaving Greg exposed from the navel down. As a medical professional, she'd surely seen plenty of naked men. What was one more? "I'm trying to identify this man," I told the nurse. "He was carrying someone else's driver's license in his wallet. I have a sneaking suspicion he might be a missing person we've been looking for."

She arched a skeptical brow. "And you can identify the missing person by his privates?"

"No. I had no idea he wouldn't be wearing underwear. I was hoping to ID him by his outie belly button and appendix scar."

"Oh. I see." The nurse tilted her head to take a gander at the man's surgical scar and navel. "Well, he's got both. Does that mean he's the man you're after?"

"I'm not sure. Maybe. Do you have any idea about the percentage of people who have had their appendix removed?"

"I don't know the statistics," she said, turning to check the man's IV drip. "But it's a very common surgery. We see appendicitis patients all the time here in the ER."

When in doubt, Google. I ran a quick search on my phone. The Internet shared its infinite wisdom, informing me that approximately seven to nine percent of the population had undergone an appendectomy, a higher percentage than I would have thought. Data showed that children aged ten to nineteen were the most likely to suffer appendicitis, that males had a slighter higher risk than females of coming down with the affliction, and that appendicitis tended to be more common in the summer months, just in time for bathing-suit season.

I performed a statistical analysis. Taking into consideration that around ten percent of the population sported outie belly buttons, and assuming conservatively that seven percent of the population had lost their appendix to appendicitis, only 0.7 percent of people would have both a protruding navel and an appendectomy scar—less than one in a hundred. Given that such a small portion of the population would have both of these characteristics, plus the fact that this man appeared to be in the same general age range as Greg Olsen, I had both an inkling and statistical evidence that this guy could very well be the missing man.

I whipped out my phone. "I need to get photos so his next of kin can ID him. Mind covering his privates?"

She yanked a poofy blue disposable cap from a box on the rolling table next to the bed and situated it over the man's gonads. Once it was in place, I snapped a photo that showed his appendicitis scar and his navel. I also took a close-up photo of his face, which was bruised, swollen, and partially covered by the white bandage around his head.

As the nurse left our curtained-off quarters to check on another patient, I called the Studio Suites Hotel and identified myself to the clerk. "I'm the cop who was just there. Can you tell me when Mr. Leftwich checked into the hotel?"

Clicking sounds came through the phone as the clerk

apparently tapped some keys on his computer keyboard. "February fourteenth."

Valentine's Day. The same night Greg Olsen disappeared. That increased the odds that the man lying in the bed before me was Greg Olsen, didn't it? Of course, the only way to get a positive ID would be to have the police lab run a blood test or have Shelby take a look at him. The latter would be much faster.

"Thanks." I ended the call with the desk clerk, returned my cell phone to my pocket, and used my radio to request an officer to come keep watch over the guy. Summer was still tied up with booking the three juveniles, unfortunately, so she couldn't do it for me.

Derek's voice came across the radio. "I'll babysit the stiff."

Such professional language. "He's not a stiff," I said. "He's still alive." For now, anyway. I wasn't sure how bad his head injury was, whether his brain swelling might get worse. If this guy was indeed Greg Olsen, he just might end up dead, after all. That would be ironic, huh?

While I waited for Derek to arrive, I reached into my pocket to retrieve my cell phone so I could call Detective Jackson with an update. To my surprise, the device vibrated and rang with an incoming call. On hearing the sound, Brigit glanced up from her place on the floor, as if wondering herself who might be calling. The readout on the screen told me it was Detective Jackson. I jabbed the button to accept the call and put the phone to my ear. "Hello, Detective. I was just about to call you myself."

"Give yourself a pat on the back and buy Brigit a box of her favorite treats on me. You two nailed it. Sample twenty-three showed trace amounts of an antibiotic that wasn't found in any of the other blood samples. The other samples also varied in their glucose and potassium levels. They were obviously drawn at different times. Hollywood's got nothing on Greg Olsen."

So Greg's death was scripted, after all, a scene in a fictional live-action drama. Only in this case, the lead character had inadvertently suffered a real injury. *Should've used a stunt double.*

"Problem is," Jackson continued, "we can't arrest the guy when we don't know where he is."

"Maybe we do know," I said.

"What are you talking about?"

"Just a second." I pulled the phone from my ear and sent the pics of Greg's face and abdomen to her. Returning to the call, I said, "I'm in the ER at John Peter Smith, waiting for Derek Mackey to come keep watch over the patient in the photos. The guy was attacked tonight in the parking lot of a hotel where he's been staying since Valentine's Day. He had a fake ID in his wallet. It belonged to a local man who confirmed he lost his wallet at the Take Two Theaters in November."

"Glory hallelujah!" she cried. "Looks like we've got a Lazarus on our hands. Back from the dead. As soon as Derek shows up, meet me at Shelby's."

FORTY-FIVE
IT'S HIM, ALL RIGHT

Brigit

Brigit lay on her cushion in the cruiser, facing the back window in a puppy pout. She didn't appreciate Megan scolding her and pushing her away from that man. Sniffing privates was a natural instinct for a dog. If Megan didn't like it, then maybe she should work with a human instead of a K-9.

Before Megan had pushed her away, Brigit had already gotten a tell-tale whiff of the man. She knew he was the same man she'd scented outside the building where she and Megan had waited at lunchtime today, the same one she'd smelled at the house with the dog with the smushed face. She'd smelled the blood on his bandage, too. It was the same blood she'd smelled before in the man's kitchen. Well, almost the same. Her nose had detected very small differences among the puddles, and his blood smelled slightly different tonight, too.

Her nose detected an influx of familiar scents as the cruiser rolled to a stop and Megan cut the motor. She stood and looked out the window, flexing her nostrils for a better smell. What do you know? They were back at smushy-face's house again.

FORTY-SIX
BEEP

The Slasher

Beep . . . beep . . . beep . . .

FORTY-SEVEN
RESURRECTION

Megan

Detective Jackson climbed out of her cruiser as I parked my patrol car behind her. I rounded up Brigit from the back and met Jackson on the walkway.

She cut me a smug grin. "I can't wait to see the look on Shelby's face when she realizes the jig is up."

We walked up to the porch. Jackson raised her hand to the door and knocked fast and furious. *KNOCK-KNOCK-KNOCK-KNOCK-KNOCK!*

Shelby opened the door wearing a guarded expression and pink knit pajamas with little Eiffel Towers printed on them. Once again, she held her French bulldog in her arms. If I hadn't seen Marseille's bloody paw prints on the floor for myself on Valentine's Day, I might believe her little doggie feet never touched the ground.

Jackson jumped right in without preamble. "We know, Shelby."

"Know what?" the woman asked, her gaze shifting between the detective and me.

"About the hidden messages in the e-mails."

Shelby's eyes went wide and her skin flamed as she took a step back, her arms reflexively tightening around

Marseille. The dog wriggled in protest, but Shelby only doubled her efforts, hanging on to the dog as if she were a lifeline. Marseille stopped moving and snorted out a sigh of resignation.

"Officer Luz found them." Jackson thrust printouts of the secret e-mails at the woman.

Shelby looked down at the printouts, but didn't take them, refusing to release her death grip on her bulldog. She pressed her lips together so hard they turned white, and said nothing. *Her legal training is serving her well.*

Jackson tucked the printouts under her arm, and swapped them for the lab results. "The lab analysis shows that the samples of your husband's blood collected from your kitchen varied in relative amounts of elements. One of them contained trace amounts of antibiotics not found in the others. The test results prove the blood had been drawn over time prior to Valentine's Day, and was tossed around your kitchen that night to make it appear he'd been attacked and killed."

Shelby stared at the lab report that Jackson held up, but still stayed quiet.

"The jig's up, Shelby," Jackson said. "We've got your husband in custody."

Shelby studied our faces for a long moment, as if trying to read our minds, before she finally spoke again. "If you had Greg in custody, he would have called me."

Jackson tossed a look my way, inviting me to tell Shelby what had happened this evening.

I was happy to oblige. "Your husband got jumped by muggers in a hotel parking lot tonight. He's in the ER as we speak."

Shelby's eyes narrowed, but not before flashing with alarm. "I-I don't believe you. You're just trying to get me to admit that I had something to do with whatever happened to him. If he was still alive and was hurt, he'd have contacted me."

"He can't," I said. "He has a head injury. He's unconscious." I pulled out my phone and brought the first photo of the injured man up on my screen. It showed him lying in the bed, eyes closed. "Take a look." I held the phone up for her to view.

Shelby's eyes squinted and her head jerked forward and back as she tried to discern whether the man in the photo was truly her husband or merely a decoy we were trying to use to trap her. Her movements were much like that of the heron I'd seen on Goat Island when searching for her husband's body. She turned her gaze on me. "That man doesn't look like Greg at all."

"He would have changed his appearance. He wouldn't have risked being recognized as the missing man whose face was all over the news and the Internet." I turned my phone so that the screen faced me, and scrolled to the second picture that showed him with his gown raised, his outie belly button and appendix scar visible. "How about now? Does this look like Greg?" I turned the phone to face her.

She gasped and gaped for an instant before composing herself and leaning in to take a closer look. "That can't be him." She sounded far less sure now, her words more of a plea than a protest. "It can't be!"

Maybe I should've taken a photo of his junk so she could positively identify him.

"Look, Shelby," Jackson said. "We've got enough evidence to charge both you and Greg for conspiracy and insurance fraud. You're going to jail tonight, regardless. But if you cooperate, answer all of our questions, we'll take you by the hospital first so you can see your husband before we book you. Deal?"

Shelby's shaking head said *No*, but her wild eyes said *I don't know what to do! Are they lying to me? Am I being duped?* She was teetering on the edge of resistance and cooperation. I decided to push her over.

I waved my phone, the pic still up on the screen. "This man in the photo? He was carrying a fake driver's license. I went to the address on the license to inform them that their loved one had been hurt and was in serious condition at the hospital. Imagine my surprise when the man whose photo was on the license answered the door."

Shelby's chest rose and fell at a rapid pace and her breaths came fast. Her voice was a soft squeak. "What name was on the license?"

Jackson and I exchanged a glance. *We've got her now.*

Shelby lost it then, shrieking, "What name was on the license?!?"

I eased my hand toward the cuffs on my belt. "Samuel Leftwich."

Shelby went pale, her dog slipping from her hands as they went to cover her mouth. Marseille didn't mind. She landed unhurt on the rug and looked up at Brigit as if to say *Bon jour*. Brigit wagged her tail in greeting, and the two exchanged sniffs of their doggie derrieres.

Shelby's head began to bob, slowly at first, but then nodding frantically as she burst into sobs. I reached out and gently removed her hands from her face, pulling them downward and cuffing them behind her.

Jackson recited Shelby's rights. *You can keep your mouth shut if you choose. If you can't afford an attorney, we'll give you one for free. If you decide to say something, it could come back to bite you in the butt.* "Do you understand the rights I have just read to you?"

"Yes," Shelby said.

"With these rights in mind, do you wish to speak to us?"

"Yes." She raised a shoulder to wipe the tears from her cheek.

Jackson pulled a small digital recorder from her briefcase and pressed RECORD. "Detective Audrey Jackson here at the home of Shelby and Greg Olsen, along with Officer Megan Luz and her K-9 Brigit. We have a suspect in custody. Please identify yourself." She held the recorder toward Shelby, who softly recited her name. To ensure she had the woman nailed down, Jackson said, "Mrs. Olsen, do you admit that you and your husband conspired to fake his death to collect insurance proceeds?"

"Yes," Shelby said.

"You admit that you knew he was alive when you called nine-one-one and summoned police to your home on the night of February fourteenth?"

"Yes!" she cried, stepping toward the front door.

Jackson put a hand on Shelby's shoulder to hold her back. "You admit that you gave false statements to me and Officer Luz that evening?"

"Yes! I admit it!"

"You admit that you went to the coffee shop on Wednesday and to Burnett Park today to meet your husband?"

"Yes!" she sobbed. "Yes! Yes! Yes! Just take me to Greg! Please!"

Jackson eyed the woman, taking in her tears and anguish, before saying, "All right."

I agreed with the detective's decision. There was nothing to be gained by throwing our weight around, forcing Shelby to answer our questions here before we took her to see her husband. Besides, we already had enough to nail her and she'd likely be even more forthcoming if we met her halfway. Discretion was a law enforcement officer's most powerful tool.

Before we took our shackled quarry out to the detective's cruiser, I asked Shelby what arrangements should be made for Marseille.

"Can you call Regina to come get her?" She angled her head to indicate her cell phone, which was charging atop an end table in the living room. "There's a spare house key in the drawer. You can leave it for her in the mailbox."

I phoned her coworker, but left out the details. "Shelby is coming to the police station. Could you come over and pick up Marseille, take care of her for a bit?"

Regina agreed to pet sit, and I told her where she'd find the house key to let herself in. When we ended the call, I dropped the key into the mailbox and closed it.

Jackson buckled Shelby into the back of her cruiser, tossed me the car keys, and slid into the passenger seat. I loaded Brigit into the back, instructing her to lie down on the floorboard.

As I drove to the hospital, Jackson locked Shelby's testimony down. We learned that Greg had watched You-Tube tutorials on how to draw his own blood, and had purchased the necessary medical supplies, with cash, from a medical supply store in Oklahoma before they'd moved to Fort Worth. They'd concocted the spam e-mail communication system after Shelby accidentally made a paragraph in a legal memoranda disappear when she'd meant to change the font color from red to black, but had clicked on the white block instead. At a thrift shop in Dallas, Shelby had bought the shoes and clothing purportedly worn by the killers and later found in the garbage bag at the bottom of Lake Worth. Greg had walked around the kitchen in both pairs of shoes to make it look like there'd been two attackers. To simulate a human body, Greg had dragged a large bag of dog food through the blood on the kitchen floor, and tossed the blood-covered bag into the trunk of his car. He'd been the one to drive his car to Marion Sansom Park. The passenger we'd spotted in the security camera video had been none other than a cardboard cutout of Jason Momoa from the *Aquaman* movie, a promotional display Greg had brought home from the theater·in Oklahoma after the movie's run a couple of years back.

Now that we knew the who and the how, I wanted an answer to the big remaining question. *Why?* "What did you plan to do with the insurance money?"

"We were going to buy a place in Paris," Shelby said softly, staring out the window. "The French film industry is more about art than entertainment. Greg hoped to freelance for a movie company there, or maybe work on his screenplays and get one of them produced. People in the industry sometimes use a pseudonym. We thought he could fly under the radar there."

With prison looming, Greg might never become a part of the French film scene now. Or heck, for all I knew, maybe the Parisian film producers would be intrigued by his experience as a former jailbird once they were released—if the two could afford to get there one day. They might even make a movie about this entire debacle. If so, I wondered who they'd cast to play Brigit and me.

Now that Shelby had started talking, she was in no hurry to stop. She continued on, without prodding, as if Jackson's cruiser were a confessional. She seemed almost relieved to be getting things off her chest, or maybe she was trying to justify her actions, garner some sympathy from us.

"Greg and I work so many hours we have to schedule times to see each other. The insurance money would have allowed us to live a whole new lifestyle. My mother and sister don't like to fly, so I knew they wouldn't surprise us with a visit in France."

Despite the fact that we'd caught them, it was a well-thought-out plan, far more intricate and clever than the typical criminal could come up with. I was impressed with Shelby's acting abilities, too. "Were you really crying when we came to see you that day in your garage?"

"Yes," she said, "but it was because I'd rubbed menthol ointment under my eyes. It's an acting trick. Greg read about it on one of the movie blogs he follows."

A-ha! I knew I'd smelled the stuff.

Jackson met Shelby's eyes in the rearview mirror. "You know, if you'd told us that Greg had a drug or gambling problem, or was into strip clubs, it would've pointed suspicion away from you. Officer Luz wouldn't have taken a second look at your e-mails and you might have gotten away with your plan."

Shelby slowly shook her head. "I couldn't let anyone think bad of Greg."

She'd been brought down by love. Another irony.

We pulled into the hospital's parking garage and, while I attached Brigit's leash to lead her inside, Detective Jackson put a hand on Shelby's forearm to escort her into the building. After checking in again with the receptionist, we made our way to the curtained area and down the row. I reached out, grabbed the last curtain, and pulled it back.

While the IV stand and machines remained, the monitors had been turned off and the tubing and wires hung to the floor. The gurney was gone, along with the suspect who'd been lying on it. Derek lay asleep in a chair. He snored loudly, his mouth hanging open, his teeth and tongue tinged green by the colored gelatin he'd gobbled down. The empty bowl and spoon sat on the tray table beside him.

I was tempted to wake Mackey with another jolt from my Taser, but the chief would never let me slide for the indiscretion a second time. I settled for kicking my former partner's foot. "Derek! Where's the suspect?"

He scrubbed a hand over his face as if to wipe away the sleep and sat up, looking over to where the bed should be. "I guess a nurse took him away for tests."

"You *guess*?" Jackson snapped. "You mean you don't know?"

"I must've fallen asleep." Derek scrubbed a hand over his face again, but this time it seemed intended to hide his shame. "I cuffed him to the bed. I didn't think he could go anywhere."

"Think again." I grabbed the call button attached to the back wall and pressed it several times in rapid succession, like an excited contestant who knew the right answer on *Jeopardy!* A few seconds later, the nurse I'd spoken with earlier yanked the curtain back.

Jackson motioned to the empty space. "Where's the patient who was here?"

The woman stammered, flabbergasted. "I-I don't know."

Jackson sent a scathing glance at Derek before turning back to the woman. "He wasn't taken for testing?"

"No," she said. "They'd already run a CAT scan on him. He was being kept here for observation until he came around." She pointed to Derek. "Wasn't he keeping an eye on the patient?"

"Not a good one, as it turns out." Jackson's gaze went to the door marked AUTHORIZED PERSONNEL ONLY. "Greg must have escaped through that door."

Derek stood, as if ready to go after the guy. "He couldn't have gotten far."

My gaze went to Derek's waist. His holster release was open and his gun was gone. My gut hardened into a ball of terror and my voice was a mousy squeak. "Derek, where's your gun?"

He looked down at his empty holster. "Oh, shit."

"Holy hell!" Jackson threw up her hands. "We've got an armed suspect on the loose!"

I pulled Shelby in Derek's direction. "Can you at least hang on to her?" I didn't wait for an answer before I left them behind and followed Jackson out the staff-only door with Brigit beside me.

We drew our weapons and looked up and down the hallway, but Greg was nowhere to be seen.

Jackson pointed to our left. "You two go that way."

Brigit and I took off at a sprint down the hallway, careful to stay in the center of the corridor in case someone stepped out of one of the rooms along the way. I kept my gun pointed down, as I'd been trained to do, and issued a silent prayer that no one would die here tonight.

At the end of the hall was a perpendicular passage. I stopped at the corner and peeked around it, first one way, then the other. *There he is!* Greg was halfway down the hall, aiming for the emergency exit door at the end. He ambled alongside his wheeled gurney, weaving like a drunk, his pasty backside on display for all the world to see.

My partner and I had to act fast, before he realized we were on to him and could get off a shot at us. As much as I hated to send Brigit after an armed suspect, I knew she could move much faster than I could and was our best bet for preventing an escalation. I looked down at my partner and she looked up at me, awaiting her orders, eager to please, to do her duty.

For the second time that night, I gave her the signal

and off she went, a furry blur in the hall. Greg had just begun to turn his head when she leaped up onto his back. He cried out in surprise as she took him down to the tile floor. Unfortunately, with his wrist being cuffed to the bedrail, the gurney turned over on top of them, the wheels sticking up in the air like the legs of a dead cockroach. Brigit disappeared as the sheets and blanket billowed over them.

By then, various hospital employees had heard Greg's cry and ventured out of the doors to see what was going on.

"Back in your rooms!" I shouted as I ran to my partner. "He's got a gun!"

The medical staff disappeared into the rooms and closed the doors behind them. Banging and thudding noises quickly followed, telling me they were barricading themselves in the spaces. They'd probably learned what to do in an active-shooter drill. *What a world we live in.*

The blankets and sheets moved as Brigit and Greg wrestled and wrangled beneath them. Detective Jackson ran up from behind me and grabbed one side of the gurney, trying to right it. The frame came only partway up, anchored to Greg by the cuff on his wrist. The thin mattress toppled out of the frame, falling atop the writhing pile. I yanked the mattress away and grabbed at the bedding, pulling it back to reveal my K-9 partner pinning the injured man to the ground. Greg flailed his left arm, waving the gun about, though it seemed to be a reflexive gesture rather than an intentional one. My heart pumped blood like an open floodgate. I didn't want to have to shoot this man, but if he didn't put the gun down I'd have to.

I ordered Brigit off him and he grew still as she backed away. The hand that held the gun now lay beside him on the tile, but it would take him a mere instant to raise it. I pointed my gun down at his face. Fresh blood showed on his bandage. His stitches must've pulled loose while he'd been grappling with my partner. But he had nobody to blame for that but himself.

"Let go of the gun!" I ordered.

He looked up at me and issued a desperate, anguished wail, but he didn't release the weapon.

"Work with me, Greg," I demanded. "Okay?"

He swallowed hard, his eyes desperate, and turned his head to look at the gun in his hand.

Fearing he might put the weapon to himself, I softened my voice. "You're not in big trouble yet, Greg. All you've done so far is put on a show, just a setting and some props." I hoped he was buying this. With his crazed expression, it was impossible to tell. "You've suffered a head injury. You weren't thinking straight when you took the police officer's weapon. But if you raise that gun now, Greg, everything changes. You won't be able to see Shelby. She's waiting for you back in the ER."

His eyes brightened, the fog seeming to clear. "She is?"

"Yes," I said. "She wants to see you again. Alive. Don't take that away from her, Greg. Don't break her heart. Always and forever, remember?"

He stared at me for a long moment. Brigit stood rigid by my side, ready for orders. His dazed gaze moved from me to Brigit, where it lingered for a moment before his shoulders relaxed. "Okay," he said softly. "What do I do?"

"Release your hold on the gun," I said, my own still aimed at him. "Detective Jackson will take it from you."

He did as he'd been told, and the detective snatched the gun up from the floor. As she did, Greg's eyes rolled back in his head and his jaw fell slack.

I hollered, "All clear!" to let those hunkering down in the nearby rooms know the threat had been eliminated. I closed my eyes for a quick moment to thank the powers that be that nobody had been shot here tonight. "We need a doctor! Stat!"

A woman in scrubs rushed out of a room, performed a quick assessment, and summoned help to load Greg back onto his gurney. I gave the staff a quick rundown of the situation, and the detective, Brigit, and I followed as they wheeled him back to his space in the ER.

Overwhelmed with emotion, Shelby emitted an odd squeak and burst into tears when she saw her battered husband on the bed. She, too, seemed to teeter on her feet. Lest she also end up with a head injury, I took her arm to steady her.

Jackson addressed Derek, hiking a thumb over her shoulder. "You can go now, Mackey."

He left without a word. He didn't even ask for his gun back. Smart decision on his part. There was nothing he could say that wouldn't incur further wrath.

The ER nurse took over, reconnecting Greg's tubes and wires.

When the nurse was finished, Shelby stepped up to the head of the bed and leaned over to look into her husband's face, her tears falling onto his cheeks. Perhaps sensing she was there, he rallied momentarily, his eyes fluttering open. He offered his leading lady a small smile and reached up a hand to touch her cheek before he once again fell into unconsciousness, the scene fading to black.

FORTY-EIGHT
BEDSIDE MANNER

Brigit

Brigit wished the woman had brought the smushy-faced dog with her to the hospital so Brigit could have played with her. This place was boring. And what was with all the beeping? The sound irritated her ears. Still, she knew Megan was counting on her to sit still, so she did just that. It was her duty, after all.

But wait . . . *What's that smell?*

Detective Jackson had left the room a few minutes ago, but she returned now with a crinkly bag from a vending machine. Brigit lifted her nose to scent. *Potato chips.* She'd only gotten to lick the dust from the bag of chips she'd come across days ago at the park. She'd love to eat some actual chips. The only question now was, would the detective share? She knew better than to beg but, boy oh boy, did those chips smell good!

The woman sat down in the chair Derek had been sleeping in earlier and, while Brigit watched, drool dripping from her jowls, opened the bag. When she finished, she locked her eyes on Brigit's. "This is all for you, girl. You've earned it."

Brigit wasn't sure what the words meant, but when the detective poured the chips into a plastic kidney-shaped bowl and set it down on the floor, it could only mean one thing. The potato chips were for Brigit. *Woo-hoo!*

FORTY-NINE
REUNITED. TEMPORARILY.

Greg Olsen

"Shelby?"

What was his wife doing here? And, where, exactly was here? He couldn't seem to clear the fog in his head. To make matters worse, he felt a warm but agonizing *throb-throb-throb* on the side of his head. Another painful throb pulsated at his knee.

His gaze roamed the room, taking in the IV, the woman in the suit, the uniformed cop, and the enormous, furry K-9 who'd put her front paws up on his bed to stare at him and was making the gurney shake with each wag of her fluffy tail.

Shelby's lip quivered. "It's over, Greg."

"Over?" And then it hit him. Their plan to fake his death, collect a million dollars in insurance, say goodbye to their typical lives and humdrum existence and start a new, romantic life in France. He should have realized it wouldn't work, that the odds were stacked against them. The bad guys might have gotten away with their crimes in movies like *No Country for Old Men, Gone Girls,* and *The Watchmen,* but real-life law enforcement was often more cunning than the cops in movies. One look at the dog and the two women staring him down from the end of his bed, and he knew he'd underestimated them.

FIFTY
IT'S A WRAP

Megan

Over the next couple of weeks, while Derek was temporarily suspended without pay, Detective Jackson and I wrapped up loose ends in the two cases.

I discovered through some additional digging that, decades ago, James Thomas Perkins had worked in the Midwest as a salesman for a propane company, tasked with bringing in new residential accounts. Before extending credit, the company required its salesmen to obtain the Social Security numbers of prospective clients so that a credit check could be run. Perkins had kept a database of those names and numbers, and had later used that information to open business accounts with online banks in the names of the shell companies he'd established, also using fictitious names.

The various vehicles he'd driven were rentals he'd swapped out as needed to stay one step ahead of law enforcement and the irate customers he'd ripped off. The wedding ring, too, was a farce. While he'd been married three times as a younger man, he'd been single since his forties, when his last wife had called it quits.

Fortunately, the Stormchaser Roofing bank account

still had a sizable balance when Perkins was apprehended and the account had been frozen. His victims in Fort Worth wouldn't get all of their money back, but they'd see seventy cents on the dollar. I'd call that a victory. In light of his repeated criminal activity, and the fact that his total take added up to hundreds of thousands of dollars, the prosecutor didn't go easy on the guy. He'd offered Perkins a plea deal of five years in the state penitentiary. Last I heard, the attorneys for each side were still haggling, and Perkins's lawyer had threatened to let the matter go to court. Perkins would be an idiot to go to trial, though. Every potential juror and judge in the state had lost a roof to hail at one point or another. It was an arduous enough process without some scam artist swooping in to rip you off. A jury was likely to lock the guy away for life.

The boys who'd attacked Greg would spend several weeks in juvenile detention. They were still young enough to turn themselves around, and I hoped the stint would set them straight. A life of crime and violence would be no life at all.

Shelby and Greg were being held in separate women's and men's facilities, though they were able to communicate fairly regularly through their attorneys. Making false statements to law enforcement was only a Class B misdemeanor, punishable by a fine of up to two grand and 180 days in jail. The Olsens had lied to me and Detective Jackson, costing us time and energy that could have been applied to other investigations, yet they'd receive a mere slap on the wrist for it. Fortunately, insurance fraud in the amount of $300,000 or more was a first-degree felony. Such felonies were punishable by fines of up to ten grand, as well as five to ninety-nine years in prison. Greg was looking at an additional charge for taking Derek's weapon. The defense attorneys and the DA were working out a plea deal for the couple to pay the maximum fine and serve several years in prison. Greg wouldn't enjoy his time in the clink, but it would provide him an opportunity to work on his screenplays. Meanwhile, Marseille adjusted well to her new life with Regina, who had happily agreed to keep the bulldog and posted a dozen pictures of her adorable adopted beast each day on her Facebook page.

It was a bittersweet day when Frankie moved out of our house and Seth and Blast officially moved in. Frankie and Zach had rented a moving truck, and the four of us spent the morning loading it with Frankie's furniture and boxes of her personal items. I felt no small sense of satisfaction when the men carried out the television I'd rescued from the clutches of Frankie's former boyfriend the day she and I had met.

Frankie and I had enjoyed lots of girl time together in the house, but we were both moving forward with our lives, going on to the next natural phase. Besides, her new place was only a ten-minute drive away, and I'd see her at the fire station. Even so, we parted with hugs and tears. "I'm going to miss you," I told her.

"I'll miss you, too."

She'd given Brigit a hug goodbye, too. I'd kissed the top of Zoe's head, her fur sticking to my lip gloss, and reached out to ruffle the cat's ears. "Behave, you little stinker."

But now, Seth and I were at the florist, speaking with a woman about my bridal bouquet and the other flowers for our wedding. Brigit and Blast had come with us. Brigit had sniffed a few of the flowers before flopping over on the floor and putting her feet in the air, as if succumbing to a scent overdose. *Drama queen.*

After looking over the options and working out the pricing, we decided to go with champagne-colored roses. They'd be a nice complement to my dress, without competing with it. They'd smell nice, too.

We returned to Seth's Nova and, after loading the dogs in the back, he opened my door for me. "Our wedding day will be here before we know it."

I stood on tiptoe and gave him a kiss. "I can hardly wait!"